BEYOND THE FRAMEWORK

Cultivating Agile Growth

By: Jeremy Berriault

Contents

ACKNOWLEDGEMENTS

Writing acknowledgments for this book feels like embarking on a quest of gratitude—a journey that spans decades, carrying a treasure trove of information, knowledge, and experiences. It's as if this book could be a story—a narrative woven with insights and moments that have shaped me.

First and foremost, a heartfelt acknowledgment goes to my wife, Liz, and my two sons, Logan and Nicholas. They've been my steadfast companions throughout the past two years of crafting this book. Even in the face of my writer-ly quirks, their unwavering support has been a true testament to the power of family.

Next on my list of acknowledgments is Tom Cagley. We have known each other for years, which has been a blessing. You've been a mentor, colleague, and friend. You have given me incalculable information, shared your experiences, and supported me through a lot over the past. You were a big part of helping me get this book— the talks we had, personally, on your podcasts (SPaMCast) and at conferences where we presented have been very influential in how I see agility. It played a significant role in bringing these ideas to light and sharing them with the world.

There's someone else I must acknowledge—someone I've never met in person, yet whose impact has been profound. That someone is Simon Sinek. Back in 2011, while I was navigating the labyrinth of MBA studies, his TED talk on the Golden Circle transformed my viewpoint in a mere 15 minutes. The ripple effect of that talk shifted my focus and paved the way for the words you're about to read.

Amidst the tapestry of influences, authors, colleagues, and individuals who have sculpted the path I tread, works like "Great Big Agile," "Leading Change," "Tame Flow," "The Fifth Discipline," and many others have served as my compass, guiding me in framing and articulating ideas effectively. It's as if these books have been my intellectual sidekicks, accompanying me on a journey of continuous learning and exploration.

And here's a little secret that's probably not often found in acknowledgments: jujitsu. For 15 years, I've been immersed in this martial art, which is much more than physical combat. Jujitsu has given me a philosophy, a way of life beyond the mat. It's a mindset that helps me navigate challenges, view work and life from different angles, and find solutions even when faced with adversity.

As I reflect on these acknowledgments, I'm reminded that this book isn't just a collection of words; it's a convergence of stories, influences, and insights. Like a mosaic of appreciation, each piece represents a person, moment, or concept contributing to the bigger picture. With a touch of humor, a dash of introspection, and a heartfelt thank you, I celebrate the journey from the first word to the last, acknowledging those who have shaped its pages.

INTRODUCTION

This book, Beyond the Framework, has been developed and refined over the years, proving its efficacy in organizations aiming to achieve agility. It guides you to go deep into creating a truly agile environment and not resting on the laurels of implementing a framework.

In a business context, "agile" refers to the capacity to respond rapidly to shifting market conditions, evolving customer requirements, and intensifying competition. It requires adopting a mentality and cultivating a culture that encourages adaptability, creativity, and teamwork.

Firms need agility to remain competitive and relevant in today's fast-paced and always-changing business climate. Businesses are becoming quicker and better equipped to adjust to shifting consumer preferences. Also, adjusting to preferences in the marketplace has a greater chance of achieving commercial success than those more resistant to change.

Organizations adopting an agile environment can become more productive, customer-focused, and efficient. They can recognize and seize new opportunities, adapt to their customers' requirements, and continually enhance the quality of their products and services. Agility enables businesses to cultivate cultures of invention and collaboration, which may contribute to greater employee satisfaction and retention.

Why is understanding agility and its implications so essential?

The shift from traditional product or service delivery to an agile environment has become common for many organizations in various markets. Such a transformation is necessary to avoid becoming obsolete and to remain competitive. However, many organizations struggle to realize the total value of an agile transformation. The State of Agile[1] report highlights several challenges that organizations face, both internally and externally, when implementing an agile environment.

As we go through different markets, we find that many organizations are shifting from traditional product or service delivery to trying to form an agile environment. They see no value in conducting an old, conventional

---

[1] https://digital.ai/resource-center/analyst-reports/16th-state-of-agile-report/

way of completing work with the current rate of change. Organizations must transform to avoid obscurity when the competition takes up market share.

Unfortunately, some failures come along when doing an agile transformation. Most stats show that organizations struggle to see the total value. Many studies and documentation show those numbers; the State of Agile (16th Annual State of Agile Report) is among the most popular. One key thing that comes out of all the research is that frustrations occur internally and externally with any organization that makes the change.

The question is, why does it fail?

One of the reasons for the failure of agile transformation can be attributed to the focus on the tools rather than the fundamental principles that underpin agile methodology. Simon Sinek's Golden Circle [2]model provides a helpful framework for understanding this issue. First, we have the "why" of an 'organization's being that supports an agile environment. "why" involves identifying organizational values and customer needs; this helps create focus on the ultimate goal of the transformation. The "how" of an agile environment, which can refer to the behaviors and practices of the team, is then impacted by the lack of the definition of the "why," leading to the failure of the agile transformation.

Finally, we get to the "what" that has become the primary focus for organizations when they start their agile journey: the frameworks to achieve faster deliveries and meet client needs. A few examples:

- SCRUM
- LeSS
- SAFe™
- NEXUS
- XP
- KANBAN

These are a few of the over 30 frameworks organizations use, not including the hybrid versions.

The failure of an agile transformation is due to the lack of attention given

---

[2] Finding Your Why, Simon Sinek

to the "why" first. Organizations must be bold but focus on the fundamentals of an agile environment to ensure a successful transformation. Putting the "why" first helps motivate and guide the organization and creates a solid agile environment. The team members will develop the appropriate behaviors and practices to identify the right tools to meet organizational goals and customer needs. This shift in focus will foster innovation, ensure customer satisfaction, and increase employee satisfaction.

As we all know, in an agile environment, teams work in brief cycles, or iterations, usually lasting two to four weeks, and provide tangible results after each iteration. To keep the project on schedule and guarantee that any issues or adjustments are dealt with swiftly, the team members work closely together and frequently communicate. Customers' and stakeholders' feedback is prioritized in agile environments to guide the development process and guarantee that the final product satisfies their needs.

Authentic agile workplaces are renowned for their adaptation and flexibility. They enable teams to react swiftly to altering demands, market circumstances, or client wants. Agile environments, thus, make it simpler to change course or pivot direction if necessary by breaking down complex issues into less complicated ones, making them smaller, manageable chunks that provide value sooner.

Several businesses today are concentrating their efforts on establishing the best framework they can use to make their deliveries go more quickly and fulfill the requirements of their customers. The question that needs to be answered is not whether these requirements are being satisfied or are quicker than in the past but whether there is value. It is essential to remember that the framework is merely a means for accomplishing these objectives; it is not the goal itself. The next level, which is how effectively this instrument is used, is where organizations should concentrate their efforts and attention.

What is most frequently disregarded, yet is the single most vital aspect of any attempt, is the "WHY." Merely identifying the "WHY" as "getting things done faster" or "having more releases to satisfy demand" is not sufficient since it does not take into consideration the emotional components of the organization's values or the requirements of its customers. In an agile environment, businesses tend to focus on how effectively they run sprints and events; nevertheless, this is where the blinders are put on, and the tool is blamed when things don't go as planned.

For enterprises to succeed in an agile environment, they need to begin with the "WHY" and work their way outward to the "HOW," ensuring that everything is compatible with teams and leads to the appropriate behaviors for value creation. This method will encourage continued growth and stewardship and prevent the top-down command-and-control method, which can impede creativity and lead to frustration.

It will be easier for businesses to satisfy the requirements of their customers in a way that is both successful and efficient if they shift their operations from the inside out, beginning with the question "why" and finish by selecting the tool most suited to each of their teams. Teams will like what they are doing, and executives will see an improvement in employee satisfaction if they focus on being agile and having the appropriate habits. This strategy will foster creativity, and the business will be able to establish a naturally innovative environment, hence increasing the level of happiness experienced by customers.

The notion of agile evolution has developed over many years through observing and interpreting published works in the agile environment. I have dedicated substantial time to gathering insights that challenge the prevailing notion that agile maturity is the correct lens for viewing agile environments. I offer a fresh approach that identifies focal points for nurturing a perpetually evolving agile environment while not entirely discarding maturity. Striking a balance is essential.

My theory does challenge the traditional view of agile maturity and proposes a new approach to an agile environment. I believe that organizations should focus on creating an evergreen, evolving, agile environment rather than striving for a particular level of maturity. My approach emphasizes continuous improvement and identifies and addresses areas that need improvement through foundational behaviors that support agility. My insights will offer valuable information for those looking to improve their agile processes and create a more effective and efficient organization.

Evolution of Agile Organizations

About six or seven years before the printing of this book, a theory came to mind inspired by the iconic television show Pokémon (I will thank my kids for this one). In the show, there is a constant dialogue about the different evolution stages within each Pokémon character and how they grow. By talking with them more, one can discover what is different about them as they evolve, even though every Pokémon of the same lineage has similar characteristics. But like every living being, they have a particular personality, the one thing that sets them apart. Talking to them brings out that aspect and helps the trainer strengthen them through new moves and functionalities, including attack and defense strategies.

Just as Pokémon evolve and become stronger by discovering their unique characteristics through interaction and adaptation, agile teams and organizations also evolve by embracing their distinct qualities and responding to changing circumstances. The key lies in recognizing that while different organizations may share similar agile principles and practices, they, like individual Pokémon, possess unique attributes and needs. Agile evolution involves discovering and harnessing these distinctive traits to become more adaptable and efficient.

Much like Pokémon trainers help their creatures become stronger by exploring new abilities, agile organizations grow and mature by adapting to new strategies and methodologies. This process involves understanding their strengths and weaknesses, implementing innovative approaches, and enhancing their agility in response to evolving requirements.

Agile values and principles are no different from the teachings of great philosophers like Descartes, Kant, and Carl Jung. Just like philosophical teachings guide individuals to think more broadly about their actions, the agile approach also provides a framework to guide individuals and teams in achieving success. As one grows with philosophical teachings, one interprets them and moves on the best path possible to succeed and become a better person. Similarly, agile values and principles provide guidelines for individuals and teams to follow.

WHERE DO WE START?

This book will provide the guidance necessary to create a thriving, evolving, agile environment within your team or organization.

What is maturity?

Before we move on, we must talk about maturity. Maturity is achieved through reaching specific growth milestones, whether psychological, physiological or within a corporate environment. Various models can help determine maturity levels, functioning as checklists to establish these specific levels. These models are effective for pinpointing where things stand concerning established standards. However, do they assist in determining the level of agility?

Considering the creation of the Manifesto for Agile Software Development[3] over 20 years ago, and its wording doesn't emphasize reaching specific milestones or offering markers or checklists for people to follow and achieve. This raises the question: What exactly are we referring to when discussing maturity within "Agile"?

When conversing with organizational leadership and agile maturity, teams' performance within a given framework is often referenced. This may involve comparing the agility of different organizations. However, it's important to note that agility is subjective, making it challenging to quantify. Moreover, the emphasis on maturity aligns more with conventional manufacturing processes than the agility the Manifesto for Agile Software Development promoted.

The manifesto's values and principles serve as a constant reminder of a fundamental concept: whatever you create is intended for real-world use by real people in real situations. The agile approach prioritizes outcomes and individuals over processes and organizational structures.

But this raises another question: If processes don't matter, can a team be considered mature if it operates within a (supposedly) agile framework? In contrast, other teams or departments continue to employ outdated

---

[3] https://agilemanifesto.org/

management techniques that disrupt the workflow.

Unlike traditional maturity models, the manifesto emphasizes adaptation and continual improvement, allowing gradual evolution. This raises questions about whether "agile maturity" might be a hidden paradox. The debate revolves around emphasizing evolution or maturity within agile environments. However, it is not a rigid rule to choose any one of those options; organizations, teams, and individuals can achieve growth in both terms by exploring new ideas and perspectives.

The misconception

In many organizations, leaders often talk about their level of agile maturity, claiming they are mature in "Agile, " Scrum, development, or even the organization as a whole. However, their concept of maturity differs from the psychological definition of maturity, which encompasses mental, physical, emotional, and bodily growth and development. A holistic maturity, to be precise. In the business world, a concept similar to the CMMI model[4]. The chaotic, aware, enabled, managed, and optimized model (CMM) outlines different maturity levels in business processes.

Chaotic: Processes are unpredictable and uncontrolled.

Aware: Organizations recognize the need for process improvement.

Enabled: Basic processes are in place, and there's some consistency.

Manage: Processes (in place at the time) are well-documented and standardized, allowing for more effective control.

Optimize: Continuous improvement is the focus, and processes are highly efficient and adaptable.

This misconception is focused on doing agile frameworks instead of being in an agile environment.

A new approach to agile maturity (Agile x Maturity)

In its traditional form, agile maturity involves a set of levels or markers individuals or businesses can achieve. These markers are used to determine

---

[4] https://en.wikipedia.org/wiki/Capability_Maturity_Model_Integration

maturity and success in implementing agile principles. However, this approach often involves generic comparisons to others based on milestones and steps set by previous markers. While this can be useful in determining whether a business is within normal ranges, it may not be the best approach in today's rapidly changing markets.

To truly develop the organization to balance agility and maturity, we must discard the idea that agility is only about the frameworks. In the current market environment, businesses must adopt agile principles to keep up with the pace of change. Agile principles do not only apply to producing physical products or software. Services are moving into agile environments. Even the public sector is benefiting from forming agile environments. Many people are unaware that agile behaviors and methodologies were used in the military for centuries under decentralized command. Agile methods also have a long history, dating back to the 1940s with the development of Kanban. The RUP era model, Lean, and Scrum emerged in the 80s. So, it is not a new concept. Even the frameworks themselves have evolved. Nothing is in a fixed state.

The manifesto[5] was created in 2001 and aimed to develop a better way of building software based on their collective experiences. They distilled their insights into four core values and 12 principles that provide a relatively straightforward framework for implementing agile principles. Since it was built for software development, people didn't see it as a possible blueprint for creating similar environments for other parts of the organizations until much later.

Considering the principles it created, maturity in an agile environment should be viewed as the organization's ability and discipline to continuously improve and evolve agile processes rather than trying to hit a set of fixed markers. Businesses should focus on identifying areas that need improvement and adapting their approach to meet their organization's unique needs. By adopting a continuous improvement mental model and embracing agile principles, businesses can stay ahead of the curve and remain competitive in today's rapidly changing markets.

Since we aim to balance evolution and maturity, we must get a few things straight: looking at agile values and principles and trying to tie them to a

---

[5] https://agilemanifesto.org/

maturity point of view, we obtain something that does not fit.

Think about some of the areas of focus people use to state that they mature in agility:

- How well did we DO something?
- How well did we DO our Scrum?
- Do we DO our Scrum events?
- How well DO we finish our sprints?
- How well is the teamwork based on our stats? (DOING)

The answers to those questions are used to provide the false hope that they are in a functioning agile environment. Even though the questions themselves might give a false view that the organization is indeed taking both aspects in development if you analyze closely, the same answers will tell you that all that is being done is still using traditional methods and management styles and disguising them as agility.

Traditionally, it was about how well and efficient teams were when they completed work. They consider the results mature because they can meet each step faster than before or with fewer hiccups and incidents. They mix agile terms in a traditional flow and create a hybrid when discussing maturity because they can deliver something faster. This common practice of disguising traditional methods as agile only leads to the appearance of agility without embracing agility's essence. What they are doing is not agile because speed is only one of the byproducts of an agile environment. True agility involves much more than just speed and efficiency. Every aspect needs to be done within each step to move forward and continue.

In a truly agile environment, the focus is on delivering value most effectively and efficiently, using iterative and adaptive mental models[6]. Rather than just completing each step faster, agile teams constantly strive to improve their operations, learn from feedback, and adapt to changing requirements. Therefore, mixing agile terms into a traditional flow only creates a hybrid approach that falls short of achieving the full benefits of an agile environment. Using agile terms to justify faster delivery without embracing the true spirit of agility can lead to a false sense of maturity and achievement.

---

[6] The fifth Discipline – Peter M. Senge

Teamwork is more than a framework.

Any environment can be agile if the focus is on teams and not just a group of individuals following the steps of a framework. Most agile teams in software development today are matrix teams, meaning they have developers, QA, product owners, product managers, or business stakeholders. However, while they think they work as a team, they don't work as a team. It's like a table hockey game where the forwards, defensemen, and goalie can only go to a certain point. The same can be said for non-software teams in an agile environment; the only difference is what is delivered.

When organizations end up with fragmented teams, even if there is some overlap, there is still a high probability that they will run into problems due to behavior changes that did not happen in creating the agile environment. That lack of behavioral change is 'collaboration.' Without cohesive collaboration and a shift in behavior, merely following the steps in a framework will not make an organization truly agile. The focus should not just be on doing the steps; that would return to the traditional approach. It should create an environment where teams can work together to solve problems and innovate. In other words, it's about fostering a culture where teams collaborate seamlessly and are empowered to make decisions. Only these organizations can consider themselves genuinely mature and agile.

Focusing solely on the steps within a framework is where the challenge lies in achieving maturity. The desire to attain a certain level of maturity is natural and understandable. However, it's important to remember that achieving maturity in manufacturing and waterfall methodologies means creating a product quickly, efficiently, and repeatably with a decreased bottom line. However, in an agile environment, it's not just about the flow of work but also a new way of thinking, gathering information, and executing and delivering constant feedback to validate the hypothesis of the problem being solved.

Employing rigid processes isn't the agile way.

Despite agile methodologies and frameworks being around for nearly 80 years, organizations still struggle to adopt them fully. Perhaps the issue lies in the obsession with achieving "maturity" in the context of agility. While there's nothing wrong with striving for maturity in getting the job done, it doesn't work well within an agile environment. Agility is not about ad hoc changes and chaos but discipline and a structured approach to problem-solving.

Jocko Willink's quote, "Discipline is the pathway to freedom,"[7] resonates with the principles of agility. An agile team requires discipline to create more freedom and opportunities for innovation to meet the customer's needs. The more disciplined the team, the easier it is to find the right path to deliver a valuable product. Willink also discusses decentralized command with missions in his book Extreme Ownership. This concept aligns with agile principles, where the team is given a clear goal and the freedom to figure out how to achieve it within their work guidelines. This approach encourages a sense of stewardship and accountability within the team.

However, there are scenarios where traditional environments and agile teams clash, leading to frustration and a lack of collaboration. In organizations with several departments and a mix of agile and traditional teams, traditional teams follow strict hierarchies, adhere to specific handoffs and lack transparency. This can cause agile teams to be frustrated while working with them, leading to escalating issues. Additionally, traditional teams may have cognitive biases towards agile teams, thinking they are ad hoc, chaotic, and lack discipline.

Imagine a race where teams are in pairs of cars and must cross the finish line simultaneously. One car is a Corvette (a well-run agile team) with so much horsepower, while the other is a Chevette (traditional team) with little horsepower. In such a scenario, it's a recipe for frustration and inefficiency. Either the Chevette burns itself out trying to keep up with the Corvette, or the Corvette holds back its power to keep pace with the Chevette. In either case, both teams face frustration and difficulty achieving their goals. This situation is called the Corvette Chevette paradox. This paradox creates an environment that does not help anyone involved.

Gary Mottershead's quote, "A bad system can destroy good people," emphasizes the importance of allowing agility to grow organically

---

[7] Extreme Ownership, Jocko Willink

throughout the organization. Organizations risk creating a bad system that hinders collaboration, innovation, and overall success by constraining agility in specific areas. Agile teams require the freedom to work within a disciplined environment to achieve their goals, and traditional teams need to understand the benefits of agility and how to work collaboratively towards a common goal. Only by breaking down these barriers can organizations achieve true agility and success.

Evolution comes from viewing teams in an agile environment as living organisms. Different teams are different cells working together as different organs within the body. They work together to survive, succeed, and reach a level better than the day before. They adapt to the environment, much like in an agile environment; it is about adaptation.

In an agile environment, instead of the common goal of survival, the common goal is aligning with the organization's goals and values. Aligning with those goals and values, along with the teams working independently to help achieve them, ensures a smoother flow of work and ideas.

Once you have this smoother flow, you can focus on being strategic. When we move away from the tactical, things start to progress from an evolutionary viewpoint. One of the things that will help with that evolution is creating those agile values, nurturing a set of agile values unique to your organization, and creating something that is not just a copy and paste of the Manifesto but organic to the organization and its teams.

Senior leadership working throughout the organization to have the goals and guidance gives everyone a sense of stewardship to help achieve them.

Look at Google, for instance. Go to their corporate site and look at their values[8]. Could you read them in an agile frame of mind? Although they don't directly say agile within their values, they do have that view of why they are doing what they're doing. It builds out into what they develop and what they produce. It's about the engagement that helps get those agile values. Agile values are now created with much collaboration to ensure they resonate with everyone and that there is some stewardship to them. It helps motivate and gives purpose to the work done.

When everyone is involved, they start seeing those agile values, and with

---

[8] https://about.google/intl/ALL_us/commitments/

leadership also living those values, it will help improve focus on self-managed teams so that everyone is in sync with how to meet those needs.

The self-managed teams, cells that work together, work on opportunities for better continuous improvement. Continuous improvement is just another form of evolution. Teams are continuously evolving as they progress on their agile journey. Evolution is about adapting to the environment so that an organism can survive and have a good life. Where would we see that in the workplace? Employee satisfaction.

When an organism has issues with one of its internal systems, the entire body will struggle, no different than a team where employee satisfaction is low. It is necessary to ensure that self-managed teams, those individual cells, are set up and have what they need to be prosperous and healthy. That will help make things better and evolve because that evolution will help the teams get the job done.

Building an Agile Environment through evolution and maturity.

To achieve agility, it's crucial to enable teams to understand the organization's goals, strategic goals, and desired outcomes for their customers and clients. This alignment will help everyone work together towards a common goal. However, being agile is not just about following a framework or using specific tools; it's about using those tools effectively and embodying agile values.

Effective leadership in an agile environment involves providing a vision and guidance to the team while allowing them to chart their path to achieve the desired outcomes. However, there may be times when intervention is necessary to steer the team back on course or adapt to changes in the market.

Product discovery, rather than product development, is an important aspect of agility. It involves understanding customer needs and problems and developing features that address them effectively rather than simply building features and hoping they will hit the mark.

Organizations must have clear, agile values and understanding to adapt to change effectively. Failure to do so can result in stress, firefighting, and the delivery of obsolete products or services.

What if we understand how to iterate and increment through a flow and the right leadership style that can easily adapt? Having that environment makes adapting second nature. That's where the value is - accepting change and adapting to change.

So, why do we run into problems with changes? It's because the structure of the term "maturity" and its mindset can be crippling and stiffen teams up, making it difficult for them to adapt. This, in turn, makes scalability difficult. From an evolution perspective, we can become scalable by cultivating agile values, mental models, and behaviors within our organization.

By fostering these agile values and behaviors within our organization, we can enhance our capacity for scalability and adaptability. This approach will help improve teams and lead to improved success through everyone's involvement, participation, and dedication in getting the work done and moving forward.

It's important to understand that moving to an agile environment is a journey, not a destination and that agility and maturity are closely intertwined. Maturity involves reaching specific milestones or levels of competence, like checking items off a predefined checklist. In contrast, agility is about continuous adaptation and progression. The combination of the two gives birth to an agile environment that continually refines what and how it does it, demonstrating a higher level of maturity and discipline in its flexibility and ability to respond to change effectively.

If we look at the Manifesto from a philosophical perspective, everyone has different interpretations - some good and some bad. It's best to find a balance when interpreting and not take things to the extreme. Not everyone needs to see it the same way, as not everyone will agree on Descartes's meaning:[9] "I think therefore I am." There are general guidelines that everyone will see, but the approach to them will be different. It should be about what is best for the organization to approach agility to survive and succeed. Agile environments have their way, ideas, and path to get to where they want to be, and they don't chase other ways of achieving goals.

---

[9] Discourse on the Method

We have learned that the traditional mindset of maturity does not work well with the processes and flows alone within agile environments. But modern organizations still need it. What is necessary is to merge agility, behaviors, and mental models in these processes to achieve different goals and improve how things get done. To achieve success, it is essential to understand that there is no one-size-fits-all agile playbook. Instead, an organization should have multiple playbooks in sync to create an agile ecosystem. Frameworks are tools used for structure and discipline within the environment but are not written in stone. Agility is about constantly changing and improving within those guidelines. It involves changing how we deal with others to identify issues and find solutions. It aims to make things easier for organizations to grow. Treating organizations as organisms is an excellent way to understand how agility is about evolution, not maturity. Maturity is just a small part of it, ensuring the processes currently in the place are working well. It is, by no means, meant to ensure nothing changes over time. If it doesn't work, replace it with what does and then make it a part of the checklist you employ to ensure you are heading to success.

According to the State of Agile 2020 report, 95% of organizations involved would not be considered agile. Although there are many reasons why their agile transformations fail, the root cause is often hidden traditional behaviors causing clashes. Organizations must identify and deal with these hidden behaviors to become agile. They must create an organic, agile environment that will grow naturally to evolve rather than forcing it on their people.

Doing Agile vs. Being Agile

We must remember that we will focus on being agile, not just doing it. A significant difference exists between 'doing' and 'being' agile. This distinction is crucial and will aid in understanding the two concepts. Let's briefly discuss what 'doing agile' means to clarify further.

Referring to the earlier Golden Circle example, "doing agile" would be going from the outside of the circle to the inside. The primary focus is on the frameworks themselves, and the identity of the organization's values gets lost or faded due to that shift in focus.

Doing agile

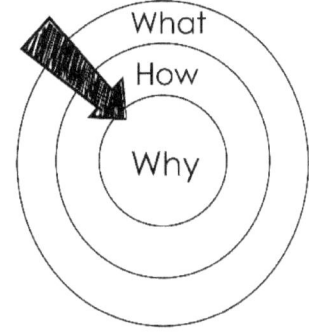

Figure Doing Agile

In contrast, 'Being agile' takes the inverse approach. We start with the 'why,' then move to the 'how,' and finally to the 'what.' This book emphasizes this perspective, focusing first on the 'why' behind agile practices, followed by the 'how' and the 'what.' Each section will maintain this focus, helping you truly understand and implement agile in a way that transforms your mindset and practice.

Being agile

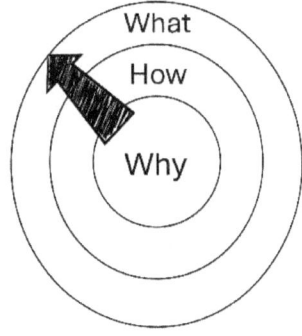

Figure Being Agile

10 AREAS TO ACHIEVE A TRUE AGILE ENVIRONMENT.

So, to build a thriving agile environment, we have ten focus areas. These areas are divided into three main sections.

Foundation

1. Start
2. Goals
3. Design

System

4. Pathway
5. Culture
6. Trust

Evolve

7. Quality
8. Evolving
9. Change Management
10. Growing.

First, you have the 'Foundation,' which lays the groundwork. Next, we have the 'System' involved, where the mechanics of the environment are addressed. Finally, there's the 'Evolvd,' focusing on expanding and adapting the approach. It's important to note that this isn't just about a product, service, or the specific framework used. It's about the behaviors and underlying actions within those frameworks expected to achieve that high value.

Although you can jump chapters to focus on different areas, reading from beginning to end on the first read is advisable. There is a flow where the previous chapter will impact the next, creating a foundation to build on. The end of the book is intended to have a plan to evolve the agile environment.

If you are about to start the agile journey, this book will give you a glimpse into the future and what is needed to achieve the benefits of agility. If teams have already transformed, this book is an opportunity to find deeply hidden anti-patterns that can cause frustration or not see the full value.

This is not a start-over initiative; it can draw a line in the sand to see where the agile environment is and define goals to improve continuously at providing internal and external value.

Workbooks

You will have a workbook section to work on as we go through each section. In these workbooks, an additional write-up on the subject and a series of questions are meant to dig deep into your team and organization, crafted to help you create an agile environment while identifying the root causes of the issues. Understanding these underlying issues and root causes will help you overcome obstacles and mature as an agile team, department, and organization to move forward continuously.

Each of these sections builds on one another, and by the end, you will have developed your agile environment. The great thing about these workbook sections is that there are sections where there will be issues and things that you can start working on right away. It also provides the opportunity to identify actionable steps within a timeline. This immediate applicability makes the workbook especially valuable, enabling you to deliver value immediately.

STAGE 1 OVERVIEW:

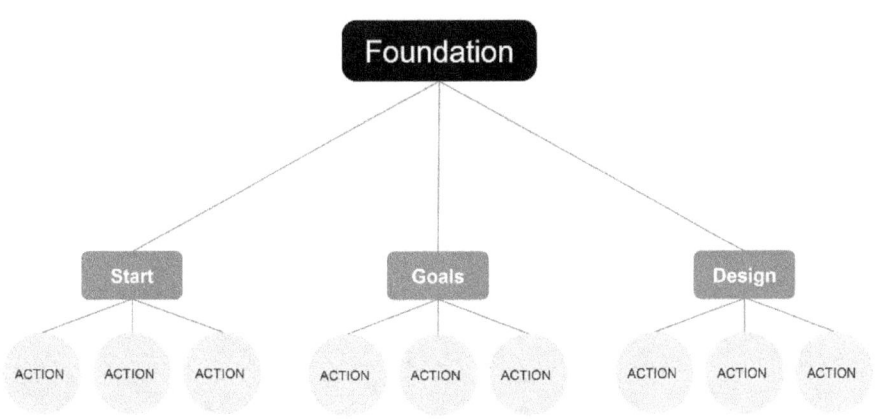

Figure Example of how the different stages are set up

So now we will go into stage one, where we look at the foundation. The foundation consists of 'Start,' 'Goals,' and 'Design.' These three stages are separate, each with its actions, and we will go through each one. In each chapter, you'll see these foundations, and we'll break them down. When you go through the workbook, you might find it long and filled with many questions. This is because uncovering those underlying issues takes a lot of work. However, once you find and resolve them and have the right setup for your team, the potential for what your team can produce and achieve is limitless.

As we go through this journey, remember that it starts with leadership. I'm not just talking about executives or senior managers or directors. Leadership is about everyone on the team. Everyone has a leadership role in what they do as a team. It's about helping everyone understand how to function and work together to be agile. Once we start on the right foot, everything will improve.

CHAPTER 01 | START HERE

How to start on the right foot with the right change mindset

Goals	Why	How	What
Have a plan to reset the understanding of agile value	The Start or Restart is important	To get the plan off to a good start.	To use for achieving the start of a strong foundation.
Leadership	**Agile Values**	**Linking**	**Value chain**
Shift to a true Servant leader	Developing tools and methods that embody agile values	The importance of linking to organization values	Important to get the full picture of the flow.

Figure 1-4

In each chapter, you're going to come across some particular goals. We aim to dissect those goals into the why, the how, and the what, so that's what we'll be looking for. By the end of this section, our goal is to have a plan to reset our understanding of agile value. Remember, being in an agile environment is all about continuously improving, so when I refer to starting or restarting, it means that if you have previously undergone an agile transformation with your teams, you're not starting from scratch. Instead, you are refocusing on the essence of being agile and adapting to necessary changes.

For those about to transform, this will give you a leg up in being agile, providing a foundational advantage for excelling in agility and ensuring minimal obstacles or impediments. The focus here is on leadership, understanding agile values, and establishing a value chain within your team and development process. The key is understanding how these elements interconnect, creating a cohesive agile environment.

START STRUGGLES:

When agile teams face difficulties in linking agile values to their leadership, it typically leads to three common issues:

- There's a force of habit,
- The old way of doing things
- Trying to put a square peg in a round hole.

Addressing these issues has proven effective, so that we will incorporate these solutions into our agile environment. Another challenge we often face is looking in the wrong direction. By this, as an example, the product team tends to view development teams more as enablers rather than integral parts of the value chain. We will explore a value chain example later in this chapter, illustrating that this perception is mistaken. Development teams are crucial to the value chain and should be recognized.

So, our goal is to shift from the ineffective approach of forcing a square peg into a round hole and looking in the wrong direction to establishing a solid foundation for achieving real value. How are we going to do that? Well, there are three actions:

- Leadership Understanding,
- Determining Your Agile Values
- Understanding The Value Chain

After implementing these three actions and applying this function at the start, you'll establish a solid base for your environment. It's crucial to understand that if leadership doesn't grasp the 'why' of an agile environment, they'll struggle to realize its total value. To address this, we're going to break things down further.

Much like any evolving environment, fostering an agile culture demands the presence of a catalyst—a driving force that not only initiates change and drives transformation but also sustains it. In an agile context, it is something that is aware of the surrounding environment and is focused on success. The following pages aim to give you an understanding of this crucial concept concerning agile values, taking them beyond the Manifesto and emphasizing their relevance to teams. It is still the same concept; we will see how it helps teams. We will explore how these agile values serve as the guiding 'why' for your team, steering them toward successful outcomes and instilling the right agile behaviors to get the job done.

Agile methodologies offer a flexible and iterative approach to project management, enabling teams to respond swiftly to evolving requirements and deliver high-quality results. However, it's important to emphasize that creating such an environment requires more than just adopting a set of practices. It necessitates a catalyst, which serves as the driving force that initiates the needed change for those practices.

Your goal is to evolve into a true servant leader. Why? Because teams can be agile and successful in everything they do. How are you going to achieve this? By embodying agile values, creating the right environment, and establishing a clear vision. It boils down to the fact that you are an agile leader who is pivotal in steering your team towards agile success.

Leadership Understanding

Without leadership understanding and accepting the why of agile, they will never achieve full value.

Goals	Why	How	What
Shift to a True Servant Leader	empowering teams to be agile and successful in all their endeavors	I aim to demonstrate my commitment to agile values, foster an agile environment, and collaboratively establish a clear vision	As an agile leader
Base Line	**Shift**	**Engage**	**Future state**
Need to understand where you are before you can evolve	Paradigm shift from traditional to agile management	Develop an engagement plan that will set a transparent team	Develop a clear cultural plan for the team

Figure 1-5

Understanding the catalyst

The first step is to understand the significance of this catalyst; only then will we know what that catalyst is. I refer to understanding it as the initial step because its interpretation varies from one company to another. The needs and goals change, which is why we need to gain a deeper understanding of their impact on teams and the organization. So, how will you find out what it is for your organization? This catalyst compels us to introspect and assess how things are currently being done at the team level and within the broader organizational context.

Baseline

"It is important that we know where we come from because if you do not know where you come from, then you don't know where you are, and if you don't know where you are, you don't know where you' 're going. And if you don't know where you're going, you're probably going wrong. " - Terry Pratchett.

Let's establish a baseline to understand our current position before moving forward. When organizations undergo an agile transformation, they often view it simply as implementing a framework. They might have a general idea of their actions, but their focus is usually more on progressing with the framework. This approach sometimes lacks proper documentation or a definitive baseline. One often missed is the absence of a SWOT analysis before the transformation, which is crucial to understanding potential outcomes, strengths, and weaknesses in the team's agile capabilities.

A key aspect that is frequently overlooked is the lack of metrics. Teams might recognize that things are getting done faster, but the specifics, such as the degree of speed improvement, quality enhancement, and overall productivity, are not adequately measured. How can we assess success without these metrics? In a future section, we will discuss this aspect more - metrics, the right perspective, and the blend of qualitative and quantitative data needed to truly understand the value being delivered. Without establishing this baseline, measuring progress becomes challenging because you don't know where you started.

Shift

Retrospectives aren't just for the team; leadership should reflect on how things progress. But let's save that dialogue for another topic. The key takeaway is that agile environments require more than sending emails or putting motivational posters or quotes on digital message boards. It's a more profound commitment. And we must understand that agile values are not set in stone; they're more like stickies. They can be moved, removed, changed, and evolved. They serve as guidelines for agility, allowing you to adapt and make your team more efficient.

Unfortunately, the tendency for "command and control" behaviors is deeply ingrained and challenging to eliminate from any workplace. This is especially true in business settings where leaders' compensation often hinges on achieving tangible results. Consequently, many leaders must closely monitor operations to ensure their efforts benefit them personally.

Leaders often prioritize short-term gains over long-term strategic thinking in pursuing personal gain. Simon Sinek's book, "The Infinite Game," highlights the misalignment between these leaders and the creation of a lasting legacy that extends beyond their careers. By fixating on control and immediate outcomes, leaders inadvertently set in motion events that reverberate throughout the organization.

One significant consequence of leadership changes is the subsequent transformation within the organization. When new leaders assume their roles, they typically introduce changes aligning with their vision of success. These changes can be drastic, reshaping how work is done and distributed among employees. The resulting upheaval can contribute to a short lifespan for senior leaders in their positions, including those in C-suite roles. Harvard Business Review states the average tenure of an executive is just over seven years[10]. Intriguingly, this phenomenon mirrors the average term of employees within a company, suggesting a potential correlation.

The potential reason behind this correlation lies in the tactical nature of leadership, which prioritizes self-interest over broader organizational considerations. As leaders secure what they need to achieve personal goals,

---

[10] https://hbr.org/2019/11/the-truth-about-ceo-tenure

they may inadvertently create an environment where employees grow dissatisfied and seek better opportunities elsewhere that align with their goals and values.

However, imagine if leadership were to shift its focus towards more strategic behaviors and actions. What if leaders genuinely grasped the essence of agility and its long-term benefits? In such a scenario, leaders might be more inclined to invest their energy in building a sustainable and adaptive organization. This shift could foster an environment that promotes longevity, not only for leaders but also for employees.

While the prevalence of such leadership practices is limited, various studies have demonstrated the positive outcomes associated with energized, exciting, fair, and equitable work environments. Employee loyalty is linked to these factors, and they have been found to drive higher levels of productivity and innovation.

To overcome these tendencies, leaders must recognize the importance of staying true to the agile principles they initially embraced. They need to constantly remind themselves and their teams of the benefits of agile mental models and the need for servant leadership. By doing so, they can create an environment that encourages autonomy, collaboration, and continuous improvement, allowing teams to fully embrace and embody agile practices.

Shifting from a "my way or your way" mentality to a symmetrical collaborative approach is essential to drive successful agile transformations. Leaders need to change how they perceive and behave concerning agile environments. In the book Agility Leadership by Bill Joyner and Stephen Josephs, leaders must move out of the "Heroic" set of behaviors and move to the "Post-Heroic" behaviors. "Heroic" Behaviors in traditional views of leadership often involve bosses dictating tasks, while newer perspectives encourage leaders to work alongside their teams.

However, a third perspective is "leading from behind," which can be valuable. Leading from behind involves guiding the team and allowing stewardship and responsibility for work. It is comparable to a shepherd guiding a flock of sheep, where the shepherd doesn't lead from the front but instead supports and guides from behind.

It is vital to recognize that every individual within an organization has a leadership component, whether implicitly or explicitly. Everyone has a role to play, and when they fully accept and embrace their responsibilities, a fully functioning agile environment can emerge. An evolutionary change can occur by helping individuals understand how to contribute to the collective effort, fostering collaboration, and promoting mutual support. This shift towards a more agile and inclusive culture sets the stage for a positive transformation that benefits everyone involved.

Embracing a set of strategic behaviors and true agility in leadership can extend leaders' tenures and create a more fulfilling and loyal employee base. By breaking free from the constraints of short-term thinking and focusing on long-term sustainability, leaders can foster an organizational environment that thrives on adaptability and continuous improvement. This way, in turn, drives productivity, innovation, and overall success.

Agile mental model

To optimize productivity and efficiency, teams are shifting from merely following agile practices to embracing agility through the right behaviors. This shift requires us to understand the "why" behind our actions and make decisions based on that understanding. By reading this book, you have already demonstrated your commitment to a more agile path. The workbook section will include questions and actions to help you build a foundation for this journey. Some of these actions can be implemented immediately, allowing you to take meaningful steps toward agility.

Many books and resources emphasize the importance of adopting an agile mindset, but a rigid " fixed attitude, disposition, or mood"[11] may not be suitable for achieving true agility. Instead, agility is about being adaptive and open to change. In this context, understanding idle time in software development becomes relevant. Embracing agility means acknowledging that idle time is not necessarily wasted; it can allow team members to reassess, collaborate, and adjust their approach.

Without addressing leadership first, all other aspects of agility will suffer. Critical areas will fall to neglect, metrics will be lacking or misused, and the organization will struggle to embody agility truly. Building an agile environment begins with establishing trust and eliminating fear. We must

---

[11] https://www.dictionary.com/browse/mindset

acknowledge that "my way or the highway" is not the path forward. Instead, we must adopt a collective set of behaviors that values learning and improvement, allowing us to advance continually without becoming stagnant.

It is crucial to create an environment where everyone believes in and supports agile values. Alignment and effective communication across the organization enhance this process, enabling everyone to understand what must happen and prevent stagnation. Agility is not a fixed state but an evolving journey. As we progress, our understanding of agile values deepens, and we gain insights into our position within the value chain. Identifying bottlenecks and areas for improvement becomes an integral part of this process, supported by a robust metrics program.

Engage

Any transformation involves a change in behavior, and leadership is no exception. Typically, there are three paths that this can take. Firstly, there's a situation where leaders fully trust and provide everything necessary for success, truly embracing agility. However, about 95% of the time, the situation either veers left or right, often driven by fear.

When veering right, leaders aim to be agile and successful. But in stressful situations or when things start going wrong, they return to their old ways, reverting to command and control because it's comfortable. This is how they used to handle things. Alternatively, veering left happens when teams practice agile, using frameworks like Scrum, SAFe™, or LeSS, but leaders still micromanage and command, resisting the agile philosophy. This creates a division between 'my way' and 'your way' rather than fostering an 'our way' mental model.

The transformation required is in how leaders feel and behave with agile. Traditionally, the boss tells you what to do. The newer approach involves the leader working with the team. A third, preferable approach is leading from behind, like a shepherd guiding a flock of sheep, not leading from the front but from behind. This is not to suggest that employees are sheep but to emphasize the stewardship of leaders who provide guidance, letting the teams work through what needs to be done independently.

To effectively create and implement agile environments within an organization, it is essential to not only establish a conducive environment that fosters learning and encourages teams to embrace agility but also to develop tools and methods that enable the cultivation of agile values and ensure a clear understanding of organizational agility across the entire organization, not just within individual teams.

Future State

We need to ensure continuous engagement and understanding of the future state. Having the right engagement plan to maintain transparency is important to ensure a clear perspective on the future state. Keeping with the flow detailed earlier, we do not want the future state seen as what you want, how you want things, and why you want them. Remember, this is the wrong order.

The future state is essentially about why we aim for our goals, how we plan to get there, and what actions we will take. This future state is deeply connected to your mission, vision, and agile values, which we'll discuss later. An identified future state helps drive continuous learning and improvement, guiding teams to move forward, not backward. Learn from issues and mistakes without fearing failure. Future states must create an environment where there is no deriding of anyone for failure; instead, focus on learning and succeeding.

So, the workbook you will find at the end of this chapter is designed to help you gain understanding. It prompts you to look inward at your teams and the wider organization regarding how things are being done. Now, we want to identify and articulate those agile values clearly.

Determine agile values

Without specific agile values that fit the team culture there will be no dedication to being agile.

Goals	Why	How	What
Tools and methods to develop agile values	ensuring that teams grasp the organization's expectations regarding agility	I aim to work collaboratively to establish, implement, and maintain agile values	As an agile leader
Creative Values	**Alignment**	**Communicate**	**Maintain**
Determine the values that resonate with the culture and teams	Alignment to enterprise values mission and vision	Develop a communication plan to distribute values	Recognize values may change and evolve

Figure 1-6

In an ever-evolving agile setting, tailoring the agile values to align with your teams is vital. Simply copying generic agile values won't address your organization's unique requirements and obstacles, leading to confusion. This lack of precise alignment causes problems in many organizations, ultimately affecting quality. Teams often feel frustrated when they know the work they must do from an agile perspective but lack a clear understanding of the underlying purpose. These agile values will guide how work is done and determine the tools and methods used.

We aim to create these agile values and learn from them. Consider Figure 1-4: it's broken down to highlight the goal of developing tools and methods that embody these values. The objective is to establish an environment where agile values naturally emerge, ensuring both the team and the organization grasp the expectations of organizational agility. So, how do we start? We need to create values that resonate with the teams, providing them with guidance. From my experience with teams, before defining agile values, they often felt frustrated and lost the "why" behind their work. This loss of purpose led to frustrations and issues impacting the product.

Some techniques used to help drive out the collective agile values were open-space meetings for mind mapping and brainstorming. This collaborative process, involving activities like mind mapping and brainstorming, helped team members collectively articulate what an agile environment meant to them. The goal was to identify guiding principles and values that align with their unique context. Engaging team members in this process enhanced synchronization and shared understanding, empowering the team to work together effectively towards their goals. The aim was to extract words that encapsulated what agile meant to them and provided guidance.

For example, consider Google. Google has numerous values, but if you look at its core values, like "focus on the user and all else will follow" and "do one thing really well," it doesn't explicitly mention agile concepts. Yet, suppose you align these with agile principles, such as prioritizing customer collaboration over contract negotiation. In that case, you can see how Google rephrased these values to fit its team dynamics and overall work approach.

Alignment

Next, it's crucial to ensure alignment. You want the agile values to seamlessly fit with the organization's values, vision, and mission. Google, again, serves as a prime example of this perfect alignment. Clear messaging and alignment significantly empower teams to move forward more effectively.

Therefore, it's essential to ensure that agile values align with the organization's and team's values, fitting into the overall vision and mission. This alignment enhances the team's ability to accomplish its goals. Conversely, teams might face difficulties without this alignment, making collaboration and task completion challenging for everyone involved.

Communicate

Effective communication is essential, too, and by communication, I mean more than what is often done by management, such as merely sending out a memo stating, "Here are our agile values; be agile." It's much more profound. You want to nurture, grow, and manage the team to succeed and flourish. Supporting individuals is crucial so they, too, can thrive and achieve success. Consider the concept of Obeya rooms. If you're unfamiliar with Obeya rooms, they are spaces where visual anchoring occurs. These rooms don't just display values; they promote transparency by visually linking different aspects.

In this day and age, you can have an Obeya room as a virtual space, like a Confluence page or Mural/Miro, accommodating remote or geographically dispersed team members. This virtual space lets everyone see how things are interconnected, emphasizing visual information management. This approach is far more effective in communicating agile values than motivational posters or a tagline in an email signature. The goal is to create a space where everyone can see and understand how agile values align with the team and the broader organization transparently and engagingly.

- **Walk the talk**

"Walking the talk" is essential, especially for managers and senior leaders in leadership roles. Reflecting on an experience with one of my clients, we successfully created agile values but encountered a major challenge: the leadership didn't walk the talk. They worked through the process, we created those agile values, and the teams established the workflow, but then the leadership just stepped back and stayed in their offices. They weren't actively communicating with the teams, not engaging in 'gemba walks' or holding 'Lean Coffees.'

The essence of walking the talk is going out to see how things are being done and engaging in discussions like Lean Coffee, akin to a small town hall meeting with a few people. This is where topics are discussed, issues are worked through, and the servant leader role is played to support and improve the team's environment.

When leadership walks the talk, and everyone does the same, it creates a unified language within the organization. Communication improves, and things flow more smoothly. This approach can reduce common problems in many organizations, like frequent escalations requiring the involvement of senior management. With everyone on the same page, trying to resolve issues becomes a more streamlined and effective process.

Maintain

When you create a transparent environment, and leadership fosters this transparency, it grows and becomes agile. This allows everyone to focus and efficiently get the work done. Maintaining agile values is one of the things that needs to happen constantly from inception. By 'maintaining,' I mean ensuring things are continuously moving forward. If you 'set it and forget it'—establish agile values and then disengage—you're not learning or improving, and everything becomes stale. Without continuous flow, there's no progress.

Techniques like retrospectives are essential to ensure continuous improvement. This isn't just for the teams; leadership must also participate in retrospectives, such as a heartbeat retrospective, to evaluate how things are progressing. We'll go deeper into this in another discussion. But it's important to understand that being agile isn't about sending an email, displaying a motivational poster, or sharing a quote on a digital message board.

There's much more to it. These agile values are not set in stone but more like stickies—they can move, change, and evolve. They serve as guidelines for being agile, not rigid, and processes to be strictly followed. The goal is to continuously improve as a team, adapting what fits best to enhance efficiency. In our next discussion, we'll also talk about the value chain.

A value chain contains valuable information to make effective decisions on what can be worked on.

Goals	Why	How	What
Understanding the importance of value chains helps with being agile	So that we have a clear picture of where more value can be found	We want to have a clear understanding of the entire flow,	Value chains

Value Chain	Current State	Future state	Plan
Understand the value of value chains	A deeper understanding the current value stream	Collaborative work effort have an understanding of where they want to go	A plan to how to get there with help from the agile values.

Figure 1-7

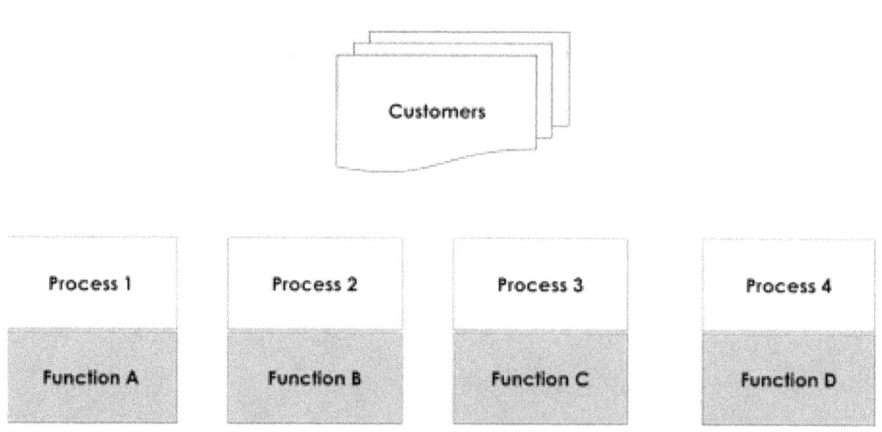

Figure 1-8

The value chain is a powerful tool that can greatly help organizations, and it's a common practice for most to employ it. However, the key is understanding where improvements can be made within the value chain.

It helps provide some root cause analysis of where issues may lie, identifying those bottlenecks. Our approach will go through the value chain to understand current and future states. We won't be breaking it up; instead, we must focus on understanding it.

To illustrate this, consider an example from the book 'Value Stream Mapping.'[12] This example will help us see how value chain analysis can be applied practically, providing insights into streamlining processes and enhancing organizational efficiency.

You have your customer, and then there are various processes like Process A, which functions through to Process B, then Process C, and finally, to Process D. One crucial point to understand is that Processes 1, 2, and 3 aren't isolated; they are interconnected within the larger framework. For instance, Process 3 could involve the actual development of the product. This includes activities like scrum sprints, daily meetings, processing of the user story, testing of the story, and then progressing to the next phase.

As we progress, you'll see that one of the key elements within a value chain is metrics. There are three basic metrics within a value stream:

- Process Time,
- lead time
- percent complete and accurate.

Our process time is the duration from input to output, essentially your work time. For example, when making a coffee cup, the processing time starts when the ceramic is handed over to the person or team. It continues as they work on shaping, painting, and drying the cup until it's ready to be shipped.

Lead time, on the other hand, refers to the total throughput time. This includes the processing time, the time spent waiting for inputs, and the time until the output is ready to be handed off to the next stage. Lastly, your percent complete reflects the quality of work and the extent to which work is being returned for rework or corrections.

Some additional metrics are:

---

[12] Value Stream Mapping, Karen Martin and Mike Osterling

- Your work in progress,
- Number of people being work that is working on it
- Number of hours are being worked on it.
- Process effectiveness
- Demand rate
- Work trigger.

Understanding metrics is critical in identifying areas for improvement, especially in an agile environment. Depending on whom you discuss it with, metrics are being used. Some may not work through them all, not understand them, or feel they don't need them because they're being 'Agile.' As we will see, we can gain a lot of valuable information from metrics.

Taking the example we discussed earlier from the value stream mapping book, the lead time is one day, and the processing time is 10 minutes, but the quality is 50%. This means that 50% of the items being processed are sent back. The total process time to complete these items takes half a day, even though the process is only five minutes, resulting in 75% quality after reprocessing.

These metrics highlight areas for potential improvement. For instance, the initial 50% quality rate prompts questions about why it's so low. One solution might be working with partners to improve the quality of incoming items. Overall, for this particular value chain, the total lead time is about seven and a half days, the processing time is 65 minutes, and the activity ratio—which is the amount of process time to lead time—is 1.8%, with an overall quality of 68%.

Regarding the activity ratio, you might say that's pretty low for the amount of work being done. But, if you look through it, the average idle time is between 95 and 98%. Consider this: in most baseball games, the ball is in play much shorter than the game's duration. This doesn't imply everyone is idle in the remaining time; it's just that different aspects of work take varying amounts of time. For example, in software testing, creating a test case might take a day, but running it only a few seconds. Understanding this difference in the value chain was a shift for me, too. It's not about idle time being wasteful; it's about recognizing the different elements of work that contribute to the final product, even if they don't directly involve building it.

Looking at the current and future states is a crucial part of this analysis. If the current state shows a lead time of seven and a half days, perhaps the goal is to reduce this to five days, a 29% improvement. Maybe we aim to decrease the processing time and increase the activity ratio from 1.8% to 4%, improving overall quality. These are just targets based on what we believe we can achieve. It's not just one person but a team and collaborative event. That's where we get into planning.

Plan

When planning your value chain and identifying desired improvements, it becomes clear that the value chain is essentially another aspect of your 'why' in agile. It integrates into a broad, team-collaborative environment. This contrasts with organizational values, where employee involvement exists but may not extend to a broad team environment. Typically, vision and mission are driven by senior leadership. But if you see within the teams, they have a good idea of how to get the work done and what it means to them to be agile.

Creating your value chain involves several steps and can be a lengthy process. Some parts will progress quickly, while others will take longer due to being required. This is where the rubber hits the road. We all know that a plane uses most of its fuel during takeoff, and once it reaches cruising altitude, fuel consumption is considerably less. It's similar to a car at a stoplight using more fuel in a short period than when at cruising speed. In being agile, we aim to continuously move through processes efficiently to consume fewer resources and get more output.

Review

As a review, we want to shift from merely 'doing agile' to truly 'being agile.' This means understanding the 'why' before the 'what,' moving from a superficial approach to a more foundational one. These foundations are critical in achieving this transformation. It starts with leadership, as behavioral changes at the top ripple through the organization. Without this, achieving the full value of an agile environment becomes difficult. You miss out on critical spaces and metrics necessary for progress, leading to a struggle in maintaining agility. It's about creating an environment of trust and understanding, moving away from the 'My way or the highway' approach to an 'Our way,' where learning and improvement are continuous. This prevents stagnation and fosters an environment everyone believes in.

Creating agile values that everyone can support is crucial, as it benefits the individuals and supports the organization as a whole. When there is alignment and clear communication throughout, it significantly enhances the agility of the team. Being agile means everyone is 'walking the talk'[13] and speaking the same language, understanding what needs to be done. This prevents the environment from becoming stale as the team and the agile values evolve.

Understanding where we are within the value chain is crucial. We need to identify how things are placed, locate the bottlenecks, and pinpoint where improvements are needed, as this forms part of the metrics. A whole metrics model for an agile environment is available– you can find many on Google. But I encourage you to wait until we cover the section on continuous improvement. We will discuss using and creating an effective, robust metrics program.

For now, this lesson focuses on aiding leadership. Remember, leadership is not just for senior executives or managers; it encompasses everyone on the team. Every team member is a leader in their own right, and it's about how they collaborate based on the 'why.' When this understanding is in place, everything starts to align and improve.

So, we have a choice: to continue down how things are or take the path of how things should be. Your homework will involve a series of questions and actions in your workbook. These exercises are designed to help you build a roadmap for this journey. You'll find that some aspects can be implemented immediately.

---

[13] Great Big Agile, Jeff Daulton

WORKBOOK - 01

Leadership Understanding

Any time a transformation is needed, leadership is needed to ensure the expected behaviors for the change. Plenty of studies show that any change's success starts with leadership.

In 2018, an article in Leadership & Organization Development Journal: Implicit Change Leadership, Change Management, and Affective Commitment to Change[14] details the implicit leaders most involved in making change happen. The explicit leaders must show the same qualities expected for change; that is the foundation.

When we talk about leadership here, we mean all aspects of leadership.

- Having the right competencies (Strategic and technical) to understand why the change is needed and become champions.
- Execution competencies to ensure the change is successful. In this chapter, we discuss baselines and paradigm shifts and engage in and work on future states. If teams and individuals do not understand where they are, where they need to be, and how to get there, it will be challenging to achieve the expected value.
- Social competencies - an agile environment's social component is far different from a traditional organizational setup. Leaders need to recognize that there is a different interaction dynamic across the organization that is required to be successful.
- Character—Everyone must be "walking the talk." Being an agile organization is more than using an agile framework. The agile characteristics of delivering in management should not be overlooked.
- Resilience is one of the critical things needed for any agile transformation. When things get tough, it is natural to fall back to the old way of doing things. It is easy to go back to a familiar pattern of doing things. We must avoid this. Stay vigilant and use

---

[14] Ma Regina, M. H., Caringal-Go, J., & Magsaysay, J. F. (2018). Implicit change leadership, change management, and affective commitment to change. Leadership & Organization Development Journal, 39(7), 914-925. doi:http://0-dx.doi.org.aupac.lib.athabascau.ca/10.1108/LODJ-01-2018-0013

agile methods, techniques, and behaviours to continuously improve, grow, and evolve.

1. Is there a documented set of delivery processes? (Pre agile transformation)
2. Is there a RACI for each process?
3. Was a SWOT analysis done on the team before the agile transformation?
4. What led the organization to embrace agile values and practices?
5. What level of team involvement in transformation?
6. Do you have any productivity metrics that are measured against?
7. Can you add any items for any other baseline item you feel needs to be a part of the definition? It is better to have too much than not enough.
8. Does leadership engage with teams often? (3-5 times a week) Use of Gemba walks, Obeya rooms, and lean coffees as examples)
9. Do the teams drive the work? Can the teams complete their planned work without leadership interruption?
10. Does leadership understand agile/performance metrics?
11. Does the leadership work with teams on training needs?
12. Does leadership track improvements?
13. Does leadership have an agile workflow? (I.E., Published Kanban board)
14. Does leadership allow for team agreement (Not consensus) and input before making changes?
15. Is leadership transparent with teams?
16. Do the teams have involvement in defining their governance for delivery?
17. Think about and write down ideas and action items for each question with no answer to help leaders transform. This can be a difficult task, depending on the leadership. It is about treating others as you want to be treated. If it has to be small steps to show the value and let it grow organically, then so be it. Remember, there are three levels of leading: Up, Down, and Side to Side.
18. How would you engage leadership to develop an engagement plan that best suits the team's culture?
19. What would the future state of the agile environment you want to see?
20. List the gaps in engagement within and between the team and

leadership.

21. Think of an Engagement schedule. Based on your answers and thoughts, determine a plan to improve engagement between teams and leadership. The engagement schedule should include:

    a. Workshops: Workshops are great for a team to work through issues and determine the best action to resolve them. It is also a great opportunity to reinforce the agile values and tie them to the organization's mission and vision.

    b. Expectations for leadership engagement: Working with the leadership, they need to understand and accept that they need to be more than someone in an office who sends emails and talks at town halls. A couple of techniques they could use to engage teams are Gemba walks and Lean Coffees. There are more that can be used to improve engagement.

22. Engagement Plan

    a. Your engagement plan is key to everything in the future. Without a good plan, all messaging will be lost, and the team will never evolve.

    b. Sending out a memo or putting up posters is NOT an engagement plan. It is about using all communication channels, including conversations, to get the message out.

    c. c. The engagement plan should also include how everyone, including leadership, will exhibit agile values and be agile in their day-to-day work lives.

    d. The future state should be a component of the organization's Vision statement. It does not have to include metrics or numbers; that comes later. It would be best to have a series of statements to guide you to measurable improvements later.

Determining Agile Values

Creating a unique set of team values that align with organizational principles is essential for fostering a cohesive environment. This approach transcends merely adopting the values outlined in the Agile Software Development Manifesto, especially as agile methodologies expand across various industries and disciplines. Organizational, departmental, and team-specific agile values should be interconnected yet appropriate for each level.

In "Aligning Organizational Values in Systems Development Projects" (Management Research Review, 2012)[15], a qualitative study synthesized data from empirical studies to explore this concept. It highlighted that while "agile" is often perceived as a method for rapid task completion, it encompasses much more, including integrating a complex array of organizational value dimensions. The goal is to simplify complexities by categorizing tasks into manageable pieces tailored to everyone involved. Here are some key organizational value dimensions:

Adaptability: Capacity for internal change.

Aggression: Focus on power, competition, and perfectionism.

Bureaucracy: Emphasis on hierarchy, systems, and control.

Clans: Control through shared beliefs.

Concern for People: Fairness, collaboration, and trust.

Consistency: Individual conformity over voluntary participation.

Constructive: Collaboration and support.

Innovation: Challenge and risk-taking.

Involvement: Ownership and responsibility.

Mission: A clear sense of purpose.

Pragmatism: Customer-focused rather than organization-focused.

Results-orientation: Emphasis on achieving goals.

It's crucial to note that not every value dimension needs to be represented. Understanding these dimensions is part of an iterative process that helps ensure tasks are completed effectively and efficiently. This alignment fosters better opportunities for collaboration, engagement, and

---

[15] Aligning Organizational Values in Systems Development Projects" from the Management Research Review (2012), and concepts adapted from Leidner and Kayworth (2006)

involvement across teams, ultimately leading to enhanced solidarity and supportiveness among members.

1. What is the company mission statement?
2. Vision Statement?
3. Are there documented Organization/Team values?
4. Plan out how an "Open Space" meeting would work to create agile values.
5. What tools and techniques would you use?
   a. When creating agile values, it is essential to remember that this is a group work function. Creating agile values in a management vacuum will not give the desired results of an agile organization, as it is viewed as a command and control activity.
   b. There are plenty of techniques to use: Brainstorming, mind mapping, and games to make it fun.
6. Do you think your team's culture and the organization's vision differ?
7. Would there be a large undertaking to get alignment?
8. How would the team react if the values did not discuss speed?
9. Do you think leadership would take over the creation of agile values? If so, what could you do to have them as a part of it and not direct it?
10. Agile value alignment issue items (What do you feel could impede or stumble the process)
   a. Organizations struggle with aligning agile values because leadership feels they could leverage off the manifesto. There is more value in leveraging those values and creating something specific to the team to motivate them through the stewardship of those values.
11. How does your leadership communicate changes?
12. How does your leadership track productivity?
13. Would it be difficult for leadership to have Obeya rooms?
14. How would leadership react to "walk the talk"?
15. Different communication pathways that would work with teams to promote agile values that are currently used.
   a. Agile values should never be communicated by email or a motivational poster. Document some additional behaviors

you would like to see in communicating agile values. Remember, anything is on the table and could provide value.

16. How would you plan on maintaining the agile values?
17. How often do you think you would revisit them?
18. What would your message be to revisit them?
19. Where would you keep agile values?
20. What would happen to the organization's change process to maintain agile values?
21. Determine the gaps between the organizational change process and a new agile change process.

Understanding Value Chains

Everything has a value chain, and having one document can give the understanding needed to create an effective agile environment. Gertner's publication[16]The Value Chain and Value Creation in Advances in Management details the value of organizations with documented value chains.

Effective management and team tools to become competitive, productive, and innovative. A value chain creates a better understanding of all stakeholders and the impact everyone can have on creating a product or a service.

Fearne et al. documented:[17] The dimensions of a good value chain and enhanced value throughout the process.

Three dimensions

1. The boundary of analysis is intra-firm, inter-firm/chain, and external stakeholders. Many aspects need to be considered when creating a product or service.

---

[16] Gertner, M. I. (2013). The value chain and value creation. Advances in Management, 6(10), 1-4. Retrieved from http://0-search.proquest.com.aupac.lib.athabascau.ca/scholarly-journals/value- chain-creation/docview/1462207621/se-2?accountid=8408
[17] Fearne, A., Marian, G. M., & Dent, B. (2012). Dimensions of sustainable value chains: Implications for value chain analysis. Supply Chain Management, 17(6), 575-581. doi:http://0- dx.doi.org.aupac.lib.athabascau.ca/10.1108/13598541211269193

Third-party vendors, other teams, or departments within the organization. It is not a linear path of one team's work.

2. The scope of value is considered: cost/waste reduction. Consumer and customer value. shared value

It is more than just the money and the value to the customer. Analyzing a value chain should take a broader scope, such as employee satisfaction and the social components of changes made. Cutting costs in one area can create negative impacts down the road.

3. Governance: relationships not considered, channel power, collaboration

Creating a value chain is a team event, and all stakeholders' Involvement only increases the value. Here, the antithesis of agile management - Command and Control mustn't be exhibited.

1. Where do you think this would not work in your organization?
2. What do you feel is needed to document the current state?
3. Do you have the pre and post-processes after development?
4. What issues could you see with conducting a walkthrough?
   a. Do not drill down into the steps of the processes. One key thing to keep in mind when developing the flow is to remember that it is about a main input that is worked on by the team and provides an output.
5. What issues do you see happening in determining future state?
6. What tools and techniques would you use?
7. Understand that when doing value chains, there should be one flow. Additional flows could be part of the chain, and teams must determine whether they are part of it or can be separate.
8. The future state is where time can be taken to examine the processes more deeply and determine what can be cut, merged, or changed. This would require a lot of planning and some sessions/workshops to find possible improvements.
   a. With metrics, techniques, and availability, what would be a wish list of things to add to the value chain?
9. The process itself could take weeks or months. Use this opportunity to have a high-level change management plan.

CHAPTER 02 | GOALS

Get the value your team and customers expect with identified goals

Goals	Why	How	What
Develop goals that will provide guidance to delivery higher business value	Everyone has a better sense of what to expect when clear goals are identified.	Understand needs over wants.	Improved relationships between everyone.
Innovation	**Understand**	**Find needs**	**Synchronize**
Innovation does not have to be with just a product.	Understand your product/service how it is used and to be used	Discovery over Development	Improved relationships with clients and teams.

Figure 2-1

In this chapter, we will move to the next step of the category 'fundamentals,' which focuses on goals.

This is not just about understanding individual, team, or product goals. We will touch upon those, but this chapter is more all-encompassing. Essentially, it's about understanding the 'why' of goals. As we discuss this element, we will continuously discuss agile in relation to the 'why' of goals. Keeping every aspect connected to the core of agile is crucial, which means focusing on the 'why,' if you aim to create a creative and innovative environment. To do so, fostering an environment focused on creativity and innovation is essential, not just speed.

FOCUS ON QUALITY, INNOVATIVE DELIVERY, NOT SPEED.

This leads to another crucial aspect of this chapter: understanding that speed is not an outcome but a byproduct in an agile environment. Speed should not be the main reason for adopting agile; this is one of the biggest misconceptions about agile environments. Many people think, *'Oh, we're agile, so we can move as fast as we want to build as quickly as possible.'*

However, this perspective misses the broader picture. This mindset can lead to failure without understanding what an agile environment entails. It's important to recognize that agile also involves mitigating risks sooner and improving our areas of expertise to ensure we deliver value. We want to develop goals that provide guidance and deliver higher business value. We want everyone to have a clearer understanding of what to expect. Once they have clear goals, they have objectives they feel compelled to understand and meet.

To thoroughly grasp the concept of goals, we will explore the following important areas of focus:

- Innovation
- Understanding
- Finding needs
- Synchronize

Goals Struggles:

Several struggles are involved when discussing goals in the context of teams. One thing that happens is that teams tend to implode because of these struggles. Why?

Here are the main reasons:

- **Goals are unattainable**

You've set goals for your team that seem so far-reaching they don't feel are achievable. The aim is to be faster, better, and deliver higher quality. But what do these objectives mean? Is their meaning clear to you and your teams? What exactly does it mean to be faster, to have better quality, or to be more efficient? Simply stating these goals isn't helpful unless their purpose and meaning are clear. Without this clarity, it doesn't instill a sense of determination or achievement.

And I know some will say all those things to have that blanket goal and leave it out there. This is not the way to go and certainly wouldn't yield the results you expect.

- **Misunderstanding innovation and mixed messaging:**

What exactly does innovation mean to you? I see a lot of misconceptions around this, but let me clear up one thing: Innovation is more than just delivering that big wow factor for our customers. And with everything we've discussed in the last section, where leaders don't walk the talk, mixed messaging causes team issues in understanding goals. This hinders the innovation factor along with it.

So, the first thing you need to ensure is to move from struggling to understanding. It would help if you had clear guidance for delivery, whether it's software, widgets, or front doors for houses. It's all about understanding those goals that teams can use as guidance to achieve the success they want, the success everyone wants to achieve. Once that's clear, we move to innovation. It is not a separate element but rather an interconnected one with the goals.

Understanding Innovation

Without innovation there is no evolution.

Goals	Why	How	What
Understand there is more to innovation than just what is delivered	fostering an environment where innovation can flourish organically	I strive to ensure a comprehensive understanding of innovation across the team	As an agile leader
Definition	**For Clients**	**For employees**	**Value**
What is innovation	What do clients see as innovation	What do employees see as innovation	What is the value of innovation

Figure 2-1

What is it?

"Innovation is the creation, development, and implementation of a new product, process or service, with the aim of improving efficiency, effectiveness or competitive advantage." - Dr. Ken Hudson.

We need to grasp the essence of innovation. Innovation isn't just about creating something that will astonish clients or significantly improve their lives. It's more nuanced than that. As an agile leader, you must comprehend the true nature of innovation. This understanding will enable you to set your goals in a way that fosters organic innovation. When goals are set to be attainable and are accompanied by clear guidance, innovation arises naturally. There's no need to force teams to innovate. If they understand their objectives, they will devise methods to achieve them.

What I mean by understanding innovation is that you want to have a definition not just for your customers but also for your employees, and you want to see the value within it. You want to ensure everyone sees there's more to innovation than what's being delivered. It could be in how it's being delivered, the change in values, or changes in the market that help drive innovation and change.

In an agile environment, you can transform and change more effectively and efficiently than in a non-agile one. Organizations that provide mixed messages, where teams implode, where you're "doing Agile," not "being agile," and lack clear guidance to have a truly agile environment will struggle. We'll talk later about hitting the mark, becoming innovative, and finding those innovations. We must understand that innovation in our product/service is simple. It gives everyone that 'wow' factor, something the customer understands and thinks, 'Oh geez, I could use this. This is great. Why didn't anyone think of this before?' But making that possible involves a lot of backstage work. That's why I say it's more than just achieving that wow factor. Unless you know the 'why' behind that goal, you won't fully grasp the 'how.'"

That leads us to our next point: There is also innovation in processes within teams, which is one of the key aspects the Manifesto for Agile Software Development brought forward. It's about continuously improving and becoming more effective and efficient in what's being built. Understanding how to enhance this process is crucial for future success. It ensures a smooth workflow. By smooth processes, I don't mean eliminating the need for employees once these processes are in place. A common misconception is that fewer employees are needed if processes become more efficient. This misunderstanding often leads to employees fearing innovation in processes and being concerned that these improvements might replace them.

However, there's a reality to consider. In my experience with various clients, process improvements have led to more efficiency and effectiveness but not to layoffs. In fact, such improvements often result in more work and the ability to deliver even more to clients. I recall one client who experienced layoffs, but this was due to budget constraints, not the efficiency of processes. Other factors at play contributed to their situation. Yet, this challenge forced them to become more efficient with the teams they had. They innovated their processes to improve. We worked with them to enhance their operations. This case demonstrates that innovation can be either external or internal. It's essential to embrace innovation, not just in products or services but also in the processes and practices within a team.

UNDERSTANDING WHAT IT MEANS FOR THE CLIENT AND CUSTOMERS

Definition for clients

Everyone on your team needs to understand that innovation is about more than just creating a new, cool app for ordering food from most restaurants in your area. Indeed, that's what clients often want, but we also need to understand innovation from our customers' perspective. Clients have varied perceptions of innovation. For many, it's about significant time savings, like cooking a turkey in 10 minutes instead of waiting hours. Time is precious to them, so providing a solution that saves time is key. There could be anything that could provide them with that, and your teams need to decide what they will provide to their customers as a solution.

Think like your customers: How much time does an innovation save in what I do? How does it automate processes so I can focus on other things? How can it reduce the effort required to get work done? Often, it's the simple things that can make a significant difference over time. Small changes can lead to significant improvements. For clients, understanding that even minor tweaks in a product can greatly enhance their lives is crucial. Thus, while we make our processes efficient, we must also align them with our clients' views on innovation. In the next section of this chapter, we will look into understanding and identifying needs, creating an environment that fosters this understanding, and helping to recognize those needs.

Definition for Employees

For employees, the concept of innovation should be viewed differently than it is for clients. While employees must understand innovation from the client's perspective to deliver what the client desires, the delivery process should differ. Employees often equate innovation with high-tech features: big touchscreens, full automation, voice control, AI, etc. These are the elements typically associated with 'innovation' in their context. Sometimes, this perception is reinforced by what I call 'conference hangover syndrome,' where attending a conference or webinar exposes them to cool new tools that promise easier work.

However, it's crucial to recognize that innovation doesn't always have to be grandiose. Small, practical changes can also bring significant improvements. Examples include standing desks, computer monitors with integrated CPUs for less bulkiness, and flexible work policies like the ability to work from home or remotely. These adjustments can greatly improve team performance and efficiency.

Interestingly, the COVID-19 pandemic forced many organizations to adopt remote working, a capability they had all along but hadn't fully embraced. The pandemic-induced shift was more a behavioral change forced by circumstances, even though remote working was feasible long before the pandemic hit.

I recall engaging in remote work in the early 2000s, yet it wasn't widespread because of the prevailing office-centric culture. The pandemic, however, normalized remote working, proving its viability and benefit in enhancing employees' lives. That's a prime example of innovation in action. We need to understand and value these changes as true innovations in the workplace.

FINDING NEEDS

Take the iPhone as an example: we've seen people eagerly lining up for the release of each new model. With its innovative approach from the beginning of the millennia, Apple has created a market phenomenon characterized by long queues of customers anxiously waiting to get their hands on the latest product. This level of excitement is what you want to replicate with your innovations. Your goal should be to make customers enjoy and feel excited about possessing your products. When they see a feature or a new product that elicits a 'wow!' reaction, it indicates that you've successfully tapped into something they needed or desired.

Customer Qualitative Data

So, innovation should be about meeting those needs, not just the wants. This type of value is qualitative. This is where you get those good reviews, those positive comments. This is where you see customers with their iPhones, declaring it's the best iPhone ever. This is the best app on this phone ever. And they tell their friends, who then want the same experience. And so it goes on. That word-of-mouth promotion, which you didn't pay for, is invaluable. You can measure sales, the bottom line, the revenue improvements – these are quantitative. However, from an innovation perspective, some of the best value you can observe is qualitative.

Quantitative Data

The same principle applies to employees. Employee satisfaction scores rise when employees take stewardship of their processes and how they get work done. Their work becomes more productive. It's about embracing a new way of doing things, allowing teams to find their working methods. They become innovative in their own right. It's no longer solely up to leaders or managers to provide solutions. Teams and individuals are capable of doing this. When you achieve this, you reach the best metric within an organization: profits. This is your quantitative data; you're improving revenues, decreasing costs, and increasing the number of features that can be sold. You'll notice this trend as it progresses.

We've discussed how reducing costs doesn't necessarily mean reducing staff; it's about making things more efficient so that teams can handle more work. Think of it like a garden hose: the thinner the hose, the harder it is for water to flow through. Open up the hose, and more water flows out. It's simple, right?

Understand what you deliver

Organizations can spend years producing a product or service without really understanding the full value it can provide.

Goals	Why	How	What
Understand how your products/services interact with customers	ensuring the delivery of valuable solutions	I aim for agile team members to actively participate in planning and crafting high-quality products/services	As an agile leader
What is it?	**Who wants it?**	**Communicate**	**Elevator pitch**
Have an understanding what is the product or service	Do you know your customers?	Everyone should be able to talk about the product/service	Anyone can sell the product or service in 60 seconds.

Figure 2-3

Understanding what you deliver is another crucial component. Many organizations struggle with this. In an agile environment, asking whether everyone truly understands their product is essential. I worked with an organization where several teams were developing a web product. They understood bits and pieces of the product but not the whole picture at once. This led to additional unused features being added. The product owner was providing features that customers neither wanted nor needed, creating redundancy in work. Part of this issue stemmed from a lack of understanding of the product and what they were delivering.

Understand what the product/service is

We need to understand the product/service. Without grasping the values, the mission, and the vision of an organization, along with agile values, understanding the product can be challenging. This can lead to frustration in trying to discern what clients want and need. Consider the earlier example: the team knew the product and their clients, but only in fragments. They understood various components but not how these elements worked together to provide true value to customers. Gaining insight into all the different features, components, and their interplay is crucial. This holistic understanding gives a clearer picture of the product. When these pieces are assembled, you end up with a product/service that everyone can utilize effectively.

Back to the cloud product example, there was a part where they needed a report section for government compliance. They created a story for this report's feature. During refinement and discussion, the only solution they could think of was creating a new report, which would take weeks, almost two sprints, due to its complexity.

However, by asking questions about the purpose and requirements of the report, what it should display, 'why' it's needed, and how it's expected to be generated, we got a deeper understanding of the need. We looked at how it's generally expected to be generated. Once we understood that, we found a simple solution. It was just a matter of adding a filter to the report application. They could generate the required report by putting a specific filter on. Instead of taking almost two sprints or four weeks to create this new report, creating the filter and generating the needed report took just five minutes.

So, it's about understanding how all these pieces fit together. Take the report example: if they had understood how the features worked, they could have generated that report immediately. There wouldn't have been a need to wait for a developer to create and test data from scratch. So, when we look at products/services, we consider the *Golden Circle:* Why is it made? How is it made? What needs does it resolve? Understand the components that are built together. What is it? Regardless of your role, can you provide that elevator pitch about what the product/service does?

Outside the Golden Circle, the final part concerns how the customer uses the product/service. This is where many organizations struggle: understanding how customers use their products. Returning to that report and the client, there were other instances where the Product Owners thought they had an idea of how the product was used. It wasn't until they introduced consistent and detailed customer interviews that they realized one of their features was not being used as they thought it would be. They had made previous changes to improve it, only to see customers struggle to use the feature as the Product owner intended. It didn't fit their needs and caused more problems, leading them to create workarounds for those features.

Who wants the product?

So, understanding how clients use the product/service and why it is made helps guide the entire process. It's also about understanding who wants the product, the services, and the processes. By clients, I mean internal and external: those using processes and tools within the team and the clients who want to use the product. Sometimes, the teams have blinders put on; they're not willing to see a broader scope of clients. They focus on a certain set of clients and cater only to them. They don't understand the needs or wants of others. So, when they focus too hard on just one set of clients, other clients get overlooked, and the product changes could cause more headaches for everyone. They're looking at the particular wants of those clients, not everyone else. They're not looking at the needs of everyone else.

One mistake many make is thinking they know what the customer will want and like without actually talking to them. That's where a lot of things fail. A key indication of this is if someone starts a sentence like this: "I think the customer would….". One of the central agile values is customer collaboration. Look at Google's reference in the first chapter. They talked to the customers; they understood what their needs were.

In the previous example, the product team focused on a scattershot view mindset in providing features, throwing out a bunch and hoping it would hit the target several times or once. They found that some of those features were just not being used or used as they should have been.

Understanding your customer avatar and knowing who your client is is crucial. Understanding that helps foster conversations and create and broaden the spectrum of meeting client needs. There are several ways to get to know your customers: Interviews, case studies, testimonials, site visits, etc. Remember, "being agile" is about having the customers in place to provide feedback. It is not just external customers I'm talking about. Internally, in "being agile," everyone must work together to understand their needs to get the work done. That's what will help improve the organization.

You want to be able to communicate efficiently. You want to know everything about your product and service. It's not enough to think you know; you need actual knowledge. Knowing means understanding how customers use your product. It's important not to rely solely on the perceptions of individual departments. For instance, the finance department may see customers as billpayers; support teams may view them as people with issues needing resolution, and product development may see them as a source of demands and expectations. What's essential is to have an overarching understanding of everything going on. This comprehensive insight leads to overlaps between all teams, helping you understand everyone involved in the process and their impact on each other.

At the center of this overlap is the product and service. This is the understanding you need about the functions of every team involved and their impact on the service or product. It's where you can communicate effectively about the product as a sales team, not just about the features but also about how it's developed and supported and how leadership backs both the product and the teams. This overlap represents the WHY of your product, the elevator pitch that everyone should be able to understand and communicate.

Everyone should have the same elevator pitch regarding the product. Maybe a slight change in how they do things, but the essential context of it should remain the same. Think about it if you can easily explain what you deliver. Can you explain it to someone without their eyes glazing over? If you had asked me this question a few years ago when my niece asked me what I did for a living, you would have had the same reaction as hers. I explained that I manage a team, I do this and that, and I lost her somewhere in the middle. It wasn't fascinating, as you can imagine.

If I were to bring up the products and how we meet customer needs, our elevator pitch would have probably fostered a better conversation. Similarly, you want to create an environment where you can sell within the team, like saying, "Yes, I could use this if I were a client." I think this would improve things; it would help improve employee satisfaction as they feel pride in their work and provide value. You want to understand that customer and employee satisfaction are linked; there is a correlation with it[18]. And you want to ensure that with higher employee satisfaction, you have a good chance of having higher customer satisfaction because now you're able to provide what everyone's needs are. So, we look at employee satisfaction and discuss self-managed teams in our next discussion. We've talked about leadership providing that servant leader style that helps with employee satisfaction. Instead of just providing that big new shiny tool, thinking that it will make the team happy, maybe there are small things that can help drive productivity. You want to provide an environment where the teams can complete the work. There are studies out there that show that when leadership provides the right environment, there is higher employee satisfaction.

Customer and Employee Satisfaction

With concurrently high customer and employee satisfaction there will high value evolution.

Goals	Why	How	What
Have a link between customer and employee satisfaction	ensuring that clients value what we provide, and employees find value in their work	I will contribute to fostering an innovative environment	As an agile leader
Employee	**Customer**	**Future of innovation**	**Plan**
Understand how employees interact and function with innovation	With knowledge of customers and understanding needs leads to loyalty	Determine the goals going forward with innovation in mind	A plan to how to tie goals with employees, customers work together

Figure 2-4

---

[18]   https://decision-wise.com/resources/articles/empowering-business-success-how-employee-engagement-shapes-customer-satisfaction/#:~:text=A%20study%20by%20Harvard%20Business%20School%20found%20that,employees%20are%20more%20likely%20to%20create%20delighted%20customers.

Employees Satisfaction

In my career, I've had the opportunity to work with various companies. I vividly recall an experience with one organization where I spoke to an Associate Vice President about a situation that needed improvement. I was genuinely invested in enhancing our work and was eager to find solutions. However, things weren't falling into place, and I was struggling. The response I received was far from what I call a "servant leader" comment. It was simply, "At least you have a job." It reminded me of Sir Richard Branson's quotes on employee management. As Branson wisely puts it, "As soon as something stops being fun, I think it's time to move on. Life is too short to be unhappy." It's true; if employees are stressed, unhappy, or unappreciated, it affects their work and commitment to the job. When employees experience low satisfaction levels, it often leads to turnover, and people usually leave because of poor leadership rather than the job itself.

Another quote from Sir Richard Branson: "I have always believed that the way you treat your employees is the way they will treat your customers and that people flourish when they are praised."

He clearly recognized the connection between employee satisfaction and customer satisfaction. Considering customer satisfaction in the context of innovation, we see its reflection in end products that customers eagerly queue for hours to obtain. Studies have shown that creating value for employees fosters loyalty. We must consider that we want them to listen to customers, not just hear them truly. Let me explain this difference with an example.

Remember the movie from the 90s, "White Men Can't Jump"? There's a scene where they discuss the difference between hearing and listening to Jimi Hendrix. When you're hearing Jimi Hendrix, you're just hearing the music, not understanding the meaning behind the words, the music, etc. But when you're listening, you focus on the intricacies of the song, the music, and the lyrics. It moves you. This is akin to listening to your customer; when you really listen, you pick up on their needs and can make the right changes. This leads to those "Oh, wow" moments when you deliver.

So, what does the future of innovation look like? It involves understanding needs over wants. You aim to become a discoverer of products or services, go beyond mere hearing, listen to the customers, and see value in everything, not just the product or service you provide but also how your teams deliver it.

PLANNING FOR INNOVATION

Now, let's consider planning for innovation. In reality, you don't plan for innovation. Rather, you should have a strategy to discover and act on what you can do. Adopt the simple 'Plan-Do-Check-Act' cycle because not having a solid plan for innovation is like hindering the capacity for creativity. Innovating just for innovation's sake isn't beneficial. Instead, aim for evolution, which in turn promotes true innovation. True innovation should meet clients' needs and implement the right changes.

The best example dates back to the 1980s. Consider the case of Coca-Cola: They introduced a new Coke flavor, discontinuing the original. Despite their expectations, the new flavor was not well-received. It might have been a marketing ploy, but who knows? Some articles out there suggest it was.

They were confident it was a great move and pushed it out. But it tanked. Nobody liked it. Subsequently, after a brief period, Coca-Cola reintroduced the original as 'Coke Classic,' eventually phasing out the New Coke flavor entirely. It seems they thought change was a good idea for the sake of change. The old product was still popular and selling well, but they wanted a change, and it didn't work out. [19]

Now, let's reflect on what we've discussed so far. It's all about being creative and innovative within a framework. Establishing a clear and achievable goal is crucial, and ensuring everyone understands what it means to be innovative and push forward. Goals should be easy to understand and attainable. You need to understand what innovation means, what you deliver, and how it links to customer and employee satisfaction. Innovation should highlight that even small changes can lead to significant impacts. The most important thing is that the focus should extend beyond just client and customer needs.

---

[19] https://time.com/3950205/new-coke-history-america/

WORKBOOK: 02

Understand Innovation

Innovation is closely tied to creativity, but the practical application of ideas truly defines innovation. Let's explore this concept further.

Innovation in Everyday Life

Take the evolution of cell phones into powerful mini-computers that assist us daily—this is a prime example of innovation. In contrast, reusable coffee filters, though often seen as mere conveniences, also qualify as innovations because they effectively address specific user needs.

Innovation in the Workplace

Many tools enhance convenience while driving innovation in the workplace. Examples include software coding tools, documentation software, and testing tools. These innovations streamline processes and improve efficiency, meeting the dynamic needs of professionals.[20]

Recognizing and Fostering Innovation

Recognizing innovation requires an understanding of its diverse forms. Studies show that creativity flourishes when organizations provide time and resources to nurture innovation. This environment supports both exploratory and exploitative innovation, significantly enhancing creative outcomes. For example, research on the effects of collectivism in Chinese organizations indicates that fostering an innovative environment positively impacts employee creativity.[21]

Creating Value Through Innovation

By understanding and promoting innovation within an organization, companies can deliver significant value to all stakeholders. Fostering a

---

[20] Jansen, J. J., Van den Bosch, F. A., & Volberda, H. W. (2006). "Exploratory Innovation, Exploitative Innovation, and Performance: Effects of Organizational Antecedents and Environmental Moderators." Management Science.

[21] Zhou, J., & Su, Y. (2010). "A Missing Link in the Relationship Between Collective Orientation and Individual Creativity: The Moderating Role of Team Context." Journal of Organizational Behavior.

creative environment drives meaningful innovation that meets the needs of both employees and customers.

1. What is your primary product/service?
2. What is your definition of innovation in your market?
3. What is the most innovative thing in our market in the past five years?
4. What does the organization do well, and what must it improve?
5. What are the most innovative things in your life from the past five years?
6. Do you get excited when news of products that are soon to be released comes out?
7. Did you get a small product or service because it made things easier? (example: Reusable coffee filter)
8. What are the most innovative things from the past five years in your work life?
9. Were there any external process changes that made things easier?
10. Have employees made any changes within the company that made things easier for everyone?
11. Describe how product vision aligns with customers/users and is updated over time.
12. How do you measure value?
13. When innovations within your organization, internal or to customers, do you measure the value they provide?

Understanding what you deliver

Sometimes, fully understanding a product's capabilities can be difficult if there are many variables and components. However, that does not mean it is unachievable within an organization. A knowledge-sharing environment can help everyone understand what products and services offer.

There is a Venn diagram where there is an overlap where everyone has that understanding—setting up an environment to increase that overlap while also putting the puzzle pieces of different components together to understand.

Improving customer service: Understanding how employees and innovation hold the key to Strategic Direction provides an understanding of how that knowledge enhances customer service and innovation. When organizations have that knowledge-sharing environment, everyone benefits.[22]

Knowing who you are providing the product or service is essential, and having a broad understanding could create missed opportunities within markets. That comprehensive understanding would come from an individual's perception of who the clients are without actually knowing. An environment that is indeed client-focused, where there is an understanding of products and their use and meets the client's needs, has more excellent value than thinking what the client's needs and creates compelling development opportunities.[23]

1. Describe your product or service.
2. Why is it made or provided?
3. How is it made or provided?
4. What is it? What documentation or knowledge-sharing is there?
5. How does the customer use it? Is that knowledge readily available?
   a. Explaining what they do or what their organization provides can be difficult. While some are straightforward, this doesn't really describe their value.
6. Do you have one or a set of customer avatars?
7. Who is your primary customer?
8. Are changes forced onto them?
9. Do you keep current on customer behaviors and wants for future use?
10. Are customers using your product/service as you intended?
11. What is your communication plan for a better flow of information between customers and employees?
12. Is there an internal knowledge-sharing program (formal or informal) that all departments can leverage?
13. What is your plan to involve other teams within the organization

---

[22] Improving customer service: How employees and innovation hold the key. (2009). Strategic Direction, 25(1), 5-9. doi:http://0-dx.doi.org.aupac.lib.athabascau.ca/10.1108/02580540910921842
[23] Andreoli, T. (1995). Marketing your strengths, knowing your customer. Discount Store News, 34(10), 67. Retrieved from http://0-search.proquest.com.aupac.lib.athabascau.ca/trade-journals/marketing-your- strengths-knowing-customer/docview/228478673/se-2?accountid=8408

to dialogue the overlap?

14. What is your 60-second elevator pitch?

Understanding Employee and Customer Satisfaction

It should not be surprising to hear that employees who enjoy their work have a greater chance of higher productivity and quality. Whether through research or personal experience, there is a general sense that this is the case.

Now, some studies show a link between employee and customer satisfaction scores. Identifying a correlation between when employees are more satisfied with their workplace and a client satisfaction score relates to it.

In The Journal of Services Marketing (2012)[24]: The relationship between employee and customer satisfaction. In it, they found that empirically, there is a path for this relationship to hold.

Richard Branson quotes

"As soon as something stops being fun, I think it's time to move on. Life is too short to be unhappy. Waking up stressed and miserable is not a good way to live."

"I have always believed that the way you treat your employees is the way they will treat your customers and that people flourish when they are praised."

It is about listening to customers' and employees' needs to find innovative ways to do things and enhance products/services. Keeping everyone engaged and having a free flow of information will help eliminate guesswork about what people want or need.

1. Do you document employee satisfaction? What is done with it?
2. Do your employees feel safe speaking up professionally about upcoming changes or directions or providing ideas?
3. Is the team full of specialists or generalists?
4. How are techniques/tools/best practices distributed to individuals

---

[24] Jeon, H., & Choi, B. (2012). The relationship between employee satisfaction and customer satisfaction. The Journal of Services Marketing, 26(5), 332-341. doi:http://0-dx.doi.org.aupac.lib.athabascau.ca/10.1108/08876041211245236

on the team?

5. Regardless of the team size, genuinely knowing the level of employee satisfaction is difficult. Part of the reason is the traditional way of management and not wanting to "rock the boat." Provide some additional thoughts on ways you can improve employee satisfaction through innovation. Remember, innovation does not have to lie with a physical tool; there is leadership and process innovation that can drastically improve morale, which will organically grow more innovation.

6. Do you document customer satisfaction? How is that shared with everyone?

7. Do your customers complain a lot? How are they handled? Is there a positive flow of information (issues handled positively between teams)?

8. Is there a direct communication path between Support and other teams?

9. Do you interview customers?

10. What do you do to resolve customer issues/complaints?

11. "The customer is always right" is a fallacy. It has been well-documented how people take that term literally in recent years. That does not mean they should be shut out, either. It is important to listen to them and not hear. Think of ways to listen to the customer and effectively resolve any issue.

12. Watch this talk on product discovery over product development. Teresa Torres gives some good insight into what can lead to innovation.
    a. https://youtu.be/_BGlPaKhRSA - Becoming a Successful Continuous Discovery Team
    b. Write down your thoughts about the subject.

13. Document any potential risks of making changes, and how you feel best they can be mitigated.

CHAPTER 03 | DESIGN

This chapter will focus on Design, the third of the 'foundation.' This step is crucial as it marks the completion of the foundational section, setting the stage for constructing the foundation of a solid agile environment.

First, we looked at 'start' from a servant leader perspective. Then, we connected it to the agile values in the value chain. By now, you might have begun planning how to instill your agile values, collaborating with both leadership and teams in your organization to establish a strong base of servant leadership and set clear expectations. This preparation leads to your goals, where you start to consider how to meet clients' needs, internally and externally. How are we going to become better? What are our goals based on our agile values?

We will continue to refer back to those agile values as we proceed. These values are your guide, shining the light on the map and directing you where you want to go.

Get the team set up where needs are met.

Goals	Why	How	What
Develop high performing self-managed teams	The improved ownership stewardship of work improves quality	Creation of a self sustained continuous improvement environment	High level of trust across the organization
Servant Leader	**Transparency**	**Expectations**	**Self-managed**
How the Servant Leader plays a role in designing	Have the transparency needed to make the right decisions	Agreed upon expectations from all parties	Have the self-managed team set up.

Figure 3-1

An effectively designed environment

Design in an agile environment is fundamentally about prioritizing strategy over tactics. This distinction is crucial: strategic thinking is about looking ahead and aiming for long-term goals, whereas tactical thinking is focused on addressing immediate issues. In many organizations, the tactical aspect tends to dominate, constantly dealing with problem after problem without creating an environment conducive to strategic planning. This perpetual firefighting mode prevents the establishment of a strategic foundation necessary for progress.

In the last chapter, we discussed needs. It was about hearing them so that you can develop a high-performing, self-managed team. And that's the part of this Design: developing high performance. You want to design an environment where you have a performing, self-managed team, improve the stewardship of the work, and create a self-sustaining, continuous improvement environment. You want that high level of trust across the organization.

These pillars, returning to servant leadership, transparency, and setting clear expectations, support the development of self-managed teams. However, it's essential to recognize that designing such an environment has challenges.

Three main design challenges are:

- Matrix environment.
- You're "Agile" in name alone
- Other parts of the organization don't recognize agile environments.

HOW TO OVERCOME DESIGN CHALLENGES

Start with servant leadership

An effective leader creates effective teams.

Goals	Why	How	What
Have a Servant Leader mindset as a foundation for self-managed teams	enabling the entire organization to fully benefit from agile adoption	I aim for teams and functional areas to excel in self-organization within an agile environment	As an agile leader
Engage teams	**Create**	**Partners**	**Walk the talk**
Work with teams to have the best fit with agile values, goals and culture	Create the environment for success	Have the right partners that work effectively with your team	Show that you mean what you say

Figure 3-2

Start with Servant Leadership:

We aim to understand the transition from traditional methodologies to agile practices, begining with the servant leader concept. Previously, we discussed the behaviors of servant leaders, what needs to change, and what behaviors they need to adopt to make things work. So, looking at how they provide for teams and how they assist, we can see how this will help build out the organization and its Design.

1. Engage teams:

We need to shift from the traditional models. A critical step in this process is ensuring team engagement. We want to create a foundation for a self-managed team, and they are there to provide that help. It's about giving and helping—that's part of the engagement. We want to confirm those agile values. As mentioned, efforts to establish these collaborated and agreed-upon agile values should already be underway. If you don't have everyone agreeing on the agile values, then the 'engagement' component will struggle.

Everyone must understand what it means to be agile for that organization and the team. You can scale it up to the organization, but if we're looking at it from a team perspective, they need to understand and agree on the values that make sense for them and the leadership. You need to be able to confirm those expectations.

- What do you expect the team to do and work with?
- What does the leader's expectation look like?

The emphasis is on the leader's expectations to provide and maintain engagement. As I mentioned, one of the clients I've worked with had created their agile values, but then the leadership stayed in their offices. This does not engage the team. Despite this, the teams produced quality work, but employee satisfaction suffered. The teams would say, 'Oh, the executives are just staying in their office, not coming out.' Instead of seeing leadership actively engaging with the teams, participating in lean coffees, Gemba Walks visiting the Obeya room, and reviewing information alongside them. This level of engagement is the expectation that needs to be met. Leaders need to be present to support their teams, address their needs, and aid them in achieving success in agile environments. For teams to reach this success, servant leaders themselves must embody agility; they need to live by the agile values they've committed to. Setting these expectations is crucial in fostering the right environment.

2. Create:

There must be a culture shift to create engaging teams in your organization. You want to create an environment where actual transformation occurs. Remember, agile transformation isn't just about implementing a framework but transforming behaviors. Adding a framework is merely getting the team to use a tool. The real agile transformation involves changing everyone's behaviors to meet objectives like team trust, accountability, acceptance of failing fast, providing better quality, and improving team efficiency. This culture shift will help determine those agile values and establish the best workflow for creating an innovative and agile environment. It won't work if the culture isn't there.

One client I worked with tried to conduct the transformation themselves without a support structure with experience in effective behavior changes needed for an agile environment. They implemented a framework but struggled because they didn't address the pre-existing culture. This ties back to identifying your baseline or starting the process. They implemented the framework without addressing the 'why' for the team or going through effective change management to transform truly. They didn't change anyone's behaviors or work to create a culture that supports proper behavior change.

They tried to enforce accountability immediately, where there was previously no accountability. They didn't identify those gaps, so their transformation effort became about linearly building a product rather than embracing iterative development, failing fast, and iterating to meet needs. Essentially, their iterations were just small waterfall projects from start to finish. The culture didn't change, and the messaging from senior leaders continued to reflect a command-and-control viewpoint.

The agile environment didn't work for them because the culture never changed, which is a prime example of what can happen when transforming without aligning behaviors with the framework. The environment you're about to build is designed to address this issue. It will guide you in identifying the right behaviors and helping the team understand their value, setting the stage for "how" and "what" to come next. It all leads to it. You'll have that teamwork environment focus on the team, and they'll be able to work together. I understand there are different roles and needs within a team. It's no different than a hockey team; you can't have a hockey team full of Centers. They need to have the right mix for the team to win.

Another example of a team winning with the right mix of players is in the movie 'Moneyball' depicting the 2022 Oakland Athletics season. On the general perception of how a successful team is set up, they should not have won, let alone make it into the playoffs. But they had the right mix because of the culture they created and could work together as a solid team. Leadership helps create that; you lead by example and believe in the team.

Employing tactics such as coercion, forceful persuasion, or sending conflicting messages about expectations when completing tasks can create a toxic work environment. This can result in mixed signals and confusion, ultimately hindering employee productivity and satisfaction. Such disruptions can affect individual employee morale, team dynamics, and overall output, subsequently impacting the quality of work and customer service ratings. Establishing effective teamwork and fostering a positive work culture requires a concerted effort to identify existing norms and implement meaningful changes from the ground up. Encouraging team collaborative efforts and adopting a servant leadership approach can help align everyone towards common goals, facilitating understanding and buy-in for necessary changes.

3. Partners:

Another essential aspect to consider is partnerships. Reflecting on the value chain discussed in the first chapter, we recognized that inputs are necessary for the process. These inputs must originate from somewhere, as no organization operates in isolation. They require external contributions from the delivery team to deliver products or services to clients or customers.

Having the right partners in place is crucial. To ensure that, we have to understand that the partners, organizations, and teams chosen should share the same or similar values with the team. This ensures they can work effectively together, understanding each other's processes. We aim to meet those expectations and avoid the 50% quality issue in the example. You want the quality coming in from your partners to be high, allowing teams to work more effectively and efficiently.

Incorporating partners into your value chain necessitates a collaborative approach to their selection. This process also necessitates involving the teams when selecting partners, letting them see how the partners work, how they collaborate, and whether their production methods align with the team's work. You want to see that fit, that synchronization between the teams. Much like agile values encourage effective team collaboration, you want to foster the same dynamics with your partners, creating a strong connection that can grow and improve. In such teams, everyone is providing value to everyone; you're providing value to the partner, and the partner is providing value to you, creating a bi-directional partnership.

Clarity is essential when defining the term "Partners" within this context. Teams engage with internal and external partners, each situated differently within the organization. While this section primarily addresses interactions with external partners, the dynamics shift when dealing with internal counterparts. Internal partnerships may be complicated by organizational politics, biases, and logical fallacies, posing potential obstacles to success. However, the silver lining lies in the shared focus on achieving common organizational objectives among internal partners. This shared goal is a foundation for collaboration and mutual support, paving the way for beneficial internal partnerships.

4. Walk the talk:

So how do we get there? How do we know what we need to do? How do we create that effective team?

Well, one way we need to think about it is that the leader does not shape the team. Instead, it's the collective effort of the team that shapes itself. We need to understand that, through partnerships, tools, and the teams themselves, they are the ones who grasp how everything fits together. They need to comprehend how everything is set up so they can be more effective. It's not about the leader dictating every action. Rather, the team collaborates with the leader to meet the necessary objectives. Whether it involves a tool, a partnership, or even the processes themselves, the leader provides the support needed for success. And that's the key thing. The next part is understanding what it means to be a self-managed team.

Understand self-managed teams

Without true understanding there is no execution.

Goals	Why	How	What
Have self-managed teams continuously improving with the work they do and provide.	allowing them to achieve goals and exceed expected value without micromanagement	I aim to foster an environment where teams work autonomously	As an agile leader
Remove fear	**Build**	**Limitations**	**Guidance**
Work with teams to have the best fit with agile values, goals and culture	What is involved in a high value team.	Self-managed does not mean free reign	Values and strategies provide the guidance.

Figure 1-3

Understand self-managed teams

There is much discussion, and perhaps some misconceptions, about what it means to be a self-managed team. However, in an agile environment, self-management is essential. This principle underscores the importance of teams organizing their work autonomously, making decisions that best suit their goals without constant oversight.

1. Remove fear

To ensure that teams are self-managed and there's value provided, it's crucial to remove fear. We must understand the limitations and the guidance to ensure these self-managed teams offer value. Thus, it's important to have methodologies in place that ensure the behaviors of these teams match the expected value.

There's a common misconception that self-managed teams are a novel concept, but they have existed since the late 1950s[25]. Agile environments have taken this concept, adapted it, and made it work effectively because these environments require the values that self-managed teams embody. Self-managed teams can focus more on tactical matters, allowing leadership to concentrate on strategic issues. Yet, there's a fear among management that by adopting self-managed teams, they will lose control. This fear stems from a lack of trust in the team's ability to work independently, concerns over losing power, and fears that they will no longer be seen as leaders.

We've discussed the need for change and the limitations of command-and-control leadership, emphasizing the shift required in our approach. We've explored the concept of leadership from behind, where leaders steer their teams toward their goals without micromanaging. This brings us to many teams' concerns about self-management, particularly the fear of failure. Being self-managed and working collaboratively can be quite novel for those accustomed to direct oversight. Often, individuals feel they need explicit instructions. However, with strong guidance from leadership, it's possible to build a foundation of trust that allows teams to navigate their path effectively.

What will happen when fears are gone?

By building acceptance of failure within the team, you can foster loyalty. Leadership must recognize the necessity of accepting failure because learning occurs through these failures. This acceptance allows the team to focus more on goals and achieve higher productivity. Therefore, building the team with this understanding is essential, emphasizing learning from failures to strengthen the team's resolve and enhance its performance.

2. Build

Building teams can be stressful. You want to provide value and make it easy for everyone to reach their goals. How do we achieve this? Through collaboration. It's important to remember that perfection isn't the goal. We've discussed the concept of a team of "rock stars." A team composed

---

[25]https://www.linkedin.com/pulse/self-managed-teams-very-brief-history-rob-thomsett/

entirely of "A players" can lead to friction. The key is to construct the team thoughtfully, ensuring the right balance, which can be achieved through effective teamwork.

You want the right composition and behaviors when actively working with them. When discussing teams, some terms related to an agile environment you'll encounter are:

- Generalist vs. specialist
- Overlap in skills
- Team size and the mythical "man-month."

Some agile frameworks mention teams of about 100, which is outdated and not recommended. Agile teams should be small and self-managed, collaborating to complete the work efficiently. When considering generalist versus specialist roles, think about software development. They are all specialists in their fields, including backend and front-end developers, testers, automation testers, and product managers. They become generalists when they use their skills to help others within the team.

For example, Testers can assist product managers in writing better stories. Developers can help Testers with automation needs, and Testers can support developers in code reviews. Product owners can help developers understand design and flow.

It's also important to understand the concept of the mythical "man-month." Author Fred Brooks' book The Mythical Man-Month details how adding more people to a project doesn't necessarily speed it up. Teams have their own pace; finding the right skill overlap is crucial for team dynamics.

Self-managed teams have limitations, as does everything. Leadership has its limitations, and so do individuals. What we want to avoid is creating an environment that becomes disorganized. Being agile is about maintaining discipline in your approach. Agile environments can seem unstructured, unlike the waterfall method, which is very structured. However, it's about being disciplined differently, ensuring that work is completed efficiently and effectively.

So, it's crucial not to let the pendulum swing too far in either direction. You aim for it to stay in the middle, avoiding extremes. Too much freedom can lead to a complete loss of control, but too much control can negatively impact team dynamics. Finding that happy medium is key, and constant leadership involvement facilitates this balance. Creating team agreements about expectations and involving leadership, the teams, and partners helps. These agreements clarify what the team can and cannot do, simplifying the process of moving forward.

These agreements guide the teams on their permissible actions and direction. This is because, when integrated into the strategy, agile values enhance the organization's overall value and the value of the product and team. This strategic approach fosters a more agile environment within the organization.

A necessary change within organizations is how HR perceives teams. A move towards agility might involve discarding individual employee reviews in favor of team reviews. The logic is that team reviews encourage collective improvement rather than focusing solely on individual performance. This shift towards evaluating the team's performance helps everyone support each other's growth.

However, individual reviews can still be valuable. A balanced approach could involve team reviews complemented by one-on-one sessions between leadership and employees, focusing on personal development to better contribute to the team. This approach ensures that while the focus is on the team, individual needs and improvements are not overlooked. It supports the idea that focusing on the team ultimately benefits everyone, aligning with the principles of servant leadership and building a stronger, more cohesive team.

Strong trust foundation

Trust networks are bi-directional and symmetrical.

Goals	Why	How	What
Have a trust network that is not forced by leadership	enabling self-managed teams to generate high value	I strive to establish a solid foundation of trust	As an agile leader
Don't resist	**Decisions = Learning**	**Opportunities**	**Organic growth**
Resisting high-trust self-organizing teams stops evolution	Good or bad decisions lead to experience towards improvement	Creating opportunities strengthens the network	Trust flourishes when it grows on its own.

Figure 3-3

In building a team, you will also need to establish a trust foundation. One critical aspect of this is avoiding resistance.

1. Don't resist trust.

Don't create an environment lacking trust in self-managed teams; such a setup is doomed to crumble down to nothing quickly. Trust is essential, and many organizations have found greater success by embracing it, thanks to leadership that empowers their teams.

We've discussed the fears, like the loss of power. If you've taken physics, you'll recognize the following diagram: a resistance diagram. It's a bit nerdy, but I believe it effectively explains the concept of trust in an organization. The diagram depicts why overcoming those fears is crucial because if not, and the resistance is high, micromanaged, and command and control, teams will not shine as brightly as they can. A little guidance and the right amount of resistance will allow teams to flourish and not burn out. It's essential to sidestep selfish priorities within teams and ensure that the team works collaboratively.

Figure 3-4

Implementing this approach doesn't diminish your leadership. I have to share an experience from years ago with a team I managed as a testament to this approach. Adopting a servant leadership role, I focused on providing for their needs, offering guidance rather than 'dictating' every move. There is a major difference between guiding and dictating. I let them get the work done however they wanted, ensuring they were getting where they should be. My support empowered the team to find the best ways to accomplish their tasks, ensuring they were on the right path.

The result was extraordinary loyalty and trust from both sides, with team satisfaction scores going through the roof. Even during escalations, when the CEO called me to discuss issues, the team provided the solutions and supported the actions taken. This demonstrates how effectively teams can work together when self-management is encouraged and trust is built. So, resisting the move toward self-managed teams is a mistake; building trust is the key to success.

Diminish the resistance.

Reviewing your journey to creating an agile environment, you'll notice points where the fear of resistance diminishes as you progress. Your leadership no longer fears trusting its teams to complete their tasks independently. But to get there, it's crucial to move away from the command-and-control approach, fostering a team dynamic where leadership focuses on providing guidance and support. Only by adopting this strategy will you see an increase in productivity.

Understandably, there will be failures, but they are inevitable. See them as an opportunity to learn and grow. This freedom makes your teams more autonomous, and instead of fearing failures, they focus on how they would positively respond to failures. So, yes, you must be ready to face failures on the way. It is a part of the process of the kind of team you aim to build. The key lies in how the team responds to these failures, learns from them, and moves forward. This approach paves the way for success.

Some articles claim that agile methodologies fail, suggesting that agile doesn't work and will never be effective for us. They are right, but let me explain why those claims are valid. The failure of agile initiatives is often attributed to deep-rooted behaviors that emerge, creating obstacles for the team. A significant factor in these challenges is the lack of trust. Without a solid foundation of trust, a self-managing team struggles to function effectively.

Without trust, things tend to revert to their previous state. It's essential to recognize that the journey doesn't end with implementing an agile framework. Embracing and implementing agility is a marathon, not a sprint. After undergoing an agile transformation, continuous effort is required to sustain and build upon the progress made. So, in essence, an agile environment won't work independently. It needs a solid foundation to stand upon, and trust is one of the pillars of that foundation.

2. Decisions=Learning

Learning from your decisions, whether they are good or bad, is a principle that resonates across various fields, including sports and business. Speaking from personal experience, as someone who competes in jiu-jitsu and has participated in international tournaments and World Championships, I've embraced a key philosophy within the jiu-jitsu community: *you never lose, you learn.* This thought has taught me to reflect on every loss, understanding what went wrong, how my game plan could have been better, and what changes are necessary for future competitions.

The perspective of seeing failure as a learning opportunity makes the difference and sets you apart from your competitors. I've had much success, but I've also had many failures. But I see losses as times of growth. This approach to learning from losses rather than viewing them as failures is crucial in sports and organizational dynamics. Recognizing failures as opportunities for learning allows teams to work together more effectively. Because when you learn from your mistakes and your decisions, good or bad, you do it as a team. You reach a consequence faster as a team and devise your next step faster. This means that when you fail fast, you mitigate risks sooner. This rapid iteration and risk management process fosters innovation out of necessity as teams discover new solutions to prevent future issues.

Moreover, adopting an agile mental model, which emphasizes failing fast, identifying risks early, and mitigating them, is instrumental in creating a culture of continuous learning and improvement. Acceptance of failure and understanding that most issues are likely the result of process gaps or inefficiencies is essential for progress.

I wrote a book on root cause analysis, emphasizing that understanding and addressing process issues is key. So, we need to understand that if something negative impacts the flow of work, the issue's root is a process failure. There's no point in getting upset over a negative outcome. Instead, it's essential to identify a process issue that allowed a problem to occur or failed to prevent it. Whether it involves steps that did not occur as they should have or the process itself facilitated the issue, the focus should be on the necessary changes within the process.

This perspective involves a systematic approach to identifying issues, acknowledging that each step in the process plays a crucial role. It will happen if something is destined to happen due to process gaps. The good thing is that for a team that sees failures as an opportunity to do better next time, it serves as an opportunity to learn and adapt. Accepting failures and the likelihood of them happening encourages a proactive approach to identifying and addressing the root causes of problems, ensuring that similar challenges are less likely to occur. Embracing this philosophy of learning from every outcome, teams can cultivate an environment where growth and innovation flourish.

3. Opportunities

When discussing opportunities, it's not just about promotions or financial incentives; it's about broadening experiences for individuals and teams.

This can include implementing learning programs, whether paid or unpaid, within the organization to meet specific needs and offering mentorship programs, knowledge sharing, and coaching. These initiatives build opportunities and enhance trust in leadership and among team members by demonstrating the value of these experiences across the board.

Apart from the usual opportunities you can provide your teams, the acknowledgment that failures are opportunities should serve the same purpose: learning and growth. Some organizations are fortunate enough to have processes and may never encounter a problem. That is until something is missed and a problem arises due to that aspect of the process, and the lack of positive acknowledgment of the issue as an opportunity leads to finger-pointing and negative conflict throughout the team. Recognizing problems are opportunities allows employees and teams to look for solutions and succeed. By establishing self-managed teams on a strong foundation, we open up new possibilities and ensure trust by connecting all aspects of team management. When these teams are allowed to self-manage effectively, improvements become evident. Accepting failures and celebrating successes alike fosters an environment ripe for opportunity.

More Opportunities = More Trust In Leadership

A prime example of seizing an opportunity was when I managed a team years ago. I had an individual to whom I had to estimate work in a non-agile environment. At that time, the workload was overwhelming, and it was impossible to cover all tasks within the available hours of the day. I needed to pull someone into the team to help with the estimate. I brought in this one individual and asked her if she could do an estimate for me. She had never done an estimate before and was worried that her estimate would not be reasonable. My response was, 'That's okay. We're going to work through this together. Here are the requirements, and here's what you base the estimate on. Go through it; I'll give you some guidance, and I'll help you. When you're done, we'll review it together and see how it works.

So, we gave her one estimate to work on, and after we worked through it, we gave her another estimate. Soon, she became the person who provided the estimates for me, and I could focus on more strategic work within the group and the team. What happened afterward was that, of all the other teams that worked in that area, my team provided the best and most trustworthy estimates, according to senior leadership, managers, and VPs. At first, they did their due diligence to question each estimate, yet over time, they found the estimates to be solid, and they trusted the estimates in the future because they understood the process used and how well it was organized. That individual took that opportunity to work with others, collaborate, and communicate with leadership effectively; her career flourished, and when writing this book, she was now a senior manager.

4. Organic Growth

Drawing from the example shared, when I offered that team member an opportunity to develop a new skill set, the experience wasn't just about task completion. It was a lesson in leadership and collaboration. She could take that knowledge and experience and grow from a career perspective. So, when you take such stances, trust organically grows as you move forward. And that's the key thing to understand, to have that trust flourish. Because when that trust flourishes and you keep nurturing it, it continues to grow.

Numerous studies have validated the significance of trust in enhancing team dynamics, management relationships, and overall satisfaction. One study highlights[26] the link between servant leadership, productivity, and high employee satisfaction scores, underlining that all these benefits stem from trust. As trust expands, so does the team's potential.

So, the focus should be on intentional design: building teams and processes that align with agile principles. We need to get away from the struggles to move forward. We must move from traditional organizational constraints to a more agile set to escape these struggles. This transition requires a commitment to servant leadership, whose goal is to serve and uplift others, regardless of one's position in the hierarchy. Remember that serving leaders are not just senior management or managers; everyone needs to be able to serve and help one another become better at what they do. It would help if you kept affirming those agile values. Doing so will enhance your ability to navigate challenges and ensure that the team's growth and trust continue growing.

Don't resist self-managed teams.

As a leader, don't resist self-managed teams. Let them grow and allow this approach to flourish. Don't step in when the teams make mistakes. Rather,

---

[26] https://link.springer.com/article/10.1007/s10672-021-09389-9

they should be allowed to amend those mistakes and get the desired results. It may seem risky when teams are empowered to manage their work, mistakes, and issues, but it opens the door to greater achievements. Understand that trust is built not merely through promotions and financial incentives but through growth over time. By providing opportunities and nurturing self-managed teams within an environment where trust is the foundation, failure is not feared but seen as a learning opportunity.

You're faced with a critical decision in developing your agile environment: will you maintain the status quo or lay a new foundation to support a more prosperous future? This decision will pave the way for the rest of the agile journey's success. By building up your teams, instilling trust, and taking on the role of a servant leader, you're not just preparing for the next phase. You're leading continuous improvement driven by trust and a clear, shared vision.

With this approach, you'll see more success and be able to tailor positive change specific to the teams, the department, and the organization. I hope you recognize the potential of this strategy.

WORKBOOK: 03

Start with Servant Leader

It all starts with leadership. Without it, the teams would be on a rudderless ship, aimlessly trying to reach their destination. For the better part of history, the standard view of leading was to use a "Command and control" mindset to get teams to perform. In the past half-century, the term Servant Leader gained steam and provided a better way to improve team productivity while helping improve morale. Another term that is not widely used yet still held in this subject is spiritual leader.[27]

Fairholm mentioned an organization that can answer those questions: "The organization (community) within which we work is becoming the most significant community."

The association of community fits the narrative of how to view a workplace. We spend approximately 25% of our time in a given week at work. That is more than the average person would spend time with outside communities like churches, parent/Teachers, or hobby communities. External organizations will have a leader who is there as a Spiritual Leader. Generally, a Spiritual leader helps provide meaning to those they lead. In the work environment, this is seen as motivation, wanting to get up in the morning to go to work instead of dragging themselves to work to do the required shift.

Fairholm explains why, even though management tries to use Spiritual Leadership qualities, there is little impact on employee satisfaction. "A characteristic of current leadership texts is that they confuse dedication, mission, or vision with spirituality. Spirituality goes beyond these ideas and provides the underpinning necessary to make them work in our personal and professional lives." This comment clarifies why leaders fail to engage and motivate employees to follow them. The messaging they offer and their conduct are amplified throughout the workplace.

The servant leader is there to help the team succeed and help the organization grow and flourish without needing credit. They are there, leading employees to grow and succeed with their guidance, like a

---

[27] Spiritual Leadership: Fulfilling Whole-Self Needs at Work by Gilbert W. Fairholm from Virginia Commonwealth University. The article was initially printed from Leadership & Organization Development Journal 17, 3(1996), pp. 11- 17. Copyright 1996 Emerald Insight.

shepherd with his/her flock. With that in mind, they have very similar traits as a Spiritual leader. Fairholm provides what he calls the Foundation Stones of the Spiritual Leader, which is very similar to the expectations of a Servant Leader.

- Moral Leadership
- Stewardship
- Community

1. How will agile values be rolled out and communicated to your target audience?
2. How do you plan to determine if teams are behaving consistently with them?
3. Where do you plan to have your documented agile values?
4. Describe how you will support efforts to address impediments.
5. How do you support and embrace agile values as a leader?
6. What process in place will you implement to review actions on needs and how they will be provided?
7. There are plenty of techniques to be a successful Servant Leader. One technique is "Leadership from Behind," and another is "Leading Without Authority." It is about treating others as you want to be treated. Over our careers, we have had good and bad leaders. Write down the good traits of previous leaders you want to emulate and the bad traits you want to avoid.
8. What are the current traits used in the team that you want to keep?
9. What are the current traits in the team that you want to remove?
10. What new traits do you want the team to exhibit?
11. How would you ensure the good and new traits fit the agile values?
12. One of the most challenging things to change in any organization is culture. One reason is years of complacency in how work is done and a lack of accountability. The key thing about cultural change is that it is a two-way street. Leadership needs to change their culture as well; everyone agrees on the culture change and remains consistent in the change. Write down your ideas and plans for changing the culture.
13. How do you identify and maintain preferred partners/suppliers to work with?
14. How do you capture and set project expectations with partners/suppliers?
15. How do you ensure outside partners/ suppliers meet project

expectations?

16. How are outside partners/ suppliers evaluated?
17. Partnerships are internal and external. Internal partnerships deal with agile values, processes, and high trust with everyone. External partnerships are sometimes made based on filling an immediate need without a deep dive to see if they can effectively work with the teams. Sometimes, there is no way around it, and it needs to be done. A good foundation will provide sufficient time for leadership to think strategically and create strong partnerships that benefit both parties. Please write down the current partnerships your team has and the pros and cons they have. See what could be changed to make the partnership equal.
18. What agile methods can you use in your workday working with everyone?
19. What must you do to "walk the talk" with teams and partners?
20. What do you think would impede you from exhibiting agile behaviours?
21. If the team does not see others following agile values, they will feel they won't have to either. It can be challenging for leadership to exhibit agile behaviours as it goes against decades of training and mindset. Even small changes can have a significant impact. Write out your ideas and their implementation.

Understanding Self-Managed Teams

Self-managed teams can take credit for saving money in multiple industries. The benefits of improved productivity, quality, and employee satisfaction are great for any organization. Unfortunately, many misconceptions can creep in and impact how the teams work and the organization oversees.

If you search through academia to understand how the misconceptions of self-managed teams have on productivity, the results may be low. Two examples are D. Emuti's Sef-managed work teams approach: Creative management tool or a fad?[28], and K.O Roper and D.R. Phillips Integrating self-managed Work Teams into Project Management[29]In a similar search

---

[28] Elmuti, D. (1997). Self-managed work teams approach: Creative management tool or a fad? Management Decision, 35(3), 233-239. doi:http://0-dx.doi.org.aupac.lib.athabascau.ca/10.1108/00251749710169440

[29] Roper, K. O., & Phillips, D. R. (2007). Integrating self-managed work teams into project management. Journal of Facilities Management, 5(1), 22-36. doi:http://0-dx.doi.org.aupac.lib.athabascau.ca/10.1108/14725960710726328

on Google, the results are different—millions of results with plenty of articles and blogs giving lists of these misconceptions.

This section identifies those gaps and has the right game plan to mitigate and remove them.

Building and setting the limits for the teams will help with this misunderstanding of working in and with self-managed teams. In some organizations, there is a mix of self-managed and typical project teams or traditional departments. There are effective ways to keep communication efficient and effective even though they conduct work differently. Having that guidance in place for everyone to be in sync is critical to continued success.

1. What scares you most about agile delivery and management?
2. What do you like about agile delivery and management?
3. How can you eliminate the fears and enhance the benefits?
4. Read https://hbr.org/2010/05/leading-from-behind. What do you think of Leading from behind?
5. Read https://medium.com/the-human-business/heres-how-to-lead-from□the-back-2a72ac44aae8
6. What is more valuable, power or loyalty?
7. It is normal to fear something new. There are plenty of articles and websites out there that say agile doesn't work. When reading or listening to those comments, remember that agile delivery and management are nothing new. It has been around for decades, and organizations in different industries have succeeded in being agile. This is the reason for this foundation section of the book. People who say it fails did not have a strong foundation before they changed. Please write down the opposing views on being agile and determine whether it is a fear or procedural issue.
8. What would be the best way for the team to communicate instantly?
9. What overlapping skills do they currently have?
10. What future skills can be added to the overlap?
11. Plan a schedule with teams to identify gaps in experience across the team members. Determine the right makeup and how they would like to communicate with each other to become more efficient. Anything that is currently not available to the team document and devise a plan as the Servant leader on how to get them, if feasible (a wish list could be that, a wish list)
12. What limitations would you put on the team?

13. Do those limitations fit with agile values? (answer now and revisit after agile values are created with teams)
14. Does HR have roles and descriptions that align with agile values? Not just a copy or a traditional role with agile terms interspersed (answer now and revisit after agile values are created with teams)
15. What would be the minimal set of limitations you want on your team?
16. How would you plan to communicate those limitations?
    a. Limitations are needed, which is lost in agile leadership. Some treat agile as a full-on free-for-all, while others see framework rules as etched in stone and include traditional governance that impacts everything. There is a happy medium where everyone has the boundaries to succeed. Work through those limitations and see where they stand with the team.

Strong Trust Foundation

An agile environment survives on mutual trust throughout the organization. With a set-up of Servant Leadership, self-managed teams, and open collaboration, trust is the glue that holds everything together. Without it, everything falls apart due to impediments, a lack of information sharing, and sometimes selfish behaviours, leading to more significant issues like high turnover and lower productivity.

Robert Littlejohn[30] lists what can create that high level of trust. Delegation

One of the critical things with self-managed teams is to let the teams manage themselves. I have trust in them to make the right decisions regarding the work they are doing. Letting teams know they are allowed to fail and improve builds trust.

Enunciate policy

Setting and agreeing to everyone's expectations helps establish limitations and allows all sides to better understand how to work with each other. Most organizations drive policy from the top down, even in agile environments, which impacts trust. A proper collaborative environment

---

[30] Littlejohn, R. F. (1982). Team management: A how-to approach to improved productivity, higher morale, and lasting job satisfaction. Management Review, 71(1), 23. Retrieved from http://0-search.proquest.com.aupac.lib.athabascau.ca/trade-journals/team-   management-how-approach-improved/docview/1309753654/se-2?accountid=8408

strengthens it.

Goal setting

Agreeing on goals for everyone to achieve and understanding how they impact them and how they can help each other achieve them goes a long way.

Decision making

Leadership's willingness to let teams make decisions and for groups comfortable making those decisions shifts to what most are familiar with in traditional setups. It is a learning process and guiding to do so, and the support must be there.

Conflict

Conflict will always exist in any environment. Understanding and agreeing on how to deal with it beforehand helps to handle it without needing leadership escalation.

1. What would trigger reverting to the old way of doing things?
2. Document ways to mitigate the triggers.
   a. One key reason any change fails is the inability to deal with and work through stressful, unknown situations. Returning to the old way of doing things feels easier because it is known. Having a high-level plan of attack when things start to revert will keep the team moving forward.
3. Do team members get frozen when making decisions?
4. If a decision does not go as planned, are there repercussions for the person who made it?
5. How would you deal with the bad decision with the team?
   a. Decisions should align with the organization or team's values. Established processes should support teams in making optimal decisions, especially when faced with challenges. Issues arise from process gaps or lack of guidance, leading to analysis paralysis. Providing clear guidance for common workflows is crucial. When encountering situations without guidance, it's important to learn, adapt, and implement changes to prevent future occurrences. Remember, the processes, not the people, need improvement.
6. Is there an incentive program?
7. What opportunities are there outside of promotions or raises?

a. Sometimes, teams like money, time, knowledge, or doughnuts. Many programs don't consider employees' needs; they only focus on their wants. Employees need the knowledge to grow and evolve the organization. This is a great way to build trust that leadership is listening to employees' needs.

Phase 2
"System"

CHAPTER 04 | PATHWAY

In the previous three chapters, we covered Phase One, and now we're moving on to Phase Two, our "System." This phase comprises three aspects: Pathway, Culture, and Trust.

Before we dive into this new phase, let's quickly review the last one. We've talked about servant leadership values, agile values, value chains, setting goals within teams and organizations for their products/services, and designing both the teams and the environment. This foundation flows into building the actual system that creates an agile environment.

Get on the same path customers are on

Goals	Why	How	What
Have a path to meeting needs and addressing wants	Customers are happy with needs met more than wants	Become a discovery shop instead of a development shop	An innovative environment
Understand the customer	**Adaptive**	**Strategic**	**Planning**
Make sure everyone is on the same page	Needs and wants change. Being adaptive is critical.	Become strategic and not tactical	Understanding risks, constraints, dependencies helps with an adaptive plan

Figure 4-1

When we talk about pathways here, we're referring not just to the pathway for the product or service but also to the path for the team, the path for individuals, and the path for the organization as a whole in terms of how it continues to function and evolve.

So, after establishing the foundation, we envision having a highly sought-after product or service—something every organization desires to achieve. The pathway component helps to build this out, not just through features and all the bells and whistles of your product but also in how the teams work to achieve this. This component is essential to consider if you want to keep making innovative products of high quality and demand for the long term.

It won't be appropriate to claim that there is a solid, one-fits-all pathway to achieve such a goal. There are multiple pathways for this, and we'll discuss these more. But throughout this phase, you must understand that your chosen pathway must be clear and defined. Without it, you are essentially going nowhere.

UNDERSTAND THE CUSTOMER:

As previously discussed, when referring to customers or clients, we consider anyone engaged with our product or service, whether directly or during its development process. This includes both internal and external stakeholders. Our primary goal is to meet their needs effectively.

We want to ensure that customers are happy with their needs being met. They want to discover, and you want to become that innovative environment. To do that, we need to understand the customer, be adaptive, and strategically plan.

There's a common misconception regarding agile organizations or teams, particularly about planning, strategy, and execution. Being adaptive in agile strategic planning doesn't mean lacking discipline. An agile environment is not possible without planning. But planning in this context means to plan at a high level. Think of it as planning a road trip between Toronto and Miami. The main goal is to get to Miami, yet there are infinite ways to get there by car. You can plan out a main route knowing that there could be times when detours might be needed. It necessitates a flexible approach, ensuring we can respond to changes without losing sight of our main goals.

Pathway Struggles:

The struggles we have within the pathways are
- Self-Interest.
- Things are not being used or not used the way they should.
- And you're not a mind reader.

Sometimes, when aiming for a target, you miss it for no apparent reason. Or so it seems. The target is there, but you're not hitting the bullseye. Moving away from teams that make guesses about features, tools, training, and processes like a scattershot approach is crucial. Instead, it would help if you strived to become a surgical unit, aiming for precision and capable of pinpointing and consistently hitting the target—achieving that bullseye every time.

And on occasions when you don't hit the bullseye, it's an opportunity to learn from that mistake, that issue, or that missed shot. You evolve, improvise, and become better at what you do.

Pathway Actions

- Understand needs over wants.
- Adaptive to change.
- Strategic focused pathway.

So, how can you ensure that you hit the bull's eyes? You need to understand the actions you must take to work through and have this great pathway, or better yet, pathways. This involves distinguishing between needs and wants, a concept we've discussed in detail in the previous section and will get into more deeply here as well in building our system.

Adaptability is our key to building an agile system. What we mean by adaptability here is dealing with changes in the market, changes in the process, changes in the flow, and changes in the team. We need to be more adaptive to any change that occurs so that we have a quick turnaround and who can make the right choices. You want to be able to be strategic when you create these pathways, not be tactical, ensuring that each step taken is aligned with the broader objectives of the strategy rather than merely reacting to immediate challenges.

Understand needs over wants

Everyone has wants, finding out the needs and meeting them differentiates between mediocre and high value.

Goals	Why	How	What
Create a model to discover, document and implement changes to meet needs	empowering teams to deliver valuable outcomes	I aim to convert needs into actionable information	As a product owner
Team needs	**Customer needs**	**Listening**	**Discovery**
The right infrastructure to ensure right tools and processes are in place	Needs are overlooked by customer and provider	Listening for the cues will lead the path.	Value can be found anywhere, and it will impact everyone

Figure 4-2

So, as we start, let's look at the needs over wants. If we look at the user story, as a valued provider, I want to transform needs into usable information so that teams can develop value. And that's important. The 'why' is about producing value by converting needs into practical information. As that provider, you want to create a model of discovery, document, and implement changes that meet those needs. Let's explore this concept further, starting with the team's needs.

Team needs

When we look at team needs in an agile environment, many people envision open spaces—no offices, no walls, no cubicles, with everyone co-located. Although it sounds good and is part of an agile environment, it is more than just physical space. Setting up a blank office space is great. It helps. But it is, by no means, the end-all-be-all about being agile. It is also about, 'Do I have the right tools in place? Can they work collaboratively, even in that environment?'

The key is ensuring that you're working collaboratively and maintaining constant communication. So now, whether through an open space or tools such as Slack or Teams, there needs to be a continuous avenue of communication to ensure that the team delivers the value everyone expects.

So, what do you think? As an agile leader, are you in tune with what's happening? Are you actually 'listening?' Are you attentive to the needs required to meet those demands to get those right behaviors? If not, you will have to start by making sure that:

- The environment is appropriate,
- The roles are clear and agreed upon,
- Everyone accepts their accountabilities moving forward.

"Beware of false knowledge; it is more dangerous than ignorance." – George Bernard Shaw.

Using George Bernard Shaw's words in the context of that agile transformation, I mean to convey that it's not just about implementing that framework or any transformation, whether it's agile environments, business, team, or anything. The word "transformation" involves behavior change, and this book is about setting up the journey to have a mapped-out behavior change within the team.

We aim to have proper change management and a good process to ensure everyone exhibits the right behaviors and actions for the right valuable outcome. We must understand that everyone must work together as a fully functioning team. It matters little whether the team operates in an open space or collaboratively via Slack remotely. As long as they exhibit desired behaviors and effective communication, you're setting up the environment to be agile.

Here is a list of things to understand what the team needs. This is from "The Character and Servant Leader: Ten Characteristics of an Effective

Servant Leader" by Larry Spears[31]. This suggests focusing on leadership qualities that help create an environment where agile principles can grow, further highlighting the role of leadership in facilitating the change necessary for a successful transformation.

1. Listening
2. Empathy
3. Healing
4. Awareness
5. Persuasion
6. Conceptualization
7. Foresight
8. Stewardship
9. Commitment to the growth of people
10. Building community

The first thing at the top is listening, which I've also discussed in previous chapters. You have to listen to everyone, not just hear them. By listening actively, you gain insight into what's happening, which enables you to understand your current situation and move forward effectively. Everything else will follow naturally once you've mastered this and truly comprehended where you stand. That's the power of genuinely listening to the people involved.

Customer Needs

As discussed in the goals section and the last few parts, the focus should be on the customer's needs, not just their wants. It's crucial to develop solutions based on these needs. This is when you start hitting the bullseye—by listening to the client's needs and translating that information into something tangible that teams can develop and users can utilize.

So, working with the user and ensuring continuous engagement is key. It's not a one-time deal to get the requirements. That's sometimes where things fall off the rails. You can have that one conversation with the user, get what they need or want, write it down, confirm it with them, and then

---

[31] https://www.regent.edu/wp-content/uploads/2020/12/Spears_Final.pdf

walk away and deliver something to them in a month, two weeks, or three weeks. That's not how it works.

It would be best if you had constant communication with the customer. You need to understand that if you don't make it a regular thing, their minds can change after they've given you the requirements of what they want or you've determined what they need. You can fine-tune the requirements by continuously working with your customers as they evolve. Then, when you do the demos or show them mock-ups of what it will look like, you can get that feedback loop to see if it meets their needs or what they're looking for.

I talked about scattershots earlier to explain this concept. Imagine taking a shotgun. If you're unfamiliar with or have never seen how a shotgun works, it contains a cartridge filled with many pellets. When you fire it, the pellets scatter. So, aiming at a target using the shotgun has many different holes around the bullseye because the pellets have spread out. You may or may not hit the bullseye directly. There is no certainty.

As a leader, you don't want to work with that uncertainty. Instead, you aim to be that surgical product owner known for precision. You want to lead a surgical product team, service team, and development team, all attuned to listening to the needs. This focus allows you to direct your work toward more succinct experimentation to deliver the highest possible value that meets your client's needs and, if it doesn't allow for better team adaptation, to find the right solution. It's important to grasp the broad view of the customer.

You're not focusing on just one individual; you're considering several and aiming to meet the specific needs of each when you deliver your work. It's essential to sidestep overthinking and cultivate empathy to meet those needs truly. This begins with listening—understanding what those needs are.

Take, for example, if you have a SaaS web application used by your clients and notice that a client prints out documents only to fax them elsewhere. A potential enhancement could be integrating a faxing feature directly within your application. This meets a direct need and saves time—

something everyone wants and values. You're saving time. It's easier to press a button to send a fax online than to print it off, walk over to the fax machine, and fax it, hoping the paper doesn't get jammed.

With that feature as an example, you could save the client even more—not only time but also money—because maybe now they no longer need the fax machine, so they can remove it. They're not paying for power, they're not paying for service, they're not paying for anything else, so it adds value. So that's when you've got to listen to those needs to see the value.

Yes, it's those small steps. Listening to and addressing these needs is where innovation and 'wow' moments come from seemingly small, tangible enhancements that save time and money, which everyone values.

Listening

Listening to needs is crucial because understanding their complexities is impossible without it. These needs are subtle, and they become explicitly clear only when we gather information and connect the dots through:

- Context: Understanding the circumstances and settings when using your product or service.
- Routines: Recognizing the daily or habitual practices of your customers that might intersect with your offering.
- Workflow: Identifying how your product or service fits into the broader spectrum of processes and activities your customers engage in outside its direct use.

This information comes from your customers, and it's up to you to create a source to extract it and then develop it into a product/service. You have to walk through their routines to understand the context of what they do and how they do it. Understand the workflow. The outcome of this whole process of using a product or service is the information you can use to develop and enhance your product. It will tell you if it can be done within the product or if you must start with a new one. This approach underpins development in either scenario, emphasizing listening to and understanding customer needs in shaping effective solutions.

If you replace customers with teams, this gives you a mental model of how to work with them for continuous improvement activities.

- **Small changes can have a big impact.**

The subtleties in customer information can give you a competitive edge. It's essential to sift through this information to discover aspects that have been overlooked until now, as these can become points of product/service differentiation if they align with customer needs. Small changes based on these insights can lead to significant impacts.

Take Apple as an example. When Apple launched the iPod, the innovation it brought to the market was the ability to store music and songs, a shift from the era of CDs to a more compact device. This change catered to the growing trend of people saving MP3 files on their computers and downloading large quantities of music. Subsequently, Apple made another transformative change with the introduction of the iPhone. By integrating the features of an iPod into a phone, Apple provided a mobile communication device and a platform with multiple apps, including those for listening to music. This small change significantly enhanced the user experience, combining communication and entertainment in one device.

Discovery

It's fundamentally about understanding customer issues and effectively conveying those insights to the teams. This involves providing a consistent message that aligns with agile values. When this alignment is achieved, it creates a beautiful environment both for the customer and the teams. It propels the teams into a discovery mode, enabling them to create innovative solutions, processes, or improvements that enhance the overall experience.

However, it's important to ensure we do not overdo and change aspects that are already functioning well and do not require further innovation or development. Some organizations and teams may feel compelled to innovate continuously, wanting to deliver the next big breakthrough every time. However, it's important to remember that if customers are satisfied with the current product or service and do not want frequent changes, such constant innovation may not be necessary.

On the other hand, this approach doesn't work in every situation. There will be situations where customers are content with a product or service and resist change, yet the evolution is dictated by the demands of the time. In such cases, innovation becomes necessary not for the sake of change but to adapt to new challenges and opportunities, ensuring long-term satisfaction and relevance.

> *"Too often, innovation leads to a different solution, not a better one. Different isn't necessarily better."*
>
> – Teresa Torres

So, understanding the importance of listening to needs is crucial, both for a customer and the team. I'm sure we've all been in situations at our workplace where something new was introduced—be it a new process, a new tool, or a new way of doing things—and it didn't pan out as well as expected. That's often because everyone starts reverting to the old way of doing things since it is much easier. The same happens when you introduce something new to the customer that wasn't needed. Your efforts will go in vain as people will revert to using the older version of what worked better.

Why does this happen? A key factor is a failure to listen to actual needs rather than wants. From a partnership perspective, ensuring that a change meets genuine needs is vital. A product is only readily accepted by its audience when it fulfills their wants and needs. Therefore, when considering new tools, changing product features, or introducing new products, assessing whether these changes align with what the team and customers genuinely need is essential. These needs must be in harmony because if a change doesn't align with the team's needs, they won't be able to implement the idea effectively.

You have to ensure that the development will improve everyone's lives. This approach creates a more supportive and productive environment for the team and its customers.

- **Understand the tacit and explicit knowledge.**

Understanding the distinction between tacit and explicit knowledge is key to grasping how things are accomplished within a team, including their routines and practices. Having explicit knowledge of a tool is great, but you also need to know how they use it. Are they using it based on their explicit knowledge (clearly defined and understood) or their tacit knowledge, including their instincts, experiences, and workflow complexities? How do customers use your product? How do they use your service?

How a tool is used to tackle problems reveals important, nuanced information. It highlights the importance of teams' collaborative efforts in devising solutions. Finding the right solution for clients does not rest solely with the product owner or business analyst. While they initiate the process, it's ultimately the team's responsibility to determine the most effective solution, leveraging the outcomes provided by these tools.

- **Work together on finding the solution.**

Understanding that there is no singular path to discovery is key. When everyone collaborates to explore different solutions, the team will eventually find the optimal way to build and implement the solution, meeting everyone's needs.

Then comes the testing. You must test everything out when you use beta testing or any feedback loop. When we talk about testing it out, it applies to any delivery framework; you have to test it out. You have to ensure that you're getting the expected outcome that you wanted. Ensuring that the outcome aligns with expectations is part of being agile, which involves continuously reviewing the features, processes, and flow within the value chain.

By doing so, you can address issues and adapt as necessary. When you do that, you work through the issues and adapt as you go along. That's the key thing: being adaptive to change. You have to ensure that no one is frustrated, not just with your product but with the teams that develop and deliver it, because that significantly impacts the whole customer experience.

From the team side, it is about testing the changes implemented to see if they resolve an issue or provide more value. It is a constant cycle for everyone to improve value.

Adaptive to change

Like water, without flowing with change you become stale.

Goals	Why	How	What
Create a model to discover, document and implement changes to meet needs	ensuring that both teams and clients avoid frustration	I aim to cultivate a team that can swiftly adapt to unexpected changes	As an agile leader
Don't panic	**Accept it**	**Plan for it**	**Execute**
The natural behavior to change is to reject it	It is going to happen.	Have the right flow in place to deal with change	Involvement of everyone impacted by the change

Figure 4-3

There are four components of adaptive change:

1. Don't panic
2. Accept it
3. Plan for it
4. Execute

Don't Panic

Since the end of the 20th century, change is accelerating quickly. Consider how quickly we transitioned from VCRs to DVDs within about a decade, then moved on to Blu-ray in just a few years, and now, we find ourselves in the era of streaming services. Everything's online. The technological advancements we live with today were mere dreams long ago.

This rapid pace of change is accelerating, not maintaining a consistent velocity, suggesting that in the coming years or even months, we'll experience even more rapid transformations. So, it is understandable why people see changes as a bad thing and why they panic. This perspective applies to teams, what they're working on, and customers, some of whom resist change. Referencing E. Rogers' 1962 "Diffusion of Innovations," he categorizes audiences by percentages and identifies the 'laggards'—those resistant to change and only adapting when forced.

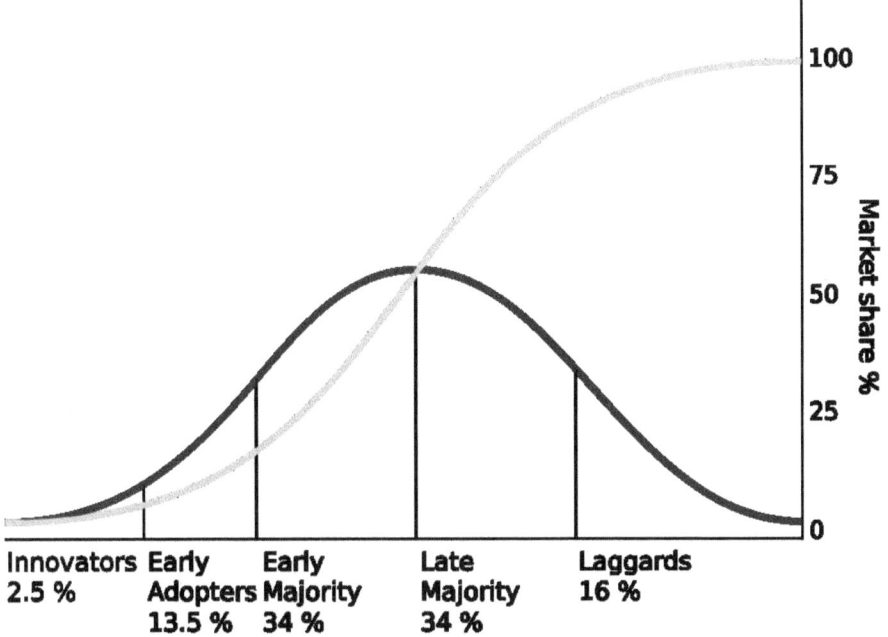

Figure 4-4 Diagram based on E. Rogers' "Diffusion of Innovations," 1962. Courtesy of Wikimedia Commons.

That's because people are comfortable with what they do and how they do it, whether a team or a customer. Let's say there's a change in the market, minimal or drastic, on a product or service that your team builds. How well would your team react to that change? They get comfortable with what they're delivering and how they're flowing. But then there's a drastic change, and they must turn left instead of right. It becomes a headache and a distraction. They don't like it because sometimes, due to experience, it blows up in everyone's face.

But we can't live in the past and keep ourselves from growing just because something didn't work out well. We must get past our comfort zone and expect and accept change. Take the evolution of cell phones as an example. In the late '80s and early '90s, cell phones were large and bulky, but then they began to get smaller and thinner, leading people to believe this trend would continue.

Yet, smartphones reversed this trend, making devices larger again, a change that has become preferred over time. But that doesn't mean it is bad because we thought it would be different. As time passed, people began to like bigger phones. So, no matter what we initially thought when their development began, the current times show that the unexpected can be a positive thing, too. It only seemed unexpected to us because we didn't 'listen.' It was only our assumption, but the companies who saw it coming and listened knew what phone development would look like.

Accept it

Did you know that there are more cell phones now than landlines? I'm sure you do. Landlines are almost a relic of the past, a prominent example of how we've adapted to the increasing use of cell phones. There was a time when smartphones were novel, and not everyone found touch screens easy to use. Some people kept an extra phone with a keypad because it was simpler for texting. How often do you see that today? Rarely.

This shows that we're accepting and adapting to change. Part of adapting and accepting change is being prepared for it. Nowadays, change is often expected; many people want to see innovation in their products or services. Therefore, when we introduce new changes and undergo a transformation, which alters behavior, there's a higher likelihood of acceptance because we're ready for it. It's crucial to understand that everything exists for a reason. We must embrace change, for innovations like cars would not exist today without it.

Henry Ford famously said, *"If I had asked people what they wanted, they would have said faster horses."*

This highlights that we cannot take changes for granted; we must actively move forward. It would help if you aimed for positive change within your teams, setting them up to embrace and implement strategic changes effectively. This will help in avoiding unnecessary complications.

Being agile is about welcoming change and mitigating risks. Unfortunately, in many organizations, changes are not adequately addressed upfront.

Often, they are dealt with later, when it's too late, leading to emergency meetings with executives scrambling for solutions that could have been easily foreseen if things were in place. So, it is essential to ensure that teams are prepared to identify the right solutions at the right time. Inclusion in the change process is the key, not just at the executive level but across the entire team. This doesn't mean gathering everyone in a large conference room for problem-solving. If you have self-managed teams, they can independently work to discover solutions. Building trust in these teams' ability to navigate challenges is key.

When the right solution is found, teams can make appropriate decisions. If the problem is significant and requires extensive effort, a larger team may be brought in to devise and execute a plan.

Considering the analogy of flowing water, consider how water adapts when a boulder is thrown into a river. From an agile perspective, the water represents adaptability, seamlessly flowing around obstacles. Similarly, when faced with change, we aim to adapt and continue our flow rather than letting change stop our progress.

- **"Why" change**

We need to be able to remove fear and evolve. Discussing change from a product/service perspective necessitates a deep understanding of the 'why' behind the change, which is key to ensuring innovation is meaningful and not just for its own sake. It's important not to change what is already working well, what clients use effectively, and what meets their needs. Therefore, changing just for the sake of change is not beneficial. We aim to ensure that your product or service backlogs are appropriately managed.

We've discussed various pathways. For your team, consider the following pathway: retrospectives, managing impediment backlogs, risk backlogs, training backlogs, etc. These must be managed effectively.

Ensuring you have that set path in place allows for adaptability. By managing backlogs and adjusting based on priorities, finding the flow becomes easier. This adaptability enables adding changes smoothly. Even if it means having to cancel a sprint to re-plan quickly and start anew, it's important to have that plan in place to ensure it gets to where you need it.

Plan for it

We've talked about plans before, but this one isn't about having a specific plan but more about setting guidelines to prepare yourself for when something unexpected happens because you don't know what you don't know. So, how do you plan for such situations?

Let's say a cell phone company has a new phone that makes coffee. It might sound ridiculous and may not meet many needs, but it fulfills some for people who are too busy. Then, it becomes the rage and the talk of the town. Other cell phone companies must adapt to this change and strategically shift. They didn't know this would happen, but they needed to have a plan for a drastic market change. They need to consider how they will move forward, how they will deal with it, and the priority of this change. Is this something they even want to address?

With change comes panic, and the goal is to remove that panic. It's about having that 'break glass in case of emergency' plan, mitigating the risk. When a few plans deal with possible triggers, there's less need for escalation to leadership, executives, or management. Teams can take the plan and adapt. When leadership understands this, they must engage with the team through Gemba walks, lean coffees, and direct conversations to see how things are going.

Instead of just sending out an email asking for a status, it's about walking over and talking to the team or, if everyone is remote, getting them on Slack or Teams for a quick conversation. This conversation builds trust. After going through this process, a quick email update on how things are progressing can be sent. Face-to-face meetings, whether online or in the office, go a long way in building trust. The plans are there for the team to move forward and execute.

Execute

Teams can effectively execute plans when triggered only when these plans are collaboratively developed with input from both the team and leadership, ensuring everyone understands the intended actions. Sometimes, you might need a quick meeting to initiate action and get things moving.

However, this meeting is no longer about dictating directions with an iron fist but acknowledging, "Okay, this has changed." The discussion then revolves around what this change means for us, where we are going, which plans we have in place to execute, and how to involve everyone in the process.

This approach is not just applicable to dealing with market changes but also to team dynamics. For example, suppose an agile team member wins the lottery and leaves the organization in the middle of delivering a critical and time-sensitive project. In that case, there might already be a general plan for handling attrition. Nonetheless, a quick meeting with the teams and leadership to understand how to move forward, assess the risks, and decide on mitigation strategies becomes crucial. Questions such as whether to adjust the scope, extend the deadline, or take other measures to meet the timeline are addressed, ensuring the team remains on track despite unexpected challenges.

- **Everyone is involved in the execution.**

  1. Keep the collaboration going.
  2. Don't shut out anyone that is impacted
  3. Understand all the risks and agree to them.
  4. Time for change

The plans that genuinely benefit your organization involve everyone. It's about maintaining collaboration and avoiding exclusion. Understanding the risks and acknowledging that change will necessitate multiple iterations and time is crucial. Once these plans are in place, there is acceptance of change, and to prepare everyone to move forward, you are on the path to creating a strategically focused pathway. This preparation positions your organization to adapt to any change.

Strategic pathway

Mission, Vision, Values and agile values light the way towards strategic thinking of products or services.

Goals	Why	How	What
Have a path of valuable work identified and effectively lined up to provide value fast	to ensure the comprehensive vision of the product or service is brought to fruition	I aim to create a roadmap, release plan, and backlog	As a Product Owner
Roadmap	**Definition**	**Clarify**	**Plan**
Understand where you are and where you want to be	Identify the priority and value	Refining the work needed for better understanding	Pulling in the work based on priority, value and capacity

Figure 24-5

Roadmap

When you create a strategic pathway, you will have your roadmap. Your user stories are waiting for you, and you have the priorities. Developing this roadmap is crucial for understanding the vision of the organization, departments, and products/services. It involves asking questions like where we envision the goal in three, six, nine, twelve, and twenty-four months.

This roadmap must be well-known among all teams involved. Each team must have a clear roadmap for their product/service; without it, they can neither pinpoint where they started nor predict where they will end.

Discussing the predicted and intended changes in a roadmap is essential. Teams must grasp the priorities and ensure alignment with the agreed-upon vision among all stakeholders. This vision circles back to the 'why' of the product/service, while the 'how' involves translating stories into actionable items.

However, a singular roadmap isn't enough. Besides the product roadmap, consider a change roadmap for your teams and an impediment roadmap, which often doubles as a change roadmap. These roadmaps facilitate collaboration between leadership and teams to foster organizational improvement. Moreover, consider the use of an organizational change roadmap. An organizational change roadmap is a great tool for engagement across the enterprise as it makes it transparent to everyone what is happening and how it relates to the overall vision.

There are many roadmaps you can build within your teams and organization. They don't have to be numerous; it's just what you need to create a strategic view of everything, pushing forward. In teams I've managed, I always had a roadmap for improvements within the team, visible to everyone. I set up little user stories on what would be done within certain times and planned them out. It helped create a good team environment for developing the products and providing the change we needed to improve things and the flow.

So, without a clear start and finish, things will be difficult. You won't be able to see your goals amidst all the changes. You need to clearly understand where you are at any point and the direction you're going—a clear understanding of product or service needs, training needs, and organizational changes.

There will always be training needs to meet market demands. But knowing what you currently have won't help without a starting point and a backlog detailing your plans. Having backlogs for your products and services, team improvements, department improvements, management improvements, and organizational risks will assist significantly. This ensures nothing gets left behind, allowing you to see the changes needed and how you can help bring them to fruition.

Definition

One crucial insight about managing change, particularly within agile methodologies, is that the key is to avoid tackling large chunks of work or information all at once. Instead, it's more effective to break down these larger tasks into smaller components. This approach makes the work easier to manage and, critically, allows for better control over each aspect and step of the process.

In software and product development, this means embracing continuous integration and development. You're working with small bits and pieces, gradually assembling the larger product. The key is understanding how to dissect complexity into manageable parts. This can be done through training changes, maintaining a training backlog, a risk backlog, and backlogs for management, departments, or teams.

For example, when faced with the need to change a large component, a deeper look and discussion might reveal smaller, incremental changes that can happen. The larger change is gradually achieved by breaking the task into smaller segments and tackling them individually. Instead of trying to clear the entire forest, you're methodically cutting down one tree at a time, paving your path through the forest rather than getting overwhelmed by its entirety. This methodical approach simplifies the task and ensures steady progress toward the ultimate goal.

- **Keep updating: It's about evolving.**

Things are not static; if you think so, you better take that thought out of your brain because it taints the whole concept of 'change.' You'll constantly be changing the process or any other aspect of your business. There will always be priority changes with the product and the features or services you provide. But this shouldn't intimidate or make you fear change. It will be easier to manage as long as you keep it visible. You can't just barge into a meeting room and say we must stop everything we're doing because of a sudden change.

Effective management involves anticipating change rather than reacting to it as an unexpected crisis. Change is rarely, if ever, sudden; it simmers beneath the surface before becoming evident. Recognizing the signs early, tracing changes to their origins, and preparing for their eventual impact prevents surprise. This foresight allows for strategic discussions about potential market shifts, ensuring everyone is informed and vigilant.

Maintaining this awareness and visibility ensures teams are on guard when changes materialize. They can adapt confidently, guided by prior knowledge and preparation. So, when it does happen, the teams are prepared and can say, "We knew about this. Let's go in this direction."

That's the kind of planning we are aiming for here.

Clarify

The next step involves clarifying expected changes. Just because something is defined or written down doesn't mean it's correct. Creating something without understanding its underlying value is a common pitfall. I've experienced this firsthand, often taking it personally when others question my work. However, it's important to recognize that the questioning is not about the work but the reason behind it and whether the value is genuinely present. Taking things personally during this process is not the way to go; it's about evaluating the ideas to ensure they add value to a product, service, or team change. This process isn't pestering or questioning for the sake of it, especially if it's planned and agreed upon.

We've discussed the importance of team charters and agreements between teams and partners. These agreements should include provisions for discussing new ideas or changes as a team to confirm their value. Ensuring that work is appropriately estimated is also part of this process. Often, people tend to equate a bit of work with how much time it will take, but humans are inherently bad at estimating time.

For instance, a personal anecdote from university involves my roommates claiming they would be ready in 10 minutes, which, based on experience, I knew to adjust to more like 30 minutes mentally. This story, while humorous, reflects a broader truth in organizations: estimating time is fraught with inaccuracies. This is why most agile methodologies will assess based on complexity and value, not time. When we understand the complexity and value of work, it becomes easier to ensure we're creating the right value within the necessary time frame.

Breaking down tasks into smaller, more manageable work efforts is essential, which is why many teams use the Fibonacci sequence for story point estimating: 1, 2, 3, 5, 8, 13, etc. This scale helps assess the complexity and effort required for tasks, with 13 often being the upper limit for a single sprint. Rating a story at 13 points strongly indicates that it can be broken into smaller, deliverable chunks. This breakdown makes it more feasible to say, "Okay, we feel that the complexity will allow us a good opportunity to achieve this within this timeframe," allowing for the reuse of resources, forward movement, and delivering value.

Regarding training and risk backlogs, the approach to estimates differs because they involve mitigating risks, so you're developing a mitigation plan against them, or you might be working to remove them entirely. Training backlogs, again from an estimate perspective, require understanding when to execute because some training could be a couple of hours a week for ten weeks, or it could be two days of in-class time. But these things need to be agreed upon when dealing with these pathways, with these roadmaps and backlogs, and planning against them will help.

How the team will approach

Now, you're going to determine how the team will approach this. You can create your team charters, define roles and responsibilities within iterations, and your agreements with leadership on what you expect and what they agree to expect in dealing with other roadmaps and work. Team charters are not extensive documents. They can be as simple as six bullet points you put up on a whiteboard. It's all about improvement. With a clear understanding of roles, responsibilities, acceptance, and agreement, you're avoiding issues down the road.

Remember, an agile environment is not a free-for-all, and planning can be made easy. It's about ensuring everyone agrees on their roles and responsibilities for that project iteration. Depending on how you work through them, team charters could be based on a per iteration basis, focusing on understanding the value of what you're providing, or can be changed on an as-needed basis. One thing to remember is that the team charter has to be reviewed consistently. That's why it's not an extensive document; you can get through it relatively quickly but achieve that agreement. A guideline I have used with teams is that the charter is reviewed at least once every three months.

Moving to stage two, the system piece, it's crucial to maintain enthusiasm about the progression. Having laid the foundation and established clear expectations, the focus shifts to understanding internal and external customer needs.

Action Plan

You aim to avoid the pitfalls of misapplying self-interest, striving instead for precision in meeting needs. It's essential to have the correct path in place for teams, customers, products, and the organization. This is achieved by distinguishing needs from wants and being adaptive to change. Ensuring that the necessary information is available and valuable is crucial. It would be best to have an environment where you can take what you hear and see and then change and create something useful for both the customer and the employees.

It's important to work closely with your customers and employees, maintaining engagement. This prevents the creation of a scattershot view of features and changes within the teams or products. Instead, you're able to pinpoint and address the real needs. By understanding the context and needs of the client and team, you acknowledge that small changes can have a big impact. However, it's vital not to change just for the sake of change. There's a fine line to walk, ensuring value in everything the team does. Collaborating to provide solutions maximizes value, allowing you to test and confirm its presence.

For a team or a customer, being more adaptive to change means avoiding fear of change, panic, and distractions. If we never accepted change, many advancements would not exist. For instance, we would still be in the horse and buggy era, and you wouldn't be reading this book right now if you had it on an E-reader. Adjusting and adapting are essential; without them, things wouldn't progress. We understand the 'why,' removing fears and recognizing the value is crucial. Even without complete knowledge, creating plans based on scenarios is possible. This involves having a mitigation plan ready to act when necessary, like breaking the glass in an emergency.

We understand what actions are needed to move forward, highlighting the importance of maintaining the right flow and keeping everyone involved. Collaboration and engagement are crucial; managing change becomes more manageable with these elements. You want to create a strategic pathway to achieve the vision. You need to know where you started and where you will go. As I said, the finish line moves because the backlog constantly fills up with new stuff to work on. It's about preparing for that, understanding the vision, and breaking down those changes and complexity to make it easier to manage. Changes are going to happen; everything evolves.

This adaptability is a core aspect of agile environments and evolutionary processes. We must ensure we evolve, not take change or new ideas personally. Agreement is possible and necessary for progress. Tools like team charters and clear definitions of roles and responsibilities can facilitate this process. Some games are designed to clarify roles and responsibilities, which can make the process engaging. It's about understanding how we will get there and sidestepping potential issues to simplify the journey so we can make the process smoother for everyone involved.

WORKBOOK: 04

Understand Needs over Wants

Ensuring the work environment is set up for success is more than allowing remote work, new laptops, and some fringe benefits (allowing pets in the office, for example). Those items would be considered the "wants." Understanding the need to complete their day-to-day work with minor obstructions is essential.

Identifying these needs and resolving them can be challenging. Budgets, training, and infrastructure, to name a few, have problems to overcome. Understanding the benefits and the ROI plays a big part, and with groups that most consider a "cost centre," not understanding their role in the value chain makes meeting these needs even more difficult.

What can happen when the needs are not resolved? If there is a lack of understanding of employee needs, low employee satisfaction scores, high turnover, and potentially lower quality could be some of the outcomes.

A case study was done in 2014[32] details the positive outcomes of working as a team to identify and implement resolutions to employee needs. They found higher staff retention and perception of the organization wanting to provide to the staff to help make their work lives easier. What needs to be kept in mind when meeting employee needs is to keep with the agile way of doing things and have it as a collaborative team involvement. To meet the conditions with a top-down approach will meet the wants more and overlook the needs.

Customer needs are essential to help create innovative products/services while providing opportunities to increase revenues. Banks have heard the needs of their clients and made innovative changes that resulted in an outstanding return on investment[33]. Product delivery organizations would

---

[32] Purayidathil, J., & Villavicencio, S. (2014). Enhancing work environment and work relationship for employee retention: A case study of project management section, jyo electronics, petchaburi: *Keyword branch*. ABAC ODI Journal Vision.Action.Outcome, 1(2) Retrieved from http://0-search.proquest.com.aupac.lib.athabascau.ca/scholarly-journals/enhancing-work-environment-relationship- employee/docview/2384089695/se-2?accountid=8408

[33] Ryerson, C. (1995). Banking on innovation: Savings banks lead the way in meeting customers' needs. BusinessWest, 11(11), 17. Retrieved from http://0-

make small changes that made customers' lives easier. The MP3 player would replace the portable DiSC players people were using after burning the music files onto discs. Was the need met? Make music more portable without carrying a large portable player.

It is about discovery over development to be innovative for customers and the workplace.

1. What components make up the work environment used by agile teams?
2. How are best practices and lessons learned currently shared across teams? How can they be better shared?
3. How are tools selected? Are tools leveraged across all teams? What can be done to streamline the process?
4. What approach is used to identify and capture training needs for agile teams?
5. What would a learning program look like?
6. Meeting team needs can be difficult as there are wants that they may not need. Go over some thoughts on how leadership can discover and meet those needs.
7. How are functional and non-functional requirements transformed into something usable?
8. How are requirements discovered? Are users involved?
9. Do those users meet the description of the larger audience?
10. After initial conversations, it is easy to think about what customers want. Unfortunately, it does not have a high success rate in meeting needs. There must be a plan to introduce the customer to a better feedback loop. Remember that customers can be internal and external. They still need to be involved. Draw up a schedule for getting involved. This is a high-level schedule and gives ideas to the team on the introduction.
11. Setting up teams to find needs can be a bit daunting as it is about listening and picking them out of conversations. Most product managers or Business analysts focus on wants only, and some that come up with ideas on changes see the application in their thoughts. Jot down your views of where things could go wrong

and what could be done to mitigate them.

12. Describe the role of the product owner/business analyst and how they participate and interact with the team.
13. What is the current interview process with customers?
14. How can the messaging be shifted from WHAT to WHY? This is the difference between a feature-based development and an outcome-based one.
15. There are workshops, training, lunch, and learnings that could be done to improve listening to the customer and work on interview processes. Provide a high-level plan and schedule of what can be done.
16. Write down your thoughts on listening to the customer needs and how the organization's current and future state.
17. Does your organization see a solution only for customers? What messaging is used for internal solutions?
18. For the remaining questions, consider internal and external solutions needing discovery. Is there team involvement in the definition of the solution?
19. Have there been times when there has been disagreement about what is being built? What was done to get the team agreement? Were there issues that happened after? To help answer, read Patrick Lencioni's book Five Dysfunctions of a Team.
20. What would involve introducing the team to work with the customer?
21. Is there a roadmap of the needs in place?
22. What is used to determine the value of the changes in the roadmap?
23. It is not just a matter of discovering the changes. It is about determining the value. Sometimes, some changes might look like there is value, yet to others building it may not see it. Without a clear understanding of the value of those buildings, it may be seen that little or no value will be discovered. Document the plan for team involvement to avoid this scenario.

Adapting to Change

In an agile environment, the one constant is change. In more traditional organizations, a change could be viewed as trying to turn a cruise ship around on a dime. It doesn't happen how we want and has issues we don't need to see.

Many factors[34] can impact the success of dealing with change. One critical thing to understand is that any change requires the right behaviors. Flexibility and a sound decision-support system are some of those behaviors necessary for success.

There is a flow in dealing with changes, whether a product change or a complete organizational change. With the right high-level plans in place that everyone knows, the triggers and processes can effectively deal with any change.

A misconception of agile development and delivery is that it can handle any change anytime. Some minor changes can happen in an iteration, which is expected as requirements/stories become clearer. What is not okay is a sudden shift or work addition in an iteration. That scenario is not simple and requires discipline for everyone involved, not just the team handling the change.

Now, there are times when a change is needed to provide added value to their clients. Teams grow, products change, disruption in the industry that requires quick organization-wide turnaround, or new product integrations that don't fit the current processes come into play. Methods and methodologies are tools that need to change depending on the job.

Using the tool analogy, if you are using a screwdriver to put screws into a board, you do not grab a hammer halfway through to do things faster. Yes, eventually, you would still get the screw in; at what cost? Frustration, slowdowns, and an impact on quality. When you could use a power drill with the right bit, sometimes seeing what others are doing could be a good thing to learn; emulating what they are doing because it is what they are doing could be costly.

1. What are the reactions to changing strategy direction?
2. How are product/service changes during development handled?
3. How are changes in the market affecting the teams handled?

---

[34] Chrusciel, D., & Field, D. W. (2006). Success factors in dealing with significant change in an organization. Business Process Management Journal, 12(4), 503. doi:http://0-dx.doi.org.aupac.lib.athabascau.ca/10.1108/14637150610678096

4. Have there been changes for customers or teams that didn't have a positive effect?
5. What is used to determine the value of the changes before creating it?
6. Work through a high-level plan of what should happen to address your responses. Some changes will happen, and panicking will put a fog in the process where understanding the value might be missed just to put a change in place. Removing the panic will go a long way with the next step in accepting it.
7. Write down some additional thoughts about panicking about change and how everyone handles it.
8. What is the messaging when introducing changes?
9. How is feedback dealt with on the change?
10. Are changes that come in a one-direction approach? (example: Here's the change, now do it)
11. Work through a high-level plan of what should happen to address your responses. We all accept change, but how it impacts what is individually done determines the level of acceptance. Going through this system, you will see how everything builds and helps drive out the strategy and guidance for the next step. Identifying needs and providing value helps determine the messaging for those who accept it. Keep the Golden Circle in mind throughout. Use the schedule for suggested changes to the current change process that fits agile values. This will change by the end of the program. It is also an opportunity to identify those quick changes that could provide additional value.
12. There is much information about how to accept change. As with discovery, there isn't one rule to get acceptance of change. Depending on the process, changes are handled differently. Identify the processes you know changes have or can happen to impact the flow, causing frustrations. Then, add some mitigation. Again, things will change over time.
13. Do you have one or multiple change plans?
14. Is there a lot of leadership involvement in dealing with changes?
15. Is there a lot of team involvement (not just team leads) in dealing with change?
16. How do teams ensure the product meets customer expectations?
17. These plans are about risk mitigation. It is sometimes overlooked

for most processes, and as such, escalations will happen. Please write down your thoughts on the recent change that caused problems and create a plan that would have guided teams to handle it effectively without escalations.

18. For any changes outside of the planned work, like the introduction of new work, change in processes, change in staff, or change in strategy (as examples), what are the general feelings of these changes, and how well are they executed?

19. If using an agile framework, what approach determines when product features and functions are delivered to the customer?

20. What methods are used to assemble product components and ensure consistency/ quality is maintained?

21. How do project team members know defined delivery events and techniques?

22. For those who are about to go through the agile transformation, take this opportunity to identify and schedule items to address these questions.

23. Those currently using agile methodologies must see how the teams work through the methodology and how it fits with agile values.

Strategic Pathways

Alessandro Di Fiore[35] provides a great example of how ING used planning to have the right strategic initiatives in place for the marketplace while continuing to have multiple agile teams work on producing products and services.

Looking at that example, you can see how a large organization with over 3500 employees can become an agile shop. People using size as an excuse not to start the effort needed are defeating themselves before they even begin. Employees will sense that, and also, though they created development teams to use agile methods to develop, they will not achieve being agile. That is another story for another time.

I wanted to point out that Alessandro shows how planning for a larger agile organization is more structured and disciplined using data collection,

[35] Planning Doesn't Have to Be the Enemy of Agile
by Alessandro Di Fiore
https://hbr.org/2018/09/planning-doesnt-have-to-be-the-enemy-of-agile

which allows them to react faster to adapt plans than traditional organizational governance. Everyone deals with "red tape" or waiting for information to go up the chain of command to get an answer on what to do. The process is slow and can turn biased, as emotions and control-driven individuals can now manipulate or exclude information to get the decision they want.

In an agile organization, senior leadership still needs strategic direction and planning. Being agile ensures that people are involved throughout and guides the teams to make the appropriate decisions so that they have ownership and take additional worries off their shoulders. For example, a good software quality assurance lead will have a high-level strategy that the analysts follow. It will guide how they can make decisions on their own to complete the work. This high-level "plan" allows the lead to focus on more strategic concerns without being distracted by tactical issues.

Another example would be an organization's vision and mission statements. Although they are unpleasant paragraphs about the organization, they guide everyone working there through a reasonable decision-making process.

In anything we do, there needs to be some planning. If not, it is a recipe for disaster in product quality, time-frames, and employee satisfaction. For senior leaders, setting up agile organizations will make planning relatively easier than traditional ones. One extensive program that I was a part of the initial "plan" was for a phase to take eight months. Two years later, it was finally completed and was only put on the shelf to collect dust five days before it went live. Initially, this program was an industry-wide initiative with an overall council from different companies making decisions. The amount of governance around it made it next to impossible to make decisions promptly.

Everyone that worked on the program grew frustrated with the progress. Once there was light at the end of the tunnel, the opening shut for good because one team did not share information on what they built. The flow of information was not forthcoming, and there was no ownership from anyone below a without a VP or higher title; there were millions of dollars wasted. Now, organizations doing agile are under the false impression that the work will be done faster and that the teams will push through the same amount of work in the scheduled timeline they provide. This type of planning kills agile because it is not agile but a waterfall.

Now, imagine that program from an agile perspective. Self-managed teams are working together with one goal in mind. Using the ING planning model, there is a steady stream of information about what other internal and external teams are doing. The sharing of information regularly and impediments they can all work together to remove to continue building the need. Risks are identified sooner, plans could easily change, and adapting to what is happening would be like a typical day. The senior leadership would be aware of the tactical work yet trust the teams to work through it while they focus on the strategy. The distractions in "firefight" meetings are a thing of the past. Disciplined planning and adaptability to working with plans will make everything work.

As Alessandro finishes, "The traditional planning approach needs to be revisited to better serve the purposes of the agile enterprise of the twenty-first century. Agile planning is the future of planning. This new approach will require two fundamental elements. First, replacing the traditional obsessions with hard data and playing the numbers-game with a more balanced co-existence of hard and soft data where judgment also plays an important role. Second, introducing new mechanisms and routines to ensure alignment between the hundreds of self-organizing autonomous local teams and the overarching goals and directions of the company."

1. What is the approach to keeping priorities in synch between the roadmap and backlog items?
2. Describe how planning is done from a Product Backlog.
3. How does the team understand their roles and responsibilities?
4. How have events and techniques improved over time?
5. Defining the work can be viewed as easy or hard, which is why agile teams have difficulty evolving. It is about finding that happy medium to provide the right amount of information where conversations on the work are smooth to ensure everyone is on the same page before pulling the work. A few techniques exist to create good user stories or requirements for understanding. Research those techniques and see how they would fit with your agile values.
6. Defining is not just for product/service features. Write a few requirements that could go in a management backlog to help remove impediments or something that could go in a team improvement log.
7. What approach is used to refine backlog items to the point where development can begin?

8. How are backlog items prioritized, sized, and assigned to a sprint?
9. Describe the role of the product owner (or manager, sometimes interchanged) and how they participate and interact with the team.
10. What approach (es) is/are used to determine how much work can be completed in a given sprint?
11. Clarifying what is about to be worked on is a tricky thing because there is a personal component people have with the work they do. That aspect needs to be taken out of the equation. This week's schedule should be about changing the teams' views that clarifying is good. As we get further out from the foundation, we will see that these schedules will be small because some issues will be addressed implicitly. Understanding what you want done to address the problems is good. Write down thoughts on what can be done to help clarify and make it about the problem to be solved.
12. How do Agile teams know when development can begin on a story? Is there a detailed Definition of Ready?
13. How do Agile teams know when a user story is completed during a sprint? Definition of Done.
14. Describe the role of the product owner and how they participate and interact with the team.
15. Describe how the team plans out the work,
    a. Planning work can be seen as easy because it has been done before and will continue. What is different with planning the work here is keeping the pull function based on priority, value, and the ability to complete the work within a time box. All while addressing the risks that come with the work. Let the team determine what work can be done within the sprint or time box. It is a collaborative process where everyone agrees on the work to be done and the expected outcome.
    b. This planning is strategic as it tries to meet the vision while tactical because it is the work to be done. Unlike the previous discussion of plans, which was relatively broad, these plans need to be specific for the upcoming work session. Priorities will change, so this type of planning must be regular and consistent.

CHAPTER 05 | CONTINUOUS IMPROVEMENT

Be better than you were yesterday.

Goals	Why	How	What
Han an environment where continuous improvement is organic and holistic	Have teams and clients experience consistently increasing value	Through ownership and stewardship of how the work is done	A structured continuous improvement program
What is missing	**Right way**	**Performance**	**Quick hits**
It is more than just Did well/Do better	Ensure the behaviors are there and still. meet agile values	It's a team effort, not an individual	Teams can effectively improve on the go.

Figure 5-1

In this chapter, we will talk about the culture of continuous improvement, the second stage of phase 2. In agile environments, creating a supportive environment is essential. A culture of continuous improvement is vital for the team or organization to succeed in an agile environment. Without it, there isn't progress in product quality, service delivery, or the development and evolution of teams.

In short, without this continuous improvement, there is no agility; you're merely conducting very short waterfall projects. This leads to ensuring the behaviors necessary for an agile environment to grow. We always strive to be better than we were yesterday, regardless of the context—at work or in any other area of life. Whether it's playing video games and reaching the next level or any other thing that you do, the goal is always to perform better than before.

CONTINUOUS IMPROVEMENT STRUGGLES

Understanding the goal is crucial to creating an organic and holistic continuous improvement environment. Forcing continuous improvement isn't the objective; we want everyone to understand its value. It's about getting the 'why'—the purpose behind continuous improvement. Once that's clear, the 'how' and the 'what' of improvement naturally follow. In this section, we'll explore what might be missing and discover the right approach to understanding performance and identifying those quick wins.

The struggles in Continuous improvement are:

- Focus On Symptoms
- Nothing Is Measured
- Leadership Driven Improvements

When we struggle with continuous improvement, it's often because we focus on symptoms. When discussing symptoms, we might say, "This is taking too much time," or "We have this many errors." The immediate reaction might be to fix them—throw bodies at the problem to address these symptoms. However, this overlooks the deeper issue that lies beneath.

The second struggle involves measurement—or the lack thereof. It's somewhat amusing when we say, "Okay, we're going to improve this or that," but what happens is that we might be looking at the wrong stats or metrics. Recalling our first lesson on the value chain, I mentioned some key metrics, like the quality metric and the input quality metric, as significant. While some might prioritize process time or lead time, improving incoming quality naturally enhances both process time and lead time because the quality of flow into the process has been elevated.

This leads us to the last struggle: Sometimes, leadership prescribes metrics for improvement that don't accurately reflect the situation or pushes for improvements based on numbers that don't align with the team's needs. We've discussed how crucial it is for teams to collaborate in driving change. Continuous improvement necessitates this collaborative effort, not a top-down, command-and-control approach.

If leadership pushes an ill-fitting improvement and fails, the blame often falls on the employees rather than the improvement approach itself. Working closely with the team to implement improvements can remove this issue, paving the way from a status quo to a team of 'rockstars.' But, again, as we've touched on with the Design part, not everyone individually needs to be a 'rockstar' Yet collectively, they are. It's about continuously pushing for and providing the highest value through the 'right mix' of team dynamics and improvements.

So, how do we overcome these challenges to achieve continuous improvement?

CONTINUOUS IMPROVEMENT CHECKLIST:

- Data Program
- Improvement Identification Process
- Where Leadership Fits

So, we have a data program and an improvement identification process, and then we identify where the leadership fits in. This checklist here is more about helping create that continuous improvement program and a root cause analysis program that fits with an agile team and your team. So, let's start with the data program.

Data program

Without the right story of measures continuous improvement is just a dream

Goals	Why	How	What
Have a program in place to measure improvements and make effective decisions.	ensuring that our agile values remain aligned as we navigate changes	I want to work collaboratively to establish a robust agile governance structure for evaluating both product and process performance	As an agile leader
Data	**Baseline**	**Story**	**Manage**
Understanding qualitative and quantitative data	Taking the data currently available to make valuable	All data tells a story. How it does depend on the audience	Evolve the program to introduce more data while keeping the value of current data

Figure 5-2

Data

We aim to ensure we have the right information to utilize data effectively since its value is well recognized. The necessary data exists in all organizations; the challenge lies in locating and harnessing it.

The data that's needed doesn't have to be complicated. Many organizations struggle with this. They might come across a software metrics book. While some books are relatively straightforward, others are similar to third-year university math or quantum physics textbooks—large and filled with complex metrics.

It's essential to avoid making things unnecessarily complicated. When things become too complex, that's when mistakes are likely to happen. After all, math is unequivocal; equations provide answers, with two plus two always equaling four. However, the situation becomes more complex when people are involved, as this is typically where errors occur.

So, we should aim to start simple and then build from there. We shouldn't be in a rush to discover the next big metric based on a book or a webinar. This is partly due to what we've previously termed the "conference hangover." While a metric may offer value, its usefulness becomes questionable if you don't have the correct data to support it.

At this point, starting with the basic necessity—a data inventory is important. This approach allows us to work through our data methodically, ensuring we don't jump ahead without the appropriate foundational information.

- Data inventory

First, it's crucial to understand what you have—label everything clearly and verify its presence and consistency. Maintaining transparency and ensuring everyone can contribute to the metric are important. I've worked with two teams focused on examining metrics and a data inventory program. They utilized Scrum methodologies, operating in two-week sprints, with their progress tracked through burn-down charts, time tracking, and other metrics, all facilitated by the software they were using.

Unfortunately, we encountered an issue: inconsistent data between the two teams. For example, story points are labeled differently in the same database—what was listed as one term for one team could appear under a different name for the other. This discrepancy was significant, but we identified the issue and created specific queries to address it. However, it required us to manipulate the data to ensure we were comparing like with like. We couldn't rely on a standard report and had to generate our tailored report instead.

- Qualitative and Quantitative data.

Conducting that data inventory before encountering problems when using a general report is always better. Make sure that the data you have makes sense. You aim to compare apples to apples, focusing on your quantitative data—those actual numbers. These numbers are significant as they help drive many measurements to determine if improvements are working. They'll point out where issues are and help identify those root causes.

Then, there's your qualitative data, based on feelings and reviews, whether good or bad. Reviews can be polarizing—bad ones are unmistakably bad, and good ones are good. Sometimes, it's challenging to determine if bots or actual people generate them. This concern is similar to what you might find on Glassdoor, where it's difficult to determine the authenticity of employee reviews. Are they genuinely reflective of the employee's experience, or are they skewed by external factors, such as being overly positive or negative due to recent employment changes?

Qualitative data interpretation requires detailed analysis to ensure the truthfulness of extreme feedback. Despite the challenges in interpreting reviews, each one holds a kernel of truth. Specifically, negative reviews on platforms like Glassdoor can reveal areas for improvement, linking directly to employee and customer satisfaction.

By examining these reviews, you gain insights into potential issues within teams, offering a starting point for improvement discussions. This approach fosters a collaborative environment, builds trust, and encourages open discussion about existing problems. Ultimately, this process helps establish a baseline for measuring future progress.

Baseline

Understanding where you're starting from is crucial because, without a baseline, it's challenging to gauge progress. Setting a baseline, drawing that proverbial line in the sand with a firm "Okay, here's the data we're starting with. Boom, done." That's the goal. You need to pick the right metrics, ensure team consensus, and then get the ball rolling by implementing them.
Some foundational metrics include:

- **Planned Versus Actual:** A comparison of estimated work versus actual completion time.
- **Cost Per Effort:** Evaluating the financial resources expended for each unit of effort.

- **Delays:** Identifying and quantifying setbacks in the timeline.
- **Re-Work:** Measuring the effort required to correct or redo work.

Especially in project management, the Planned Versus Actual metric is crucial, whether it's related to time or budget. In an agile environment, this could mean examining user stories to see if the initial workload, perhaps estimated at two story points, actually reflects a more complex, eight-story point task. This gives you a clear Plan versus Actual scenario to review and possibly refine your estimation process, be it story pointing, planning poker, or any other method you use for such determinations. Metrics like Cost Per Effort, Delays, and Re-Work can also be used depending on your goal.

These examples are just the tip of the iceberg. Several online metrics can offer value depending on your specific goals and the narrative you wish to convey through your data. However, it's important not to get overwhelmed by many metrics when building your data program.

Story

You want to start with immediately usable data and then build from there to ensure you can tell the right story. Telling the right story is vital because it enables you to ask more valuable questions to discover the issues you seek. Without the right data, you can't ask the correct questions and, thus, won't get the answers you need. Remember, math and numbers don't lie; they're the foundation. This isn't about opinions; it's about hard data.

Regarding qualitative data, the goal is collaboration, not pointing fingers or arguing based on opinions. The aim is to work through issues, avoid cognitive bias, remove logical fallacies, reach agreements, and find solutions. Telling the right story is again emphasized because it smooths the path to easier conversations. When it comes to numbers, they can be straightforward, but the way they're reported might not be.

I recall working with a VP years ago, presenting a histogram that compared defects from two different cycles; I believe it perfectly illustrated our progress. However, it led to a challenging conversation. The graph showed that cycle one had certain defects and cycle two significantly increased towards the end before improvements were made.

The VP asked, "What happened in cycle two? Why are there more defects compared to cycle one?"

Logically, especially in a waterfall model, you'd expect more defects in the first cycle, with fewer in the second.

So, what went wrong?

In these particular cycles, cycle one was marked by severe defects—severity one issues. These defects could lead to the organization being featured in the news for all the wrong reasons or, worse, result in legal action. In other words, the stakes were incredibly high, with potential for negative press.

Cycle two, however, presented defects of a much lower severity. These included issues like the color displayed on a screen, spelling mistakes, and buttons in the wrong places. When this distinction emerged in discussion, it initially led to a difficult conversation. I had to quickly adjust and explain that if the presentation of the data had been different—perhaps if I had used a bar graph to show the severity one defects in cycle one versus the minor issues fixed in cycle two—it might have avoided the confusion and made the situation immediately clear, preventing the tough discussion.

This example highlights the importance of selecting the right metrics and presenting them in a way that tells the correct story, ensuring transparency. This approach aligns with the Obeya room or information radiator concept discussed in earlier chapters. The aim is to display data so anyone can understand what's being conveyed and engage in meaningful conversations to foster improvements.

Managing

While working with data, always remember that managing it is a continuous process, not a one-time task. Even though numbers are inherently reliable, there is always the risk of corruption, making vigilant management essential. Once data becomes corrupted, you might endlessly circling back for the error. Moreover, juggling too many metrics can confuse and make data management overly complex.

As I mentioned earlier, establishing a baseline is important. It helps simplify your approach from the start and makes data management more manageable. It also becomes easier to maintain accuracy and integrity. You can consider introducing new metrics once you have a firm handle on this streamlined process. Gradually adding these allows you to explore new ways to measure improvement and progress effectively.

Improvement identification process

Without the right story of measures continuous improvement is just a dream

Goals	Why	How	What
Guidance for everyone to identify, work out solutions and implement	so that we can identify opportunities for enhancing team performance	I want to collectively assess team members' commitment to our agile values and methodologies	As an agile leader
Team effort	**Best Improvements**	**Share**	**Implement**
Improvements are made as a group to develop what everyone can get behind	Understand what best practices mean for the team	Ideas can come from anywhere. Sharing can have solutions come or they could help others.	Planning, implementing and measuring improvements

Figure 5-3

Identifying areas for improvement can be challenging. Part of the challenge comes from what we discussed earlier: the initial struggles where the focus tends to be on dealing with symptoms rather than the underlying issues. This is a key reason why many attempts at improvement fail—they aim to resolve symptoms without addressing the actual issues. The following steps can help you identify the problem and resolve it step by step.

Team efforts

It would be best if you started by guiding teams to ensure they can push through to find the issue, identify it, and then work together to find a solution. It's more than just saying we need to do better. You're looking at some deeply rooted issues in some cases. For example, one process improvement I worked on with a team involved a software development group. They faced a consistent issue that kept reoccurring. As we dug through trying to find the solution and identify the issue, we discovered an HR process causing the problem within the development process. It is related to training and onboarding. But that was the thing; initially, they looked at the individual, not at what process helped get them there.

Remember the quote, "If it's going to happen, it's going to happen." So, if your process is set up in a way that there's a gap, there's a potential for failure that no one sees; it's bound to occur. You must be prepared to deal with and respond to that change.

It's crucial that teams, not just leadership, find these improvements because they can see the different angles and a bit deeper. And you want to ensure you're not just looking at the symptoms. You have an easier buy-in when you find that issue and work together to find a potential solution. It makes the change management process smoother because everyone owns it. Finding issues can be slow, while fixing symptoms is quick—it's just putting a Band-Aid on it when an infection deep inside needs to be addressed. So, when resolving issues, remember that some solutions are quick, but others are not. There needs to be a system in place to ensure that if something reoccurs, it triggers a more in-depth improvement identification process.

This approach will further progress and help alleviate frustration. Triggering that improvement identification process is essential; otherwise, you'll find yourself attempting fixes that don't address the root cause, leading to repeated issues and inefficacy. When you run into those situations, you create a frustrating environment.

Teams become frustrated because it feels like nothing is working to make improvements, and that frustration can lead to other issues; it's going to grow, and it's going to bubble. But when you create that plan, remembering the plans from last time to trigger their process to identify deep-rooted issues, you will eliminate that panic and frustration. Because now the teams know, "Oh, there's something deeper here that we can't find. Let's work together. Let's trigger this. Let's get this improvement." This approach empowers teams to understand that underlying issues may be beyond their immediate grasp, encouraging collaboration and proactive problem-solving to initiate improvement processes.

So, we understand the need to identify the issues. There are many different methods out there for finding deep-rooted issues. It's all about finding the right way with the teams to make it fit with them. That's important because when you do that, you're looking at more than best practices and finding what works with the team to fix the issue.

So, the first part here is to identify issues. That needs to be a regular occurrence. Sometimes, you might encounter issues that may be one-time or rarely happen. One team I worked with had a server error because a pipe burst in the server room, causing issues. What do you want to do, an improvement process for the pipe bursting? Probably not.

Now, there is an improvement process there. We found a backup site and a server across the state. What they did was they just created a quick routine to ensure there were regular backups and to trigger the new backup site if the server went down. It was a test server; the production servers were located somewhere else without pipes. So, it wasn't that big of a deal, but they didn't think about using the backup site in that fashion. They just backed it up regularly just for the sake of backup, just in case something happened because there were some regulatory things we needed to do for backups, even on the test server.

We want to ensure that if something is reoccurring, we don't just sit on it. Retrospectives are great for that. They're not just there to find issues; they're there where your teams can work together to find a solution. There are some improvement processes out there that can take a while. Sometimes, a retrospective just doesn't fit in. But that's where you can start looking at your team backlog, management backlog, and risk backlog. This is information where you can get additional support from your servant leader to work through and help identify issues and find a resolution.

However, it's crucial to avoid getting caught up in the allure of new and seemingly innovative solutions—the "conference hangover—without thoroughly evaluating their applicability to your current challenges. Improvement processes can vary in duration and fit, and not every method suits every situation.

Best Practices

We aim to implement solutions immediately from a best-practice perspective. However, it's crucial to recognize that while a best practice might align well with one team, it may not suit another due to varying challenges and dynamics. Therefore, when considering best practices, assessing what fits well with the team is essential. It's about picking and choosing and adapting to ensure compatibility with the team's needs. If there are multiple teams, a practice that benefits one might not necessarily benefit another.

Measurement plays a significant role in this process. Mechanisms must be established to gauge the effectiveness of the chosen practices and ensure their benefit. This not only helps validate their impact but also fine-tune approaches as needed.

Once the best practices are pinpointed, keeping all teams in the loop is the key. Sharing this information is crucial because if a team is unaware of a practice that could address a specific issue, the opportunity for improvement is lost. It's akin to saying, "If it wasn't shared, did it happen?" This highlights the importance of a robust knowledge-sharing environment within the organization. By fostering such an environment, you're motivating improvement and enhancing transparency.

For instance, utilizing platforms like Confluence wiki pages or even Obeya rooms ensures that crucial information is visible. This is particularly effective when multiple teams work on a shared product. While team retrospectives are common, conducting broader retrospectives can offer insights into overall progress and challenges, aiding in a more comprehensive understanding and tackling of issues.

When addressing improvements and challenges, they should be managed as any other task, with specific metrics for success and the necessary adjustments. This approach ensures that improvements are implemented, tracked, and refined over time, aligning with the overarching goal of continuous enhancement.

So, the essence is to pick, choose, and adapt best practices in a way that aligns with the unique needs of each team, ensuring these practices are measurable and shared across the organization. This not only aids in problem-solving but also in fostering a culture of continuous improvement and knowledge sharing.

Implement

When all the necessary information is available and you're poised for implementation, it's time to set the wheels in motion. Planning for this change is critical because, at its core, it represents a transformation that will likely require adjustments in behavior across the board. Ensuring everyone is prepared for these behavioral shifts is crucial for smoothly adopting this change. Once the planning phase is adequately addressed, the momentum to move forward kicks in, which signals a readiness to accept and implement the new direction. Of course, as I have mentioned before, implementing change can sometimes be immediate, while at other times, it requires a more extensive involvement, potentially involving larger teams, management, and leadership.

It's essential to clarify the role of leadership in this context of improvement and change. As mentioned, we want to avoid changes and metrics that are solely driven by leadership. So, where does leadership fit into this equation?

Leadership should enable and support change without being the primary driver. They provide the guidance and resources needed to ensure the change aligns with broader organizational goals while leaving the implementation specifics to the directly involved teams. This approach ensures that change is incorporated into the process more organically within the team, creating a sense of ownership and commitment to the new direction.

Show your work

Reflecting on the principle of servant leadership, the focus shifts to supporting the teams, ensuring they have what they need to succeed, and encouraging them to take the initiative. This approach is about showing your work, asking questions, delegating effectively, and ultimately fostering a culture of trust and confidence.

In an agile environment, leadership's role becomes one of transparency and accountability, similar to solving a math problem where showing your work is required. I advocate for leaders to openly display their activities and intentions, such as through a Kanban board placed outside their office or a virtual Kanban board. This visual representation of work in progress, tasks completed, and upcoming projects demystifies the leader's role and mirrors the transparency expected from the teams.

Despite the necessity for discretion in specific tasks, the aim is to share as much as possible without compromising confidentiality. This approach not only aligns with agile principles but also enhances the collaborative spirit within the team. For instance, incorporating the Kanban board into regular team meetings can streamline discussions, making it easier to identify topics, troubleshoot issues, and plan future actions. It serves as a dynamic agenda that reflects real-time progress and challenges, enhancing these gatherings' effectiveness.

Leaders display their workflow openly[36] through physical boards outside their offices or digital tools in a remote setting, setting a precedent for transparency. This practice might require some adaptation, especially in maintaining confidentiality for sensitive tasks. However, the essence of showing what can be shared is pivotal. It reinforces agile behaviors, creating an environment where leadership and teams operate with a shared understanding and mutual respect.

---

[36] https://kanbanzone.com/2021/kanban-values-to-boost-business-productivity/

If we look at weekly or monthly team meetings, you already have topics to discuss in these team meetings and the use of this Kanban board. During the team meeting, you already know what discussions you can have because everyone is transparent. Everyone understands now that you're using that team environment to work through solutions and possibly refine what to work on next.

So, the servant leadership model, supported by practices like these, bridges the gap between leaders and teams and cultivates a culture of trust, transparency, and collective progress. It highlights the leader's role not as a commander but as a facilitator and supporter, dedicated to the team's growth and success.

Ask questions

As a leader, it's essential to ask questions. We've discussed the data program, emphasizing how asking the right questions gets you what you need. As a leader, you need to apply this principle, too. One of the best techniques I've used throughout my career is the 'five whys' process to identify an issue's root cause or pinpoint where a process breaks. This method not only helps in finding solutions but also keeps you engaged with your teams. But remember, this isn't about going on a Gemba walk and asking 'Why?' five times every time. It's more about using it to identify issues. Yes, you can work it into the conversation, but you don't want to overdo the 'Why?'. Use it effectively.

This is just one of many conversational processes and methods to drive engagement. The key is to ask questions that elicit answers, not to provide the answers yourself. You want teams to navigate their issues, building their confidence and trust in finding solutions. 'Leadership from behind' is a practical style that encourages teams to develop their answers.

After graduating high school and working in an office, my first manager used this approach. He pushed me to find the solution on my own. Usually, when I approached him with a problem, he'd respond with, 'Well, what do you think? It's not my problem; you've got to figure it out.' Through our conversation, he essentially asked the five whys, guiding me to answer my questions until I had that 'aha' moment. And once I solved it, I didn't need to ask again because I owned the solution. Even though he led me to it, he ensured I understood the process to arrive at the right solution. It's about sharing knowledge by guiding, not explicitly stating the answer. You don't need to know everything; you must ask the right questions.

Delegating

Planning is essential, as is having a plan for dealing with new issues. How will you draw out the information to find a solution together? When you find solutions as a team, you strengthen your role. Delegating is part of this, offering better opportunities and leadership growth. But delegation has limits; you don't want to offload all your work. Instead, provide stretch assignments that offer growth opportunities. You enhance ownership and opportunity when you show your work, engage in discussions, and acknowledge good solutions by delegating tasks.

Two-solution

So, we talked about the two-solution program that I like to use. This approach has created trust within the teams I've worked with, a level I've never seen elsewhere. To me, this is the best solution. I didn't invent it; it emerged through the PRACTICE model published by psychologist Stephan Palmer in 2008[37]. The core principle is that whenever someone presents a problem, they should propose multiple potential solutions; I like to use two to avoid overthinking. These solutions need not be perfect, but they should demonstrate that the individual has engaged with the problem thoughtfully.

Initially, this method might elicit some wild or extreme solutions from team members. However, it sparks meaningful conversation, where finding a solution begins. When faced with particularly wild solutions, I often challenge the team by asking if these are indeed the best solutions they can envision for the given problem, suggesting they might be a bit extreme. This isn't about dismissing their ideas but encouraging deeper analysis and asking for more information. What processes are we examining? How significant is the issue? This way, the conversation

---

[37] https://psycnet.apa.org/record/2008-02660-007

deepens, inviting more detailed consideration of the problem and potential solutions. This approach has become the norm in every team I've worked with, and individuals I've coached have carried it into their careers. They've told me it's been incredibly beneficial.

We aim for continuous improvement and value increase. It's all about triggering cultural and behavioral changes. We want to sidestep struggles instead of aiming to be a team of rockstars. For that, everyone must fit well together.

Creating an environment where teams collaborate with leadership to find solutions significantly enhances outcomes. You'll start seeing immediate value from building out this approach. This approach is all about encouraging a behavior change. Engaging in any transformation, like fostering a culture of continuous improvement, hinges on the team's ability to perceive and grasp its inherent value. Once they do, the process becomes straightforward, propelling the team towards ongoing improvement and success.

WORKBOOK: 05

Data Program

We live in a time when data is everywhere. Identifying and using what is available to measure performance could take much work. With that work, the wrong data could also point in the wrong direction.

Qualitative and quantitative data can have a lot of power in a culture of continuous improvement. It provides baselines and ways to measure

Fundamental analysis is critical in providing the organization's decision-makers with the needed metrics to make positive future improvements.

"If you don't ask the right questions, you don't get the right answers. Asking questions is the ABC of diagnosis. Only the inquiring mind solves problems" – Edward Hodnett, American poet.

Utilizing a change management process is the best way to ensure stakeholders are comfortable with change. The Why, How, and What are components recognized in most models. Communication is the link between the disciplines. Begin with why the change is needed. Once that is clear, the how and what of the process are the subsequent explanations to be shared, allowing for more straightforward utilization and acceptance[38]. A side effect of this route of action is the improved overall perception of the QA team, highlighting the group as more than test executioners. Plenty of change management techniques will provide additional suggestions for introducing change.

Appropriate use of this process prevents laying blame or placing the failure of some or all components on any individual or group, creating conflict. Negative conflict[39] decreases employee morale, creates a barrier to communication between groups, and breaks trust. Data collection is a little more complicated than identifying quick counts on issues such as code, requirements, or environmental issues. Building out that base is critical.

1. Do you have a current set of metrics to track performance? How do they compare to "best practices"?

---

[38] Finding Your Why, Simon Sinek
[39] Five Behaviors of a Dysfunctional Team, Patrick Lencioni

2. Do you have metrics to track quality? How reliable are they?
3. Describe who has access to this data. What do they do with it?
4. Are there regular reviews of the value of the data stored?
5. Keeping data is the only way to ensure product, service, and team improvements. A strong continuous improvement program all starts with data. Teams or management gets into trouble when they try to get a metric the data does not support. Partly because there is no understanding of what data is available. Once that is identified, determining the metrics and reports to help make the improvement decisions becomes easy. Start a list of data points that your teams currently store and that you feel can be used to provide productivity, performance, and quality metrics. The book Metrics and Models by Stephan H. Kan and Actionable Agile Metrics for Predictability by Daniel S. Vacanti are good sources to help.
6. How are organizational metrics identified and adopted?
7. How would you create the baseline of metrics?
8. How would you work with leadership to ensure the metrics are understood and still fit agile values?
9. Are there conflicting metrics?
10. Creating a baseline helps make the start line. Even in teams tracking metrics previously, it does not mean a new line can't be drawn to use as a new starting point. It is about keeping value in metrics to make valuable decisions. Please write down the current set of metrics used, who reports them, who uses them, and what they are used for. Then, from your point of view, mark which ones are valuable, not valuable, and not sure. This can be used in a collaboration exercise to ensure a good base of metrics that everyone values.
11. How do stakeholders know how to interpret the measures provided to them?
12. How are these measures used to improve performance?
13. How are metrics analyzed at the organizational level?
14. How do you measure project, product, team, and process performance?
15. It is all about telling a story that gives the right message to the audience. Think back to when data was misinterpreted based on how it was reported and the following issues. Think about ways

you can determine the right way to show the metrics so the specific audience that needs to make good decisions.

16. Write a high-level plan to introduce new data points and metrics and create a plan to review the value.

Improvement Identification Process

Root Cause Analysis is a group of techniques that will help determine what methods need adjusting or revamping. Much like an assembly line, the movement of data and work products follows a similar design where information from one area feeds into another. Quality throughout could be improved to increase efficiency and the bottom line for the organization. RCA will provide that data to make informed decisions on improvement initiatives[40]

One of the key elements to finding a process issue where stakeholders will take notice is to have a dollar figure attached to it. Here is where some additional work is needed when documenting saves. Depending on how the organization is set up from a time-tracking perspective, the data could already be present and formulated to provide the information needed. If not, there is a simple workaround to use with any toolset to calculate the financial impact. Three documented components are Investigation, Fixing, and Retest. As stated earlier, this process occurs throughout the entire SDLC.

Using these terms is not solely for test execution. Investigation and Fixing are universal statements for any work done throughout, while retesting would be new in some areas. The easiest way to think about retesting is to confirm that the Fix meets expectations.

1. How is performance feedback provided to agile teams to support team improvement?
2. How does the performance feedback translate into actual improvements to team performance?
3. Are there metrics used to help determine the root cause of the issue for which the team is trying to identify improvements?
4. Are specific individuals within the organization responsible for

---

[40] Slack, N., Chambers, S., & Johnston, R. (2010). Operations Management (6th edition ed.). Edinborough Gate: Prentice-Hall.

improvements?

5. Is a group responsible for overseeing improvements to the organization's methods and techniques?
6. What are your thoughts on finding the root cause of issues and how it is done within your organization?
7. What are your thoughts on best practices?
8. Is conference hangover a thing within the team? How is it dealt with?
9. How often are best practices reviewed?
10. What are the challenges with best practices?
11. Sometimes, there are best practices that are used within a team, but they have struggled with it. The reasoning is, in part, trying to copy other companies or teams. Think about times when trying other teams' best practices failed and what could have been done differently.
12. How are team outputs used to improve the organization?
13. What would a knowledge-sharing program look like with your team and others?
14. How would you create messaging and share the knowledge with others, and what can they add to the continuous improvement initiative?
15. Write down your thoughts on a knowledge-sharing environment.

Where Leadership Fits

The Industrial Revolution started in North America in the late 1700s. Over time, there have been other waves of revolution through wars and improved technologies. As we march through the 21st century, there is a need for improved agility, and technology is allowing organizations to do so. One component is just on the cusp of making that change to make things run smoothly: leadership.

As organizations move to more agile principles and methodologies, the central premise that most senior leaders miss is that the previous "command and control" structure will reduce the value potential of delivering products and services.

In Lejla Cizmic's article,[41] she talks in detail about two groups of leaders in an agile organization. Group 1 is all aboard with the agile transformation to achieve their desired value, and Group 2 masks "command and control" in their agile methodologies.

Agile Methods Are No Match For Outdated Leadership

She states, "These Group 2 leaders, in contrast to the first group, see Agile as a product delivery framework where the implementation is led by an expert (an Agile consultant or a coach) and implemented at a local, confined level. They see the Agile implementation as affecting the teams at the execution level, leaving the executive leadership and the middle management to go about their work business as usual."

Leaders that fall into Group 2 only see agile environments as delivering something faster. That is the value that they see. Yes, there is an outcome with agile methodologies that improve efficiency, producing products more quickly, yet that is not the real meaning of having an agile environment. Let's review the Manifesto for Agile Software Development, which was the starting point of this new revolution:

- Individuals and interactions over processes and tools
- Working software over comprehensive documentation
- Customer collaboration over contract negotiation
- Responding to change by following a plan

In these four lines, there is not one mention of speed. Now, let's look at the 12 principles. Again, there is no explicit mention of speed in each principle. There is, though, mention of delivering valuable software early, but the miss is the word "continuous delivery." The intent is to offer in small chunks to ensure the feature is what is needed. What is happening now is that the benefits found in agile Software Delivery are having organizations move other departments and divisions to become more agile. In doing so, they must recognize that the current structure needs to change.

Lejla says, "Implementing Agile transforms an organization horizontally and vertically. It impacts leaders and teams. It impacts the processes,

[41] https://www.agilealliance.org/agile-methods-are-no-match-for-outdated- leadership/

people, and technologies, and more importantly, it impacts the language, culture, behavior, and the mindset of everyone in the organization.

Agile as a system is akin to that of a live organism. It is like a tree that relies on favorable conditions to thrive and bear fruit."

On this cusp of a new evolution in senior leadership, one critical thing must be endocrine in everyone's mind: To quote Jeff Dalton's book Great Big Agile, " Don't do agile; be agile."

As with any organizational evolution, a fundamental shift in mindset is needed so that it is not a matter of just following steps to get something delivered. Doing that will only lead to frustrations for everyone involved and only achieve a fraction of the value possible.

Embracing agile values, continuously communicating them, having the proper alignment within the organization, and keeping everyone engaged and empowered will shatter the old ways of leading and move organizations to previously unimaginable levels.

1. Write your thoughts about how leadership moves from a Command and Control thought process to leading from behind as part of a servant leader.
2. Is delegation of work seen as a positive or negative task?
3. Thoughts on the 2-solution to one problem method. Is it something you can use? How would you implement it?

CHAPTER 06 | TRUST

Giving trust in the teams to get the work done will eliminate the need for leadership escalations

Goals	Why	How	What
Teams to deal with issues without getting an executive involved	Team empowerment that they are trusted to make the right decisions	Remove of mental barriers of "Us vs. Them"	Strong self-managed team network
Team of teams How can an organism evolve when the cells don't work together?	**Involved** Having the teams involved with what each is doing removes frustrations	**Promote** Promoting to the teams they can work together with trust they can get it done.	**Escalations** Escalations will still happen. Now they will not have conflict involved

Figure 3-1

This chapter focuses on the last stage of Phase 2, the "System" Trust. Building off the foundation we've established up to this point, this portion is about working more towards having that full-on trust network. It builds on the culture of improvement by giving teams the trust they need, trusting them to improve continuously, and in return, they trust the leadership to support those improvements.

In this stage, you're creating a strategic environment for your product/service and entrusting the teams to deliver on the product or service's vision. This involves working on the pathway of continuous improvement, changes within the leadership, and constant learning. This level of trust stems from the foundations laid out at the beginning, including starting points, goals, and design. It all feeds into this last part of the system.

Therefore, this last system component, Trust, propels everything into the next phase. At this point, teams should operate like cells within an organism, each performing its function but collectively contributing to a larger purpose. The aim is for teams to manage issues independently, without needing executive intervention, thus building this trust factor.

Why?

This approach empowers teams to make decisions and learn, breaking down the mental barriers of "us versus them." This step is also tied to the design stage, where teams are structured with both generalists and specialists to foster a trustful environment, eliminating the "us versus them" mindset. The goal is cultivating a 'team of teams,' encouraging involvement, promoting trust, and effectively handling escalations.

TRUST STRUGGLES

- Focus on "Me"
- Mixed Messages
- "What could go wrong today?"

In tackling the struggles of building trust, we initially concentrate on the individual, focusing on "me." This phase is soon followed by mixed messages among leadership teams and individuals regarding the way forward, leading to micromanagement. Another key issue I've faced with several teams is a tendency to worry about what could go wrong each day. Throughout my career, I've seen this mindset fail to help the situation and instead create a negative environment.

As we've walked through this agile environment building architecture, it should become apparent that the negative outlook is beginning to dissipate. You might notice a shift in your way of dealing with work and use an adaptive mental model approach instead of a fixed mindset, feeling the negativity fade away and fostering a more positive outlook to create an authentic agile atmosphere within the team.

Removing negativity and adopting a positive mental model transform the work environment. It becomes agile, fun, and open to challenges and changes. These challenges are anticipated and welcomed, providing opportunities for the team to learn and grow through facing and overcoming obstacles.

TRUST ACTIONS (from us vs. them to synchronization)

- Communication Program
- Guidance for team collaboration
- Understanding expectations for agile values

It is understood that to build trust, there must be collaboration and the removal of the "us vs. them" mindset. But the question is: how do you transition from an us versus them mentality to a synchronized set of teams? That's where we analyze and understand where everything fits: the actions required to ensure you have the right communication program. And by that, I mean walking the talk.

How do you communicate the agile values?

So, in building out that strong trust network, how are you going to communicate it? How will you guide team collaboration? One of the key issues with trust and those struggles is that individuals feel that it is all happening "without me" or "it's all about me." If that's how your teams collaborate, you need to change that because that's not the correct way for them to work effectively. The adage: "There is no I in team" is the mantra here.

Then comes understanding the expectations of the agile values. We've discussed agile values as an agile team's guiding principles. Well, now we have to continuously build on it because this is where the foundation of trust lies. Understanding the expectations of the agile values will get you there to build that trust network, where everything will start falling into place.

Communication program

Without achieving full use of team's capabilities, they will be speaking different languages

Goals	Why	How	What
Harmony amongst teams.	so that we can enhance the capabilities of the agile teams	I want to establish relationships and agreements between teams and partners collaboratively	As an agile leader
Know your team	**Involved**	**Promote**	**Escalations**
Understand the why, how and what on the team's communication styles	Understand the why, how and what on the partner's communication styles	Develop a communication plan that meets needs	Get everyone on board

Figure 6-2

- **Know your team**

What are we looking at from a communication program? You want harmony among the teams, within the team, and with partners. You aim to extend the teams' capabilities. Identifying relationships between the teams, internal and external partners, and suppliers is crucial.

One of the first things to start with is knowing your team. If you don't know your team, you won't get far. What you're going to provide and what's going to be communicated across won't happen. It won't work.

Picture a cohesive sports team where the coach isn't just a distant figure but is alongside the players from start to finish. They gather in the huddle at the beginning of the game, offering support throughout, win or lose until the end. Providing guidance, the coach empowers the team to execute, trusting each member to fulfill their role in synchronization with the others on the team and communicate effectively. This creates a framework akin to a team charter, guiding their actions. The team embraces this charter, understanding its significance in shaping their collective identity. With shared purposes and a clear vision for collaboration, they unite under its principles, driving their success.

Organizations will ask this when it comes to collaboration: How are they going to communicate with each other effectively? Some think they can throw a tool out there for the team. Like, "Oh, we're going to start using Slack."

Slack is undoubtedly a great tool. I've used it; I like using it. But is it the right tool that fits with the team's dynamic? That's what you should be thinking about.

It should ultimately be up to the teams who will use it to decide on a tool, not leadership. Plenty of tools exist, so letting them decide is crucial. Given the freedom to choose, they can determine what works best for them as a team. This autonomy allows them to decide how they will communicate with each other effectively. If their choice proves ineffective, it will become apparent retrospectively.

Something didn't work? No problem.

It's about collaboratively finding the right way to make it work by embracing self-governance. The roles and responsibilities are established; it's about how they exercise their authority. A team charter could be as concise as six bullet points or as detailed as one or two pages, depending on the team's size and needs. The team can discover the most effective approach with this charter as their foundation. All that's required is to trust them to develop this charter and understand their responsibilities.

As leaders, our role is to provide guidance. For instance, prompting them to consider their team charter, we might say, "Okay, you guys, when you look at your team charter, think about how you will communicate with each other. How are you going to deal with it daily, moving forward?"

Next, you need to understand your partners.

- **Know Your partners**

We've talked about partnerships in previous chapters, but here, we will discuss them in the context of collaboration and trust. With partners, you want to ensure that they are the right fit and that you have an agreement allowing effective communication. Sometimes, we skip the part about how communication will be handled or dealt with from an escalation point of view, not focusing on how the teams will work together.

The goal is to ensure they're in sync to complete the work. Check if both parties share similar agile values. Can they work together? Can they be involved in making decisions without bringing in leadership as an escalation point?

Keep in mind that it's about more than just filling a gap. There are plenty of organizations and partners that can fill that gap. It's about making sure they are the right fit. This means they should align with the team, the organization, and the vision of the product or service being developed.

An excellent example of this comes from a client I worked with. They needed to integrate a service within their application and opted to purchase rather than build it. They chose a partner because this partner offered an out-of-the-box service that met their needs from a timing perspective. Initially, it seemed to fit the bill perfectly. However, the teams involved in the project were not included in the implementation process of this partnership.

Issues emerged once the service was embedded and operational within the application. The service worked, but there were constant struggles to ensure its proper functionality. The challenges arose from both sides—how the partner-operated and how the client's team was organized. Essentially, they were not in sync.

As a result, regular meetings were scheduled with leadership to address these issues, but the teams themselves were not engaged in resolving the problems. The matters were managed by upper management, highlighting the lack of sync between the teams and the partners. This situation highlighted that the partner was chosen primarily to fill a gap without considering the deeper integration and collaboration needs. Other factors were at play, including time constraints, and the decision to select this particular partner was made at the executive level, specifically the CEO and CTO, without much involvement from the teams working with the service.

The teams were only brought into the loop when it was time to sign the Statement of Work (SOW). Perhaps, had the teams been more involved from the beginning, including during the discussions on the SOW, understanding the requirements, the necessary changes, and the potential impact on each team, it could have led to a better communication plan and a smoother integration process.

- **Develop Plan**

Developing a plan to ensure mutual understanding is crucial in a partnership, one that is based on a higher level of trust to have fewer escalations. This means speaking the same language, avoiding questions about ongoing processes, or pushing back on certain issues. Imagine two teams, one using Scrum and the other using Waterfall, working in harmony and synchronizing. Adopting similar frameworks is unnecessary, but a mutual understanding of how each team operates and stays aligned is essential.

How will the teams handle escalations? What agreements have they reached?

These questions form the basis of a partnership agreement between the teams. Perhaps introducing such an agreement when bringing in the Statement of Work (SOW) and involving the team could have worked well. Unfortunately, in the case of the organization I was working with, we never reached this stage. The organization was acquired, and the software was shelved, preventing further development of such a collaborative agreement. Could the set up of different partnership agreements, externally and internally, could have avoided such a fate for this organization? It may not have, yet it would have created a set of teams that were more in tune with each other and provided more value.

Nonetheless, the struggles experienced highlight the potential benefits of a partnership agreement for facilitating effective information sharing and workflow. An agreement is more than just an SOW. It can encompass the nuances of team deliveries and sprints, but at its core, it must outline the communication process and problem-solving strategies. At what point does management get involved? How do we collectively achieve our vision? Effective communication is crucial in answering these questions and achieving mutual goals.

- **Deploy Plan**

It is important to remember that when deploying plans, it's not a matter of setting them in place and forgetting them. Communication agreements between teams, individuals, or teammates are living documents. If you are unfamiliar with the term "living document," it refers to a document whose content is not static but evolves. This means it's something that should be revisited regularly. Each time you revisit it, you can make small changes to refine and improve it.

Guidance For Team Collaboration

Guidance to team collaboration

Sometimes it isn't the fancy new ways of communicating that are the best for the team.

Goals	Why	How	What
Have the teams collaborate on what is best for them.	so that they have everything they need to succeed as self-managed teams	I want to empower agile teams by providing them with the necessary tools and resources	As an agile leader
They will tell you	**Listen to needs**	**Limitations**	**Tools and Training**
With the increased trust built in the team they will provide the way they want to communicate	Remember wants and needs are two separate things	Understand there are limitations needed so that things are not out of control	Add to the training program

Figure 6-3

Guidance for team collaboration is precisely where leadership comes into play. Leading from behind, as we've discussed, leadership provides guidance and ideas and sets expectations. We've discussed expectations before, highlighting what teams expect from leadership and what leadership expects from teams. Communication and collaboration are paramount in the agile environment, where we focus on agile delivery, whether of a product or service.

- **They will tell you**

Guidance in this area ensures that teams will collaborate with leadership if any issues arise to understand what's happening. When there's a level of trust, you want to build it to the point where teams can approach leaders— whether it's leadership, management, directors, or senior executives—

freely, without fear, understanding that you're there to assist. They will tell you what's happening, and we need to understand that not everyone communicates similarly. As discussed in previous chapters regarding problem-solving, some might approach a leader with both a problem and a solution, while others might prefer to email and follow up with a meeting.

It's important to understand how everyone communicates and to determine the most effective path for communication to ensure information flows smoothly within the teams and with leadership and partners. Is it Slack? Is it Teams? Is it email?

A practical approach I've used with clients and teams to streamline communication is the "two email rule": if an email chain goes beyond two replies, it's time to call a meeting or make a phone call. This approach helps to avoid confusion and miscommunication that often occurs in lengthy email chains. Email discussions can sometimes become unproductive arguments or misunderstandings, partly because written words can be misinterpreted or deliberately provocative. Do an internet search for the "as per my last email" meme. We don't want any of that.

We aim for open communication, focusing on what we're delivering, the dynamics within teams, and the well-being of individuals. Establishing this trust is key to fostering a healthy, open communication environment.

- **Listen to Needs**

Creating an environment where everyone feels cordial and comfortable enough to improvise, discuss issues, and propose solutions is crucial. We've touched on how receiving criticism for your work can lead to eye rolls, frustration, and upset among team members. It's important to remember that these interactions are not personal. The goal is to work collaboratively to improve, find practical solutions, and enhance communication.

Leaders must communicate effectively with the group and understand how the group interacts among themselves. Similarly, teams should know the best ways to communicate with one another, and individuals within those teams need to identify the most effective communication strategies for their interactions. Avoiding the "I want" scenario is key—it's not the right approach. Instead, the focus should be engaging in conversations highlighting needs and differentiating between wants and needs.

Recall our discussion on wants versus needs. We discussed that it's about facilitating conversations to thoroughly understand and address these points. It's essential to keep everyone involved and informed about processes and new developments.

Understanding wants and needs shouldn't be limited to emails, Slack messages, or texts. An environment that encourages open, face-to-face conversations, whether through lean coffees, casual water cooler talks, or quick elevator chats, can greatly improve the clarity and effectiveness of understanding both wants and needs.

In most organizations, many teams are now distributed. Face-to-face meetings would be difficult unless there is a big travel budget. However, those conversations can still be conducted virtually; remember to keep the cameras on to see each other's faces.

From a leadership standpoint, starting conversations that uncover needs often starts casually, perhaps during an elevator ride, at day's end, or around the lunch table in the break room. Asking simple questions like "How is your day? How's it going?" can set the stage for deeper and open dialogue. If the conversation turns towards frustration, you can always steer it back calmly while probing deeper, trying to understand the "why" behind their communication.

Charles Duhigg's book *Supercommunicators* provides great insights on how to get the most out of conversations without seeming forced or cookie-cutter.

Why are they saying? What's the root cause?

You often get to the root of their needs by asking further questions. For example, they might desire training in a specific area, but the genuine need could be broader. Maybe it's not just training for them but for the entire team. Perhaps what's required is a more systematic approach to coaching or mentoring. You might not know initially, but you can uncover these needs through these conversations.

- **Limitations**

Understanding the needs from a research perspective is essential, as it allows you to weigh what matters more than needs.

What is that?

It's the wants that may fit a need. Utilizing open-space meetings and workshops to dive into those conversations helps work through, collaborate, and understand what's happening. This involvement is key to shortlisting certain aspects. Once shortlisted, it's then up to the teams to work together on these because they understand. Perhaps they will find a solution right away for those needs, or maybe it will take some time and more effort now that they know what they must work on and gain from it. They all agree on one thing and work on it together.

However, there are limitations to team collaboration, especially in terms of understanding the wants and needs. There are boundaries to how they communicate, and understanding these limitations is crucial. One challenge that hinders team collaboration is that these limitations are not always transparent. It could be a budget limitation, time, or any other resource constraint. Or it might be a budget issue specifically. Whatever the case, understanding these limitations is necessary so they can work within them.

It might seem like limitations are negative, but they are not. When limitations are transparent, they can foster an innovative environment, encouraging working with less to achieve more. I believe such limitations challenge teams to think creatively and find ways to overcome these obstacles. So, hiding limitations does not help build trust. When you communicate limitations, teams understand what they can do and work with those constraints.

Find out what's best for everyone.

You'll notice other limitations, too, as you start looking into them. One example is using too many tools for the same job. I saw an organization find this out when they checked all their tools and saw duplicates. They realized that using one tool for many tasks was smarter. Before, they had two tools doing the same thing, and they only noticed this by checking the inventory across the enterprise. This shows how spotting limitations helps you work smarter with fewer but better tools.

Another big limitation might be your budget. Not everything can be bought, so you need to figure out how to make the most of what you have. Staying within budget while still providing high value is crucial. This ties back to agile principles, which focus on delivering value to the team and clients. When you work together, setting clear goals, you guide the team toward maximizing value within budget constraints.

Teams will also highlight these limitations, encouraging them to identify them. At the same time, they'll also suggest how to work around these limitations to meet goals. This kind of autonomy and freedom helps everyone understand limitations better and strengthens teamwork and leadership.

- **Tools and Training**

Limitations can also be pivotal in shaping a training program—a program that not only enhances skills but also opens up new opportunities. Part of this involves integrating tools into your frameworks. Up until now, we've touched on frameworks like Scrum, SAFe, and Kanban but haven't focused on them too much. As I mentioned in the initial chapters, this discussion is more about the behaviors and actions within the frameworks than the frameworks themselves because these behaviors ultimately deliver the most value.

Tools are only as effective as the way they are used. We've explored the reasons behind tool selection and how this ties into an organization's overall strategy. Many organizations opt for Scrum, aiming for speed, which they see as the primary outcome. I'm not dismissing the efficacy of Scrum.; it does work, as does SAFe™. However, the point is that a framework is a tool that can be applied in various situations. The real challenge is determining if it's the right tool for the right team.

Often, you'll hear criticisms like "Agile doesn't work" or "Agile is a failure."

However, the issue isn't agile environments or any specific framework; the problem usually arises when organizations try to misuse a framework, similar to trying to hammer a screw. When an agile environment does not provide the expected value for an organization, it could be due to improper use of the framework or a lack of understanding of how to implement it effectively. Operating without a thorough understanding of the behaviors needed behind the framework is like trying to fit a square peg into a round hole—it simply won't work, no matter how hard you try. This misalignment leads to frustration and issues.

So, before deciding on a tool or framework, it's important that you and your team understand its purpose and how it aligns with the behavior changes your organization is undergoing during its transformation. While Scrum can be used anywhere, it has its limitations depending on the context of its usage. With over 30 different frameworks available for agile delivery, you must choose the best fit your organization's needs to deliver the highest value. This is where you have your envisioning sprints come into play, conceptualizing how a tool could work within your organization and assessing the tools in question.

Talking about tools broadly, not just frameworks, if you find that Scrum or SAFe isn't working for you, it doesn't necessarily mean these frameworks are ineffective. Instead, it may indicate a misalignment or misuse within your organization. The issue could be less about the frameworks themselves and more about how they are applied. Rather than dumping them, it's important to identify where the problem lies.

If facing challenges with these frameworks, consider changing their teams' behaviors before considering replacing them entirely. Initiating the right behaviors can make a significant difference in making a framework work effectively and driving success across your team and projects.

The current framework you're using isn't necessarily bad; it might not be the right fit, or perhaps the behaviors surrounding its usage need adjustment. Using the analogy of trying to hammer in a screw, if the screw represents your framework and the hammer your current behavior, switching to a screwdriver — that is, changing your behavior — can resolve many issues quickly.

Training can be a powerful method to change behaviors. Numerous online training programs cover different frameworks, led by experts with certifications who understand these frameworks very well. Turning to these resources can enhance your understanding of the potential of the frameworks you're currently using and others you might consider adopting. These training programs aim to foster the right behaviors within teams. A solid training program is a great starting point for building trust, alleviating frustrations, and facilitating the necessary behavior changes during a transformation process.

Transparency with your team is crucial, especially regarding training. The selection of training programs should be a collaborative effort, not solely the manager's responsibility. The team should feel empowered to suggest and request courses that will enhance their skills and provide more value.

Implementing a Kanban board for managing training initiatives is a practical next step. This allows for identifying courses and partners and encourages ongoing evaluation through training retrospectives. Having team members share what they have learned from training sessions can be invaluable, as it helps assess whether the training delivers the intended value. Additionally, coaching and mentoring within teams, alongside value assessments for selected courses, can further build trust and ensure that training efforts are aligned with the organization's goals.

Understanding the expectations of agile values

This is where the rubber hits the road.

Goals	Why	How	What
Defined Agile environment	so that they realize speed is not the priority	I want everyone to understand their roles, responsibilities, defined events, and the importance of disciplined agile behaviors in maintaining a quality agile environment	As an agile leader
Roles	**Actions**	**Techniques**	**Events**
Roles and job titles are very different things.	The behaviours that help events and techniques achieve high value.	Processes that need to be viewed as being more than just steps to do.	Events are not a rubber-stamping activity.

Figure 6-4

While you're figuring out the right training programs, it's also important to understand how your teams communicate with you and with each other. Understanding the expected communication flow, guiding how they should interact with leadership, managers, and other teams, and fostering mutual understanding among teams are key aspects of your leadership role. Your job is to communicate the value you're aiming for. You should set the expectation that value is shared and pushed forward through conversations and collaboration to resolve issues. It would be best to clarify what isn't expected, like constant escalations to leadership. It's crucial to make it known that teams are trusted to manage their responsibilities and resolve any issues that arise effectively and efficiently.

When scaled, this forms a core part of the expectations set by agile values for a team, a department, or even the entire organization. These values serve as the guiding principles for how everyone should work together. How is this accomplished? Through clear communication, setting expectations, and creating an environment of trust and collaboration that aligns with agile principles. All of these can be done by defining roles.

Roles

I've mentioned team charters before as part of agile guidance. These are the key components you need to implement to ensure your agile values are met as expected. When discussing agile components, I refer to roles, their behaviors, techniques used, and events to support value creation. If you're unfamiliar with 'events,' it might be because they used to be called ceremonies. The Scrum Alliance updated their scrum guidelines and switched from 'ceremonies' to 'events.'

You want these separate components to ensure everyone understands that agile isn't just about speed. It's about making sure everyone knows their roles and actions. This is where everything starts to click. Everything we've discussed in this book builds up to this understanding of expected values.

Talking about roles, it's essential to know that you can take on more than one role. Depending on the event, the technique, and the behaviors, you might find yourself playing different roles to achieve that value. I've had this experience myself. On one project, I ended up having nine different roles. That was a waterfall project; having nine roles wasn't fun. However, the behaviors I needed to adopt across those roles were essentially what those nine different roles required.

Don't get roles and titles confused.

In Scrum, you've got the Scrum Master, the Product Owner, and the Development Team. It's important to grasp that it's not about strictly sticking to these titles. Getting too hung up on titles misses the point. There are various roles to play, and it's all about fitting into these roles effectively. So, when discussing titles and job descriptions, you might see terms like Scrum Master, Developer, Agile Analyst, or QA Analyst. But, when you look at the roles within the workflow, you see titles like Team Leader, Executive, Scrum Team/Development Team, and Product

Owner. These roles or behaviors are what the team needs to focus on and work through.

HR plays a crucial role in transforming organizations to align with agile environments. It ensures that roles match job titles and that everyone understands the team's behaviors, techniques, and events. This alignment is essential for successfully implementing agile methodologies within an organization.

One effective strategy for fostering this alignment and moving away from rigid titles is using team reviews. These reviews have been shown to significantly enhance employee satisfaction and productivity compared to individual reviews.

A systematic review published by the American Psychological Association found that job resources and demands at the team level have strong relationships with productivity, health, and work-related well-being. This review highlights that team-based assessments often lead to better collaboration and collective problem-solving, boosting overall team performance and employee satisfaction.[42]

Research from Insperity also indicates that measuring team performance alongside individual performance helps organizations align more closely with evolving customer needs and market dynamics. This dual approach ensures that while individual achievements are recognized, the emphasis on team goals promotes a collaborative work environment, which is crucial in today's business landscape.[43]

Gallup's studies further support this approach, showing that highly engaged teams see significant improvements in productivity, profitability, and employee retention. Engaged teams reported 18% higher productivity and 23% higher profitability than less engaged teams, underscoring the importance of fostering a collaborative team environment to drive business success.

---

[42] https://hubstaff.com/blog/employee-satisfaction-and-productivity/
[43] https://www.insperity.com/blog/team-vs-individual-performance/

An example of how HR can help ensure consistency in teams' use of agile values and continuous improvement in value production is through team evaluations rather than individual ones. Much like the Agile Manifesto, it is recommended not to do away with individual evaluations or reviews but to set up team evaluations where team members support each other to improve collectively. Individual reviews can then focus on how individuals can better support their team and personal growth.

Shifting towards a team review system can help create a more supportive and collaborative workplace, leading to higher employee satisfaction and improved performance across the board.

- **Actions**

Most organizations see the agile framework as a means to an end. They focus on what must be done and consider themselves "Agile." Looking solely at the guidelines to work through the framework only scratches the surface. There's a lot more that needs to happen for an organization to be an agile environment. Understanding how everything fits together where there is an effective and efficient flow is critical.

For instance, when creating a project roadmap, it's often just the executive or a small team making those decisions. But in an agile environment, you're bringing in many more roles like product owners, the product management team, subject matter experts, and the agile teams with transparent and collaborative behaviors. They all look at the roadmap together, considering current and future capabilities. This way, everyone gets it; they agree on the outcomes and the value they represent to everyone involved. They understand what's needed, can work with it, and mitigate risks to better plan and deliver value.

You're giving everyone stewardship by involving all these roles in the roadmap. It's not just a plan made by one or two people anymore; everyone's in on it and knows how to work with it. This empowers a cross-functional group and drives continuous improvement. You get a clearer picture of how things will happen, when, and how to make them happen. When only a small group drives the roadmap, you encounter problems later. Maybe the development team doesn't see what they need until it's too late, or maybe user groups or clients change their minds during development. The lack of empathy and support for others can have far-reaching negative effects.

This goes back to the planning part we have discussed in previous chapters. You'll struggle without clearly understanding how each role contributes to value. You want to go from a scattershot approach to hitting the bullseye, improving team precision in product development, training programs, and your communication approach.

Think of it like an archer hitting a target. Ideally, they are aware of the environment and can concentrate on making the appropriate adjustments to improve their chances of hitting the bullseye. However, there are missing or incorrect actions, which will create sudden interruptions. Now, you're moving the target around, changing the bow and arrow, and constantly changing conditions. The archer will be unable to achieve the required concentration level because of the constant interruptions, which will cause a high probability of a less-than-perfect shot.

Agile environments require consistent behaviors to keep the ecosystem alive and functioning optimally. Part of that is ensuring a valuable outcome for everything done within the team. To have the core actions and behaviors for everyone to have, they are:

- Transparency
- Communication and Collaboration
- Empathy
- Support

From there, all other behaviors are built from where everyone thrives.

- **Techniques**

When you start changing or not using the right actions, you create problems that don't need to exist. You're making it harder for everyone to succeed. But when you use the right roles and actions based on good techniques, you're adding value. This means having clear roles within the teams, knowing what everyone is supposed to work on, what they're expected to achieve, and the actions they'll take to get there. Building off those roles and actions, you'll use techniques that bring out the value.

Many techniques are used throughout the workflow, regardless of the framework used to complete the work. Do an internet search for "how many techniques are used in agile delivery," and you will get many different answers. Getting the proper techniques for your team may not be straightforward to establish. Finding and tweaking what works to get the right outcome could be trial and error. Remember that it's about you doing things, such as creating a team charter, figuring out who does what in the workflow, self-subscribing, or using three diverse humans, to name a few.

The Gemba Walk is a technique mentioned in this book for leaders in an agile environment. This technique is a way to observe and understand the team and their work. "Gemba" is a Japanese term that refers to the dedicated space for collaboration, problem-solving, and ensuring a smooth flow of information. The "Walk" part is you, the leader, walking out to the team's space. This is your opportunity to have a good conversation with the team that is less formal.

Plenty of books, YouTube videos, and blogs detail different techniques. Like picking the right framework, let those using the techniques to achieve the outcome find the ones that make sense for them and fit the organization's agile values. From there, it is about knowledge-sharing and learning.

- **Events**

All these techniques set the stage for the events, highlighting their value. Yet, some organizations, supposedly practicing agile, go through the motions with these events. They treat them like a checkbox exercise, not engaging with the process.

I've got an example that brings this issue to light. I had a client who treated their events, especially the daily stand-up, as just another status meeting. Instead of the intended 15 minutes, these stand-ups would drag on for half an hour, morphing into refinement sessions for stories or, worse, turning into gripe sessions without any productive outcome. They weren't using this time to identify and plan to overcome impediments. Their demos were just product walkthroughs without engaging in meaningful feedback or integration of insights into future work. And when it came to retrospectives, they merely became a formality. They'd say what went well and what could be better, slap it on a Confluence page, and forget about it. There was no follow-up, no tracking of improvements—just continuous struggle without progress.

This approach doesn't just miss the mark on a functioning agile environment; it undermines the potential. We must respect an agile environment's full spectrum of roles, actions, techniques, and events. Leadership and teams need to honor these components and any plans in place. Acknowledging and learning from failures is a critical part of the journey toward improvement.

These are the keys that unlock true agility. It's about more than just following steps; it's about behaviors, proactive actions, and mutual trust and respect between teams and leadership. Walking the talk this way can significantly contribute to fostering an innovative, dynamic, and genuinely agile environment in which everyone wants to participate.

WORKBOOK: 06

Communication Program

Being transparent, accepting feedback, and having the right messaging for everyone to support helps build a supportive trust network within teams and throughout the organization. Issues arise when information is not assimilated with groups because it does not hit the mark.

Knowing your team and your partners, understanding how they work together, gel as a team, and function effectively, provides a glimpse into how to support and build trust. Move from traditional "Command and Control" management to agile organism management by providing the guidance needed to complete the work while allowing teams to do the job.

Use of technology[44] in employee communication: Regular and effective communication fosters a culture of openness, trust, and integrity. It provides insight into how organizations develop a plan and understand the best methods that work for the team.

There are hundreds of ways to communicate with teams, which does not mean anyone will do. Everyone is different, and the way work is done is different. Some frameworks and processes are relative and standardized, which does not mean you can implement what other organizations use.

Throughout this system, we discuss Simon Sinek's Golden Circle. With everything that is worked on, it is important to understand the why first— knowing your team and partners in the why makes everything else fall into place.

1. Are there team charters?
2. If there are, where are they found? How often are they reviewed and changed? If not, are there documented expectations of how everyone works within the organization?
3. What are the expectations in the team charter?

---

[44] Use of technology in employee communication: Regular and effective communication is critical for fostering a culture of openness, trust and integrity. (2011). Express Computer, Retrieved from http://0-search.proquest.com.aupac.lib.athabascau.ca/trade-journals/use-technology-employee-communication/docview/871588869/se-2?accountid=8408

4. Write down your thoughts on what else can be added or used in team charters to improve how teams work together.
5. Write down your thoughts on team charters with internal and external partners.
6. What is the level of communication between teams and partners?
7. Think back on introducing different partnerships with teams you worked with and write down the good and bad things that happened. From there, a high-level plan can be drawn up for use in the future.

Guidance to team Collaboration

Collaboration environments need to consider many factors to achieve the expected value.

Nina Evans goes into a lot of detail about what is involved and what could happen when it is all not in place. The creation of silos and "negative brainstorms" have impacts on productivity as well as employee satisfaction. So, creating that collaborative environment everyone needs to have is not as simple as leadership saying, "Be more collaborative," while giving tools to use.

Nina referenced these two definitions[45]:

Collaboration is a principle-based process or working together that produces trust, integrity, and breakthrough results by building true consensus, ownership, and alignment in all aspects of the organization.

Collaboration is more than working together cooperatively ('teamwork'); it is more than going along (accommodating) or getting along. That remarkable and unpredictable chaos, complexity, and creative stuff makes life interesting.

Things that need to be considered are.

- The role of leadership plays in participating and leading by example.

---

[45] Evans, Nina. (2012). Destroying collaboration and knowledge sharing in the workplace: A reverse brainstorming approach. Knowledge Management Research & Practice. 10. 10.1057/kmrp.2011.43.

- Having the right tools is based on knowing the teams.
- Using multiple and the right techniques that fit everyone.

While avoiding individual and negative cultural issues creeping in and impacting productivity.

1. Is there a current process for requesting tools? How does it work?
2. Is it the same for training?
3. How are issues typically brought to a leader's attention?
4. What are your feelings on employee satisfaction within the team? Is it used effectively? What can be done differently to get more value out of it?
5. What would you like to see different about identifying training and tool needs and the overall communication models with the team?
6. What would work to avoid "I want" scenarios?
7. How would you get buy-in for "Open space" meetings?
8. Are issues interrupting workflow brought to the leader's attention early or late? How are they handled?
9. Are agile frameworks seen as tools within your organization or being agile?
10. Do you have a learning program in place?
11. How would you work with the team to create a learning and incentive program that fits all needs?
12. What would a learning program look like? (does not have to all be paid courses; there are plenty of ways to improve knowledge.

Understanding the Expectations of Agile Values

Agile environments are not the free-for-all that most people think. There are still processes to follow with the discipline to not fall back to traditional ways when things are stressful or to become lax with the flow order when things are going very well.

Agile values provide the guidelines for meeting everyone's expectations. They provide the deeper meaning of why the teams do what they do—

guidance to the roles that everyone plays. Understand the expected value of the behaviours everyone should exhibit. Please emphasize the actions everyone takes to deliver and the events in the iteration.

"Hyperscrumamentalism" and "Cargo-Cultism"[46] are two real situations about 95% of organizations struggle with within their agile evolution journey. The behaviors that are found in these situations are anti-agile delivery and management. With the right agile keys, everything falls into place.

This section has helped identify many deep-seated issues within the team and peripheral groups that impact the total value of being agile to this point in the system.

1. How does the team know what they are responsible and accountable for?
2. How do team members know how to perform their role?
3. How does the team understand their roles and responsibilities?
4. How do you know current HR policies align with agile values and roles?
5. How do you know agile teams are exhibiting agile behaviors?
6. How are expectations related to roles and accountabilities shared with team members, stakeholders, and leaders?
7. Is the focus of agile just on the team? Does leadership have agile actions?
   a. Agile requires many actions and behaviors that are not explicitly mentioned in frameworks. Part of the reasoning is that agile is lean with processes and needs to stay that way. The difference between what we are talking about is the additional things needed to help support the delivery framework to make it achieve full value. A good example is driving a car. Get your license, start the car, put it in gear, pay attention to your surroundings, and drive to the destination. Additional "actions" to make that process flow: Gas, roads, building the car, servicing the car, etc.

---

[46] https://deanondelivery.com/the-4-isms-of-agile-failures-a40c960ace1f

1. A support network is needed to be agile.
2. Are there techniques used outside of what is in the agile framework?
3. How do teams establish standards and rules that fit within the organization?
4. Are events following the guidelines detailed in the framework guidelines?
5. Do events get skipped or changed?
6. Does it feel that everyone is just doing the event for the sake of doing it?
7. There should be value from each event that drives towards the team and organization's goals. Each event is meant to make things better than before. Just running through it because it is part of the process is worthless. Write down your thoughts on the matter and what can be done for positive change.
8. Write down your thoughts on how a team-based review system can work along with individual reviews to promote teamwork and productivity.

Phase 3
"Scale"

CHAPTER 07 | QUALITY

Quality products/services are made with quality behaviors

Goals	Why	How	What
Have quality focus overlap across teams throughout the workflow.	Have accountability across the organization	Have everyone help others better at what they do.	A quality assurance program
Understand QA	**Quality in**	**Not just delivery**	**Holistic**
QA is more than just testing products.	Having quality inputs from the start means quality output	There are aspects of information flow that impacts everyone.	Make quality and improvements holistic

Figure 7.1

We are now in the homestretch: the scale stage. In this phase, we focus on quality, evolving, and growing. Just as a review, remember that everything builds on each other. What we learned in the previous two phases covered the essentials: Start, Goal, and Design, building on top of each other, which then leads to your Pathway not just for your product but for everything else, ensuring the culture is set up and building a more substantial level of trust across all teams and with leadership.

We will talk about the "Scale" phase, starting with Quality.

In this part, we aim to improve everything across the processes, not just the quality of the product but also the quality of the teams, the leadership, and the organization. Imagine a place where everyone ensures quality meets the client's needs. Quality becomes a collective responsibility, not isolated to the test team or quality assurance. It's a team effort; everyone is involved, making quality one job for all.

Sometimes, in software development, a lot of the pressure to ensure quality falls on the test team, or sometimes, it is incorrectly called quality assurance (QA) teams only. That shouldn't be the case, especially in an agile environment. In such a setting, everyone is involved in every process, including quality assurance. Remember, we talked about how teams are like cells in an organism; they have their function, and they produce what they need to produce, but they're in sync with all the other cells within the body to ensure that you have growth, that you evolve, and that you continuously improve. So, quality is no different; it is a team thing, and everyone needs to be involved.

UNDERSTANDING QA

Definition of Quality Assurance

Without Quality Assurance there is no continuous improvement.

Goals	Why	How	What
Have an understanding the value of Quality Assurance	so that our teams comprehend what is necessary to elevate our performance	I want to collaboratively create and establish our agile behaviors and values	As an agile leader
Misconceptions	**Definition**	**Value**	**Deploy**
What Quality Assurance is not	Get an understanding of what is involved with QA	How it can be used in any aspect of an organization flow	Expand the value of QA across all teams

Figure 7.2

Quality also means ensuring we exhibit the right behaviors to achieve it. When this happens, you will see an overlap across teams, indicating everyone is involved. You want to ensure everyone has accountability because, as I said, from a software and product development perspective, typically, the most significant load of quality is on the shoulders of those who write test cases, execute them, and validate them. They ensure it's there and does what it's supposed to do, or it's built the way it's supposed to be built. But, honestly, it involves everyone from start to finish within that value chain.

Every stakeholder is involved. As we proceed in this section, we will discuss in detail what Quality Assurance (QA) entails. We aim to comprehend quality overall, emphasizing the importance of quality inputs. It's crucial to ensure that what comes in is good so that what goes out is equally robust. You'll understand that quality assurance is about delivering flawlessly; it extends throughout every process, not just when producing the next big software or having that perfect marketing plan. It's about continuously enhancing team quality, a concept discussed in detail in the previous section.

Here, we address these challenges, reinforcing that quality assurance is a shared responsibility connected to aspects of our work and process.

Here are some struggles that most people will hear about an experience in Quality.

- "I'm not a tester."
- Bottlenecks
- Constant Customer Issues

A common challenge in maintaining quality is the mindset of "I'm not a tester," which you often hear in many teams. This perspective can lead to the belief that Quality Assurance (QA) is solely a concern for testers. However, this view overlooks the reality that QA is everyone's responsibility, regardless of the industry—software, pharmaceuticals, or medical. People often assume that quality assurance is the exclusive domain of testers, who are solely responsible for ensuring everything is done correctly. But in reality, when everyone in the team delivers high-quality work, they actively participate in quality assurance without realizing it. This is a crucial shift in understanding that needs to be recognized.

Additionally, bottlenecks can exacerbate these challenges. Recall the value chain example we discussed earlier, highlighting a bottleneck where inputs accumulate, increasing lead times for subsequent teams. Such disruptions in the flow can impact overall quality, prompting a closer look at QA as a strategy to prevent future issues. This approach helps mitigate potential problems and ensures smoother processes down the line.

Our final challenge lies in handling customer complaints. Quality struggles can trigger these complaints, and how they're addressed can make all the difference. They can spur the team into swift action, plan adjustments, or demoralize individuals and teams. I recall an experience with an organization where, shortly after product releases, the support department would be inundated with customer problems. This continual stream of complaints stemming from quality issues can severely affect team morale despite their efforts to deliver a quality product, resulting in a demoralized state that can escalate into a snowball effect.

So, how do we transition from constantly finding these issues to achieving a flow of high quality? How do we reach the point where we produce, validate, and mitigate? Quality is not just about producing the product at the end; it involves the entire process from start to finish. We want to avoid the 'garbage in, garbage out' scenario. We aim for high-quality inputs, whether information, hardware, or products, to ensure that high-quality work goes into producing high-quality outputs for the next phase or the client.

QUALITY ACTIONS

- Definition of Quality Assurance
- Understand Changing Priorities
- Product/Service Value is a Team Accomplishment

As we consider our QA actions moving forward, we'll define what quality assurance (QA) really means. We will explore how changing priorities can impact quality and discuss strategies for adapting in an agile manner. Understanding these shifting priorities is crucial to maintaining quality and preventing issues before they arise.

Moreover, I previously mentioned how quality involves everyone, not just a select few. We'll cover this aspect from an action-oriented perspective, ensuring that every team member across various departments, like finance, sales, or marketing, understands their role in producing a quality product. It's important to recognize that it's not solely the development team's responsibility. Everyone has a stake in this process, contributing to the overarching goal of quality assurance and producing a quality product.

DEFINITION OF QUALITY ASSURANCE

Without quality assurance, there is no possibility for continuous improvement. We've already discussed the importance of building a culture focused on continuous improvement, and now it's time to develop this foundation further. Quality assurance is a key component in this ongoing process. As we move forward, teams must understand how quality assurance fits into the bigger picture. We aim to help teams see how they can elevate their performance levels through dedicated quality assurance practices. This understanding is essential for integrating quality assurance into their daily activities and overall strategy, enhancing continuous improvement.

- **Misconception**

Let's start with the misconceptions, as I've briefly touched on this topic before. There's a common misunderstanding that quality assurance (QA) is merely about finding bugs or pushing a button to see a defect emerge. That's not the case. When we look at quality assurance, there is a broader spectrum. If you do a Google search for quality assurance jobs, you will see some job postings that are more in-depth than just testing or finding issues. Some job descriptions show what quality assurance is and what the expectations are. These descriptions aren't abundant, as perceptions of QA can vary significantly across industries. If all sectors looked at Quality Assurance in the same way, for mitigation, and not just finding bugs, it would go a long way in improving everything.

The encouraging aspect is that quality assurance is already a part of many people's roles; it's just not recognized as such. The persistent struggle and the familiar refrain of "I'm not a tester" stem from the misconception that QA is about Testing, which it is not.

- **Definition**

When defining Quality Assurance (QA), it's essential to understand what the term entails. To set the stage, let's differentiate between quality assurance and quality control, two terms frequently used in software development, pharmaceuticals, and medical fields.

A general definition of quality assurance is:[47]

"Quality Assurance is known as QA and focuses on preventing defects. QA ensures that the approaches, techniques, methods, and processes designed for the projects are implemented correctly."

Essentially, QA is about setting up systems to prevent future defects or issues. For example, when we discuss continuous improvement, if an issue with a process is subsequently fixed or addressed with a solution to avoid similar issues in the future, that intervention is a part of quality assurance. QA involves various strategies, such as probability analysis, to proactively set things up for successful project execution.

On the other hand, Quality Control (QC) is more about Testing and validation. Whether it involves a tangible product, software, or documentation, QC includes reviewing and testing to ensure the final output is high quality. QC is the process of validating the quality of the product to ensure it meets the required standards.

- **Value**

There is value in both quality assurance (QA) and quality control (QC). Instead of merely focusing on defects, the goal is to prevent them. A defect represents something unexpected, often carrying negative connotations like error, wrong, or mistake. To soften the language, some groups opt for more neutral terms like "variance," suggesting a deviation from what was expected rather than an outright error. Having focused on QA for much

---

[47]https://www.invensislearning.com/blog/what-is-quality-assurance/#:~:text=Quality%20Assurance%20%28QA%29%20is%20like%20the%20foundation%20of,is%20about%20always%20finding%20ways%20to%20improve%20products.

of my career, I believe that the terminology itself isn't the most critical aspect—my goal has always been to improve and correct, regardless of the words used. Some people react strongly to words like "defect" or "error," which can raise defences unnecessarily.

We've discussed previously the importance of reviewing stories in the Pathway, where the focus isn't personal; it's about ensuring quality. The words used shouldn't matter as much as the intention behind them. In QA, our focus is on prevention.

In our discussions about process and continuous product improvement, we've touched on the importance of looking beyond symptoms to ensure that issues are recognized as process issues, not human errors. This is a point worth repeating from our conversations about building a culture of continuous improvement. It's essential to understand that it is not about human error. Focusing on individuals or teams when things go wrong can destroy trust, decrease morale, and lower employee satisfaction. This can lead to a negative spiral affecting the product or service quality, which may lead to customer complaints and further issues.

So, leadership and stakeholders must understand that any issues that arise are typically process issues. Recognizing this can significantly improve the working environment and help maintain a focus on quality across all aspects of an organization.

Now, I know you might be thinking, "Well, Jeremy, what if there's this one individual on the team who is just a hot mess? They can't do anything right; maybe they came in under false credentials," or "it was a bad hire," or something along those lines. Think about why that individual ended up in that situation. Go back and consider why they are messing up.

For instance, let's take a developer who keeps making spelling errors in their code and syntax errors. Ask yourself, why were these syntax errors not caught? Perhaps there were code reviews. Maybe we have a tool that performs these code reviews. Then, ask, "Why did the tool miss it?" Perhaps it wasn't in the library. Next, why wasn't it in the library for detection?

This method of questioning, often called the "five whys," helps dig deeper into issues. You typically look at a process issue by reaching the fifth why. Even if you initially think it was a bad hire, ask why it was a bad hire. Was there a breakdown in the hiring process that allowed this person to slip through? You mentioned false credentials; is there a method in place to verify credentials during the hiring process? Many organizations now require a coding test to confirm a developer's abilities. This approach helps ensure their skills match what they claim. Here, you're looking past the symptom to the underlying process issue.

When we previously discussed continuous improvement, we emphasized the need to "do this, do that, look at those stats." Since we are going deeper into recognizing the issues, we must see beyond mere symptoms. Often, the issues aren't within the team but stem from external factors that trickle down and cause problems. That's why, from a quality assurance perspective, you need that broad scope to investigate. If issues aren't addressed, they will impact processes downstream.

Consider the children's story "Princess and the Pea," in which the princess can feel a pea under a stack of mattresses, bothering her despite all the layers of soft mattresses, preventing her from sleeping. Think of each mattress as a different level of process leading up to a problem. Quality assurance is about peeling back those layers and mattresses to find the underlying issue, that small pea. For instance, in the example of a bad hire, maybe improvements could be made within the HR process to prevent similar issues.

Quality assurance looks at the full spectrum of actions, from upstream to downstream implications. It examines the entire cycle, identifying a problem, broadening the scope to understand it fully, and pinpointing the process break that caused the issue. This approach allows you to deploy the right quality assurance program effectively.

- **Deploy**

We've discussed continuous improvement, asking the right questions, and finding issues. Now, it's about deploying quality assurance. What I mean by deploying here is fostering another behavior change, to move away from misconceptions about quality assurance and towards a more team-oriented and organizational approach. We want to ensure that we're focused on being better within the QA team and with everyone. Everyone should be helping everyone become better. This is one of the key principles of agile, and as we've discussed before, this overlap helps teams support each other. Support can help out with finance, sales can assist with delivery, and so forth.

This overlapping support within teams is really what quality assurance is about. You're helping each other become better at what they do. This approach is from a conversation I had years ago, and it resonates with the whole process of what we're doing here, especially in an agile environment. We're here to help everyone improve and avoid going down the path of negativity where there's finger-pointing and escalation. We don't want that. We want to maintain a positive, supportive atmosphere.

It's about looking at the process, focusing on the issue, and working together to resolve it. When an issue arises, it's natural for those involved to feel disappointed or frustrated. There's no point in dogpiling on top of that, making people feel worse about the situation. Everyone collaborates to solve the issue in a quality assurance and continuous improvement environment.

Often, the individual who caused or encountered the issue may have the deepest understanding of what went wrong and potentially hold the key to the best solution. The results are significantly more effective when teams work together to harness this collective knowledge and drive toward a resolution. This fosters a sense of ownership we've discussed before. It's about changing procedures and transforming how we perceive and discuss these issues. It's about shifting from a blame-focused mindset to one that values constructive collaboration and mutual support.

Understand changing priorities

Changing priorities can negatively impact quality as teams try to shift.

Goals	Why	How	What
Have an effective and efficient team to deal with changing priorities	so that my teams take ownership of the expectations and are accountable for organizational agility	I want to collaboratively define, deploy, project, and sustain agile values	As an agile leader
Expectations	**Definition**	**Value**	**Deploy**
Expectations of change are light years faster than decades ago	Everyone should be prepared to act right away instead of getting caught up that it happened	Water changes direction when suddenly obstructed teams should do the same	Agile values, charters and servant leadership ease anxiety over changes in priority

Figure 7.3

One of the key factors that can significantly impact quality is a change in priorities, particularly how we adapt to these shifts. When we discuss changing priorities, this could mean several things: increasing the number of teams from two to five, reducing teams from five to two, taking on additional projects, or experiencing a loss of work. It's crucial to understand that priorities encompass more than changes in features or products based on market or customer demand. It's about comprehensively understanding these priorities and being able to plan in response to them strategically.

- **Expectations**

We've discussed the importance of having flexible plans to respond effectively and efficiently when triggers occur. This requires expecting change as part of our preparation, adjusting our workflows accordingly, and relying on agile values to guide us through shifting priorities. It's crucial to have a team ready to act swiftly when necessary.

Looking at the user story, we should work backward from the 'why' to the 'how' to the 'what.' This approach helps the team understand what's expected regarding organizational agility. It's essential to recognize that changing priorities often stem from organizational decisions rather than team-level ones. Being prepared to handle these shifts from an organizational perspective is vital.

We've observed that the expectation for change is happening faster, and people increasingly demand this rapid adaptation. Over the past few decades, companies have had to keep up with significant technological advancements. For instance, in the 1980s, CDs replaced tapes, which had been popular for decades. The 1990s brought us the internet and DVDs, followed by flash drives and camera phones in the 2000s, which were revolutionary in terms of data storage capacity. By the 2010s, innovations like Uber and artificial intelligence had emerged. The ability of companies to adapt to these changes using agile principles is crucial for their success.

A prime example of a company struggling with rapid change is Zenith. Once a major player in electronics, selling TVs and even VCRs, Zenith found it challenging to keep pace with innovations such as flat-screen TVs in the 1990s. Despite attempting to follow market leaders with similar products, LG's inability to maintain quality while trying to match the speed of industry changes led to its acquisition by LG in 1995[48]. This example highlights the challenges faced by American electronics companies at the time, which often struggled to compete with Japanese products, a common topic of jokes in late-night TV shows during that era.

This is a common scenario for many organizations: if they fail to keep pace with innovation and priority changes, they often either shut down or are acquired. Keeping up with the market is essential for competitiveness because customers increasingly expect more, and they expect it faster. A compelling statistic from one study indicates that 65% of consumers will abandon a brand due to quality issues, and most of these customers never return[49].

In the case of Zenith, when their products began to lag in quality, consumers turned to alternatives like LG, which offered TVs with better

---

[48] https://en.wikipedia.org/wiki/Zenith_Electronics
[49]   https://www.tcn.com/newsroom/press-releases/tcn-consumer-survey-reveals-significant-increases-in-brands-being-abandoned-for-poor-customer-service/

features and reliable DVD players integrated into them. LG's ability to meet customer expectations with higher quality and innovative features drew customers away from Zenith, which, despite its efforts, couldn't match the pace of industry changes in innovation and quality.

- **Preparation**

In addition to that, it's important to address the management of rapid growth or team attrition within your organization and develop strategies to handle these transitions effectively. Preparing for these changes is crucial, as well as ensuring that communication remains fresh and relevant and steering clear of repetitive or overly ceremonial approaches. That's the key. When priorities suddenly shift, it can trigger panic or anxiety. In an innovative environment, even if there is a sudden change in the market, teams and organizational priorities may still experience this sense of panic and confusion. Planning for this and understanding that, "Hey, if something happens, this is what we're going to do," helps mitigate anxiety because everyone understands their roles, expectations, and behaviors.

When you effectively mitigate these issues, the quality of work, the team, and the organization are unaffected. You're prepared to say, "Okay, let's go this route now." It's all about preparation. We prepare for emergencies, like fires, floods, and power outages, by having a three-day emergency kit in our homes. This, on an organizational level, is no different. Preparing for sudden changes in priorities at work is just a matter of pulling out the plan and executing it. This preparation can be critical because, for some teams, it might take weeks to adjust to a change in strategy. One of my clients had three strategic changes within a year before we started working together. The teams took weeks to adjust, re-plan, and move forward. Just as they hit their stride with one change, another strategy shift occurred. This lack of a clear checklist to guide them decreased employee satisfaction; teams were frustrated and struggled to maintain high quality.

This environment led to several issues over six months with the released product. Despite their best efforts, things slipped, including code reviews, creating downstream impacts that were not initially visible. Part of the problem was their haste in adapting to new strategies without a proper plan.
While some issues were relatively small, they still led to customer

complaints. The story changed dramatically when I worked with them to identify how teams could better adjust. After the final strategic change, they completed 80% of the work in just ten months—work they initially estimated would take two years. This success was mostly due to having a solid plan, which allowed them to remove anxiety, pressure, and stress and execute the work without impacting quality.

- **Change in flow**

It's important to recognize that there is a change in flow when it happens. At the same time, we need to understand that our role is about guiding, not directing. The high-level plans we've discussed, focused on objectives X, Y, and Z, outline the steps, but it's up to the self-managed teams to navigate these steps effectively. They know how to collaborate and achieve their goals. However, they may require management support. This is where the servant leader concept comes into play: working alongside the teams to ensure they have what they need to adapt to the changing flow.

Expectations will shift as situations evolve. The diagram below illustrates that while initially, you might see three points, the framework expands, and now you have 12 sides, then 49, and so on. Change is constant; managing these changes to maintain consistency and quality is challenging. Remember, our goal is to improve by 1% each day. The teams you worked with yesterday are not the same as today, and they will continue to evolve. It's crucial to provide ongoing guidance to support this evolution. There are multiple paths to achieving your vision, but collaboration is a constant requirement because it ensures that the teams can find the most efficient path. Your role is to provide the guidance needed for them to succeed.

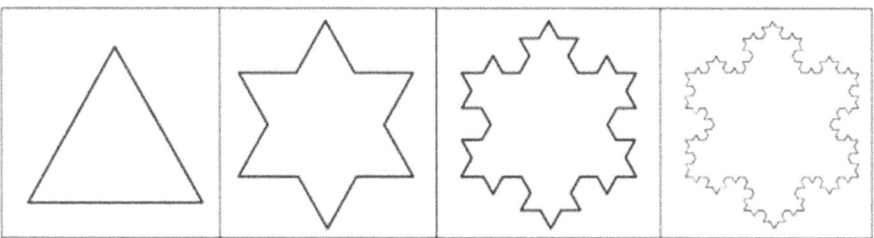

Figure 7.4

- **Agile Values**

Guidelines are important for setting the right expectations and preparing for changes in flow. The great advantage here is that the Agile values are already in place. While there might be bumps in the road that slow things down, the guidance and principles we've established over the past six weeks are designed to handle such challenges. With the roadmap we've developed, we're looking at temporary fixes and a full transformation—behavioral and actionable changes that continually improve the quality of the team, the individuals, the product, and the service.

This growth will organically extend beyond our immediate scope. Up to this point, you've set everything up perfectly. Now, we're just reinforcing and building upon the existing foundation. You're constructing something that will be beautiful but also efficient and effective, involving everyone. This process enhances the value of the product and the service, making it a collective team achievement.

Product/service value is a team event

Ownership of value is spread across the organization.

Goals	Why	How	What
All team members take ownership of product/service value.	so that we can build a thriving agile organization	I want to establish and communicate a vision aligned with agile values	As an agile leader
Commitment	**Create**	**Deliver**	**Confirm**
There must be commitment across teams to value	Work as a team to create the quality solution to meet needs	Have a delivery plan for all changes that works with teams and customers	Have a set of events and activities that confirm the delivery is as expected

Figure 7.5

- **Commitment**

When I talk about 'team thing,' I don't just mean the development or service-providing teams. I mean the entire team, everyone involved, all the stakeholders. They are the ones who demonstrate the value. You want a commitment from everyone to ensure that what is being built or served meets the clients' or customers' needs. It's about understanding the work that's coming in, both planned and unplanned, and how we will manage it. It involves maintaining quality in everything we do and ensuring that the commitment to quality, improvement, and the team itself is upheld. All these factors together create that quality.

So, how do you secure this commitment?

We've discussed using team charters, relationship agreements, self-subscription, and understanding what needs to be done. You're committing to the work, helping each other, improving, and identifying issues. This type of team commitment is far more effective than an inspirational poster on the wall that everyone ignores. You ensure that all teams are accountable for quality—not just the team that develops it, but also the sales team, marketing team, support staff, and leadership. Everyone is involved in maintaining quality, eliminating any finger-pointing by fostering a shared team interest.

We've also discussed the overlap of services and knowledge, which is crucial when creating an elevator pitch for teams. The more there is an overlap of understanding and knowledge among team members, the better the shared interest in quality. Everyone understands what others are doing, which enriches their perspective. For instance, someone from the finance team might not switch to supporting roles directly, but the more they understand how support functions and its impact, the better. This knowledge is beneficial. Although a finance professional won't code or operate machinery, understanding the processes involved allows them to offer impactful suggestions or ideas that can enhance quality and production.

- **Create**

  o Break down a solution into smaller solutions
  o Transparency of flow
  o Review the work
  o Identify improvements

You want to be able to break down the product. We've discussed this in the context of user stories, training logs, and backlogs, emphasizing the importance of managing the workflow transparently. This approach is fundamental to an agile environment—taking tasks in smaller chunks to deliver value in shorter periods, incrementally building upon them. Many groups I've worked with often included several 13-point stories in a sprint. Typically, these high-point stories consume considerable time due to their complexity, potentially hindering complete delivery within the sprint.

Could these 13-point stories have been divided into smaller, more manageable pieces to be incrementally added in each sprint? Most likely, and this would have certainly reduced frustration. Maintaining flow transparency is crucial in product development, service development, training, or dealing with impediments. Equally important is the simplification of complexity to ensure manageability.

A practical tool for maintaining quality is the stand-up meeting. This meeting is designed to quickly share updates: what was done yesterday, what is planned today, and what obstacles might impede progress. It's not the time to delve deeply into issues—that's reserved for follow-up discussions where leadership, such as the scrum master, and the team collaborate to remove any impediments. However, stand-up meetings should be time-boxed to 15 minutes or less. Allowing them to extend to 30 minutes or even an hour can be demoralizing and inefficient, mainly if the content isn't relevant to all attendees, leading to wasted time.

It's a matter of breaking things down because we aim to foster a team environment. Everyone shares the load. The greater our transparency, the better the development and the higher the quality. Improving quality also enhances value. Moreover, discussing value and the team is more than just the product itself. Meeting the customer's needs is one part of the value. How it gets done constitutes another crucial part of the value. What initiates all this—your 'why' and your agile values—essentially helps create this environment, which is equally important.

- **Deliver**

Next, we're focused on ensuring delivery. It's about more than just what we provide to customers; it's about how the team collaborates, how we enhance processes, and ensure transparency. Below is a burn-down chart that illustrates this. It tracks work over time and predicts when it will be completed. I've worked with a client whose inconsistency resulted in a burn-down chart resembling a cityscape; instead of a smooth decline, it fluctuated, never showing consistency. This was partly because the team was gaming the point system, inflating points to meet random and inconsistent targets set by leadership.

This approach to scheduling and task management gave the illusion of agility, allowing the team to take on more work mid-sprint in response to customer issues. As a result, the chart showed peaks and valleys instead of a consistent decrease. Typically, at the end of a sprint, there would be a drastic drop when, say, 20 points of work were suddenly moved to the next sprint. This manipulation of points and lack of transparency resulted in a disorganized product.

Working with them, we almost started over. We instilled the right behaviors and understanding of why and how tasks should be performed. We rebuilt their foundational practices using their existing tools, enabling proper iterative building applicable in development and across all departments—HR, sales, marketing, and support. This holistic approach allows continuous integration and development across various functions, creating a cohesive and effective workflow.

- **Confirm**

The last thing we need to do is to be able to confirm. It's not just about Testing. As I have mentioned earlier in this chapter, this is about everyone agreeing on what quality and quality assurance are, and on the improvements they will make based on the continuous improvement program that will be built using quality assurance. Right mindsets and behaviors are crucial to identify and resolve issues and to help mitigate potential future problems with the right processes in place to improve workflow and readiness for drastic changes, such as a strategic shift that changes the flow. Recall the example of a boulder entering a river we discussed in the previous chapter: the river flows around the boulder, molding itself. Similarly, you want your teams to be able to navigate obstacles, work around them, and still achieve the vision.

We are done with the quality part of the "scale" phase. Next, we will move forward and build on the continuous improvement. Looking ahead, we aim to ensure that from a quality assurance perspective, we are equipped to mitigate, avoid, or fix persistent issues with the right solutions to meet needs. Otherwise, we risk stalling and running in place without making progress. You decide to improve by this point within the framework and the system.

WORKBOOK: 07

Definition of Quality Assurance

Software Testing is the last step in the software development process for the sole purpose of quality assurance; the product is delivered as close to fault-free as possible and meets the expectations of the Business. Although the testing group within an organization has multiple partners throughout the process testing group, the most important linkage is with the business group because they are the key stakeholders. This group typically requests information system changes. Communication between these two groups must be fluid and bi-directional, with each group trusting and valuing the other's input.

The Testing group needs to understand what the Business group wants, create work products to meet those needs, and provide assurance that the product functions as expected with little risk of failure. Like the Testing Group, businesses must understand the Testing group's role and requirements to provide a quality product. Unfortunately, there is a gap between these two groups, causing a disconnect and resulting in a lack of knowledge sharing, trust, and value for each other's roles within the organization. In a project environment, these three focal points of the relationship contain multiple sub-components that can create a strained connection if not understood by both groups. In a team environment, trust is important to the success of any initiative. Clear communication regarding the work effort and costs involved is necessary to ensure buy-in by both parties to produce a quality product. Loss of trust can cause decreased value for one group over the other.

Although Testing groups provide more value to the organization than executing test cases and reporting issues, frequently, the business group does not identify their role in other terms. The business group's lack of knowledge generates a perception that the project's testing phase creates a bottleneck in production and is related to Testing's inefficiency. Information sharing with businesses is needed to understand the testing process required to ensure reduced organizational risk.

Testing also must fully understand the value of their contribution to quality assurance and prevention of organizational risk. Testing must market itself to its business partners. The most important aspect of any relationship is understanding the stakeholder. Without that appreciation, all forms of relationship-building will fail. Each group must be aware of what each group is capable of and understand how their production partners communicate and their priorities. Testing groups can improve the quality of changes early in the process and ensure the value of future projects through quality assurance processes. If Testing cannot identify with Business groups and convey their messages effectively, then the opportunity for knowledge sharing is lost[50].

1. Does your organization see Quality Assurance as Testing?
2. Are there processes and policies in place that would fall under Quality Assurance yet are not identified as QA?
3. How is quality measured and tracked throughout the organization?
4. Testing is only a small part of QA, and for decades, it is what most people think, mostly in software and hardware development. Other industries will see things differently. What are your thoughts about QA? How would you change and deploy views?
5. How would you add the definition of quality assurance to the team's workflow?
6. Write an agile value that involves the team and everyone performing quality assurance without explicitly stating it.
7. Write down processes in other departments that would be deemed Quality Assurance.
8. Write down your thoughts and difficulties that could occur, getting others to understand the definition of quality assurance and how it impacts their day-to-day work.
9. Is there a detailed root cause analysis program in place?
10. What is the message of the value in quality from leadership? Is it only product-focused, or does it include employees?
11. Is that message backed up? What could be done to improve messaging?
12. How would team involvement in quality assurance look?

---

[50] https://dtpr.lib.athabascau.ca/action/download.php?filename=mba-12/open/BerriaultJeremy.pdf

13. What would you like to see in 3 months?

Understanding Changing Priorities

Today's environment has interruptions at every corner. How we deal with interruptions will determine the quality of the work produced. Most see agile methodologies as adding whatever they want at any point, especially in the current iteration. Doing work in this fashion creates a stressful environment as the sudden change in direction impacts the plan for the team to get the job done.

Sudden shifts will impact quality either because of the added work creating an overcapacity of the team or work that is already completed or partially completed is impacted due to potential negligence because the focus of work is on the new priorities. It is essential to have plans and agreements on what to do when handling changing priorities, short and long-term. It is not expected to be a detailed, line-by-line plan to execute. It should be an agreed-upon set of distinctions and steps to deal with changes as they come. Something that is agreed upon by all the stakeholders when something comes in.

A good example is if there is a production problem that requires attention[51]. Is the problem impacting customers financially? Is it a data breach? Are they able to continue work? These questions will be examined, and a proper plan for how everyone deals with them will go a long way. Most companies will add the issues to the current iteration and expect all the planned work to be completed simultaneously. Creating version control issues, duplicate work, and added stress to complete.

In some teams, they will work together to prioritize and shuffle work)if needed) and plan how and when things will get done. Understanding that some of the initial planned work could be removed or shifted to be completed for another time.

1. What is the general sense with the team when there is a sudden change in priorities?

---

[51] Cunningham, M. L. (2017). Effects of visual cues and task prioritization on recovering from multiple interruptions (Order No. 10275240). Available from ProQuest Dissertations & Theses Global. (1914685957). Retrieved from http://0-search.proquest.com.aupac.lib.athabascau.ca/dissertations-theses/effects-visual-cues-task-prioritization-on/docview/1914685957/se-2?accountid=8408

2. Are long-term changes handled effectively?
3. How does the team anticipate priority change? Is there a flow?
4. Change should not come as a surprise to anyone, especially in an agile environment. How teams flow with the changes can have consequences impacting everyone down the road. What are your thoughts on the team's expectations for change?
5. Does your team have problems when there is a change in priorities?
6. Are there increased support calls after the deployment on a release impacted by changing priorities?
7. What is the general mood of teams after a strategy change?
8. What are the biggest obstacles in changing the workflow to prioritize and change work?
9. What are the impacts on other teams? How would workflow changes effectively work with non-agile teams?

Product/Service Value is a Team event.

It is not just the team that creates the product or service that provides value. It is a comprehensive organizational event. Nicholas del Carlo[52] states that a team is only as strong as its weakest link. Most organizations see only the group itself and the links within as valuable, when, in actuality, the organization is the team. If some other departments or teams do not provide value to what is being produced, they are the weak link at any level of involvement.

As an example, the HR team. They help support the employees and ensure they understand their roles and the available training. They have a part to play in the value.

Teams like Support, Sales, and marketing all have a role to play, yet the connection is not as strong as they are outside.

The greater the involvement, the greater the value.

Transitioning the IT work process from waterfall to agile scrum produces

---

[52] Nicholas del carlo, agile coach at ODManagement.com. (2019, Jan 04). PR Newswire Retrieved from http://0-search.proquest.com.aupac.lib.athabascau.ca/wire-feeds/transitioning-work-process-waterfall-agile-scrum/docview/2163014209/se-2?accountid=8408

a high-performing team and product. Nicholas del Carlo stated: Scrum is a simple-to-understand yet hard-to-master framework that team members can use to tackle complex problems while delivering minimal viable products of the highest possible value. Scrum can be applied to big, complex software and product development and everyday life challenges by breaking large and complex problems or goals into small chunks more attainable within a 2-week sprint.

1. How do you foster a common vision among teams' activities?
2. What approach (es) is/are used to determine how much work can be completed in a given iteration?
3. How does the performance feedback translate into actual improvements to team performance?
4. Commitment to work is sometimes forced onto teams. They are told what is expected of them through a command and control way, which goes against agile values. Although it may not impact the output's quality, it impedes the quality of work life within the team. It also impedes the quality of agile growth across the organization. Write down your thoughts on forced commitment and self-managed team self-subscription, transparency, and collaborations with other teams for work and commitment to organizational improvement and effectiveness.
5. How do leaders and stakeholders engage with projects?
6. What methods are used to assemble product components and ensure consistency/ quality is maintained?
7. What approach is used to identify lessons learned and improvement opportunities at the end of the sprint?
8. An expansion of the team needs to be created with teams. There is too much focus on creating products and services and not a lot on creating an agile environment, building off the commitment that everyone must be involved in creation. Whether it is the creation of opportunities, improvements, or a fun environment to work in, as examples, Thoughts?
9. How do agile teams ensure the product meets customer expectations?
10. How is performance feedback provided to Agile teams to support

team improvement?

11. Doing anything in an agile environment is never a "set it and forget it" behavior. Anything that is done must be confirmed that it is working as expected and providing the value everyone deserves. Setting this up within a team and those that work with them can be difficult. Doing so needs the right mix of leading and coaching. Thoughts?

CHAPTER 08 | EVOLVE

Evolution is constant, the speed of which it happens depends on surroundings

Goals	Why	How	What
Evolution of teams' delivery.	Have an exciting, engaging work environment	Through continued demonstration of value and improvements	A process that provides information to make appropriate decisions
Easy Acceptance	**Easy removal**	**Tools**	**Team focused**
The work done to this point in the roadmap will have created an environment wanting to mature	What was once frustrating dealing with issues is now welcomed opportunities to learn.	Have the right tools that fits with team's agile values and how they want to achieve value.	Productivity and evaluations are based on teams not individuals

Figure 8.1

This chapter focuses on evolution, and maturity is integral to it. At the beginning of the book, I talked about maturity, but I did not get into much detail about it. What needs to happen for a truly agile environment to succeed is the ability to adapt, and to keep the habit of adaptability consistent throughout the process of evolution, you have to "mature" your teams.

So, in this sense, maturity goes beyond simply becoming faster or doing more work within a framework; those are just side effects. Here, the focus shifts from short-term gains to sustained progress and innovation. Evolution in agility, in relation to maturity, means consistently improving, utilizing tools effectively, and ensuring accurate information dissemination. These factors collectively contribute to overall improvement.

Reflecting on our journey in this book, we've seen a continuous evolution. Everything evolves, and refining our processes to evolve delivery is essential. As we evolve delivery methods, we also grow the teams themselves, requiring acceptance of change, seamless adaptation, access to the right tools, and an increased focus on the team.

MATURITY STRUGGLES

So, what are our everyday struggles with maturity in agile environments?

It is a well-recognized issue that organizations often face difficulties with agility and maturity. As mentioned a few times, research shows that 95% of organizations studied experience clashes between traditional and agile methods[53], which impedes their maturity. Additionally, there is a prevalent misconception that merely implementing an agile framework is sufficient for achieving agility. However, as you have read, much more is involved.

In discussions about organizational maturity, the emphasis lies on maintaining consistency in processes. Each maturity model tier functions like a checklist to ensure adherence to predefined standards. However, this approach often reflects a rigid mindset, diverging from the adaptive ethos advocated in the Manifesto for Agile Software Development.

Our journey to this point aims to move away a little from maturity and keep focus on evolving and growing. This will assist in driving the maturity of the behaviors. We will discuss further what defines an agile environment, understand that frameworks are merely tools, and establish procedures to ensure everything is synchronized. This includes within teams and with any external parties that impact the process.

---

[53] State of Agile 2020

EVOLUTION ACTIONS

What constitutes an agile environment

Go from doing agile to being agile.

Goals	Why	How	What
Looking past an agile transformation to evolve the teams	so that I can help teams move away from traditional management methods	I want to embrace a broader perspective of agility	As an agile leader
Acceptance	**Change**	**Maturing**	**Evolving**
The basics in behaviors and use of agile actions.	Evolution of behaviours to increase value by including more strategy in value creation	Involve more than the team to using agile values	Organically transform teams within the organization and have partners in sync with agile values

Figure 8.2

WHAT CONSTITUTES AN AGILE ENVIRONMENT?

We aim to look beyond the agile transformation and evolve the team into a truly agile environment. As the title of the book states, this is Beyond Frameworks. Implementing a framework is merely scratching the surface. There's much more to it. We must ensure we exhibit the behaviors necessary to move forward. In understanding what constitutes an agile environment, we recognize there is a natural progression to building an agile environment. Below, we go through four components: Acceptance, Change, maturing, and evolving. Comprehending each stage is crucial for the next step in our evolution.

This isn't about having certain processes and maturity levels that work in sync. It's about understanding different levels and behaviors to achieve that evolutionary stage. There's no magic checklist for this journey. Consider acceptance, change, maturing, and evolving like throwing a pebble into a pond. When you throw the pebble, it creates ripples. The first ripple represents acceptance, which expands with change, grows further with maturing, and broadens with evolving.

- **Acceptance**

So, we're setting things up to allow for the organic growth of agile delivery. This growth isn't limited to the team but grows through interactions with other individuals and teams. From there, it will continue to expand. The struggle is that they focus solely on following the steps. These struggles often stem from attempts to merge traditional and agile management styles, including our delivery methods.

So, it's essential to understand the fundamental behaviors that align with our values. You want to capture, inspect, and adapt performance, ensure that tools and automation are available, and meet training needs. It would be best to have backlogs—not only product backlogs but potentially training, impediment, and risk backlogs. The product vision should reflect functional and non-functional needs, fitting into the overall roadmap vision. Teams should be actively involved with the backlogs—these are the behaviors and actions that facilitate adoption.

Furthermore, you're baselining everything so your agile values are understood and used as guidance. They should be demonstrated in plans, techniques, and events. Basic metrics should be established to enhance transparency. It's crucial to ensure a good team mix and for teams to develop their standards, rules, roles, and responsibilities guided by servant leadership.

You want consistency through regular coaching and continuous evaluation, including conducting retrospectives. This consistency will show the acceptance of the journey. Evaluating the team's ability to finish the work at the end of each iteration through retrospectives or cadence reviews is crucial to see how they can improve. Identifying training needs should primarily be the responsibility of the teams themselves rather than the leadership. While leadership can be involved and offer suggestions, it's ultimately up to the teams to work alongside leadership to pinpoint these needs. Additionally, having mentors within the teams and throughout the organization is vital to help improve and maintain this consistency.

- **Change**

Change is about shifting the focus from individuals to the group. This involves engaging stakeholders more and ensuring that leaders participate in agile events. While Scrum guidelines typically advise against leadership involvement in daily stand-ups, as these are for teams to coordinate daily tasks and progress, leadership should be engaged when issues that require support arise. This engagement is essential for addressing impediments identified in these meetings, as leaders can consult with Scrum Masters to review the impediment log and provide necessary assistance.

Use clear communication channels effectively to promote agile values. Defining frameworks and organizing events are critical components of this. It's also important to ensure you continuously capture feedback, including maintaining logs for impediments, employee satisfaction, and customer satisfaction. For example, feedback during sprint reviews involves product demonstrations to understand the following steps, potential strategic shifts, or priority changes that may need to be addressed in the next sprint. Ensuring a well-prioritized and properly sized backlog is crucial for team efficiency. Additionally, shared metrics should be established to enhance leaders' understanding of team dynamics and performance.

We've discussed creating a communication plan emphasizing agile values and outlining strategies for promoting them. You've expressed the importance of using transparent team charters, as visibility will be key to their effectiveness. You also want to focus on strategic planning, utilizing a backlog to define the state of future performance. Additionally, you have the team's SWOT analysis, which will vary depending on whether it's focused on a specific department or the entire organization. You aim to ensure that everything is aligned and expanding outward.

When creating your foundation, the backlog must be visual and transparent. A critical component of this journey is addressing culture change. You aim to create a culture transformation release plan as part of this process. This involves ensuring that training is provided universally and establishing agreements between teams and partners based on agile values. It's vital to capture and transparently measure improvements against the appropriate product roadmap. Other plans, such as your release plan, should also be visual and designed to reflect customer needs through the product or service features. Shared accountabilities are crucial, and from a performance perspective, you'll monitor team productivity and the value produced, continuously reassessing whether the agile values still meet the team's needs for development and output.

- **Maturing**

The maturity here concerns the team's level of discipline to not only support one another but also stay within the guidelines and continue to exhibit the expected behaviors of adaptation.

As we progress, our next goal is to increase the number of truly agile organizations. We aim to overcome the barriers that have traditionally hindered most organizations. This journey will guide you through the necessary steps. You'll start integrating engaging agile values and methodologies into your daily work, allowing your values to evolve. Leaders will better collaborate with internal and external stakeholders. There will be constant evaluation of your space and tools to ensure you're moving down that evolutionary path.

All these plans we've discussed in previous chapters are adapted, kept up to date, and refined. The product vision and roadmap are consistently updated and refined; you're finding those improvement techniques. You're improving consistently, not just in what's being delivered but also in your team dynamics and processes. You'll now be able to have cross-team performance measurements. Impediments will be identified and dealt with.

Additionally, you can have other types of retrospectives, like the technique called 'heartbeat retrospectives.' These are regular meetings, distinct from team retrospectives, where everyone gets a clearer view of the organization's pulse—not just a basic town hall. You'll get more involvement. By this point in the journey, within the organization, you'll have created a collaborative environment where all fears are removed. I've seen town halls where leaders sit up front on a stool, talking and providing status. Then, when they ask for questions, most people sit there; only a few come up to ask questions. When you hold a heartbeat retrospective, it changes this dynamic.

The culture you've created within your environment has successfully eliminated fear. People now feel comfortable coming forward to ask pertinent questions, seeking to understand and learn from mistakes without assigning blame. Overall, you've enhanced the processes and instituted evaluations for your partners to ensure they remain the right fit. This includes checking if they meet your needs, maintaining the appropriate values, and verifying that their contributions are effective and efficient. They must also integrate well with the team.

If your organization manages multiple products that need to be synchronized—like a reporting project or a sales platform, for example— then it's essential that the product backlogs across teams are aligned. Whether multiple teams are working on separate product backlogs or all are contributing to one large backlog, the key is that these teams are in sync. They must fully understand what is being developed and ensure collaborative efforts to deliver the highest value possible. Furthermore, if you have multiple teams, consider holding a large team retrospective, sometimes called a Scrum of Scrums, to ensure all teams are aligned. This broader retrospective is crucial for maintaining synchronization across all teams.

- **Evolving**

Once we finish the acceptance, change, and maturing components, it's time to focus on growth. When you work through each component, you've created an innovative and creative ecosystem that will grow and thrive. This sets the stage for you to start outpacing the competition. You'll experience levels of efficiency and effectiveness you have never seen before. This is because everything now follows the Agile way; you're employing the right behaviors and actions to evolve.

Understand that frameworks are only tools

Go from one tool in the toolbox to many

Goals	Why	How	What
Recognize that multiple tools are needed to build strong agile teams	so that we remain flexible and not restricted to a single framework.	I want our agility to be guided by our values	As an agile leader
So many tools	**Confusion**	**Hammer and a screw**	**Add to the toolbox**
Understand the tools available to increase value.	Why is the belief that after a framework is introduced to a team that they are agile?	Why one framework will not work for all.	Using multiple frameworks is not a bad thing.

Figure 8.3

- **So Many Tools**

When we use the right behaviors, we understand that frameworks are the tools that help us achieve our goals. As I mentioned before, it's like using a hammer to put in a screw; the right behaviors is to use a screwdriver for the task. The key understanding about tools and frameworks is that you don't want a toolbox with just one tool. You want to ensure you have all the tools your team needs to be effective, and the same goes for frameworks. When we look at tools, we see that many different ones are available, and some of these frameworks can be in sync.

For example, BDD can be used in Scrum, XP can be used in Scrum, or they can be used in disciplines like DAD (Disciplined Agile Delivery) or SAFe™. Many things can be added to provide value, and it's about understanding which ones to use and which work well together. It's up to the team to help decide which tools and frameworks are in sync and most effective.

Confusion

There is confusion because teams often feel that only one framework is needed when creating an agile environment. Currently, the two most common frameworks in use are Scrum and SAFe™. Both focus on ensuring faster delivery. Delivering faster is an output—your 'what.' The agile values help determine the 'why'(your center), which will then help determine the 'how,' guiding the choice of tools and outputs.

You can use multiple outputs and tools but must ensure that the tools fit the team and provide value. I'm not suggesting that if you're using Scrum, you need to change it. Scrum is an excellent framework to use. It's about understanding the right behaviors and using Scrum more effectively and efficiently. This might include adding other tools, techniques, or frameworks to enhance its effectiveness and efficiency.

- **Hammer and a Screw**

The point is to move from the hammer and screw and focus on establishing the right behaviors. No single framework fits every scenario. For example, there's a framework called P4, which many may not have heard of. P4 works well with agile teams delivering hardware products. While I won't go too deeply into it, it's important to note that such a framework exists. Teams can still use Scrum to create hardware, depending on their needs.

Each team and what they deliver is different. Ensuring no loss of value or interest is crucial because losing these leads to believing that agile doesn't work. If teams change their behaviors and use the right tools, they can make the framework work effectively. This shift might prevent them from saying agile doesn't work.

- **Add To The Toolbox**

We need to add behavior to the toolbox as well. However, we don't want to overflow the toolbox. We don't want to be like the amateur home improvement enthusiast who goes to the hardware store and buys every tool, thinking they'll use them all at some point. Instead, we want to work with teams to have a suitable set of tools in place to be effective and efficient.

Decisions should be made through team charters, considering your culture, agile values, and workflow. These elements will help determine which frameworks and tools are best suited to meet the needs of the team and the client. When picking the right tools, many factors must be considered to ensure they add value and maintain interest. This holistic approach will help teams avoid misusing agile methodologies and ensure they are genuinely effective.

This section may feel repetitive, but there is a reason. It is critical to emphasize that being truly agile is about opening your mind to opportunities and not being fixated. Work to find out what is best for you and your teams. Collaborate and grow.

Synchronization with everyone

Evolve teams with maturing delivery

Goals	Why	How	What
Have a strong knowledge sharing environment to decrease the knowledge gap	so that we can foster growth and continuous improvement.	I want everyone aligned with our agile values	As an agile leader
Learning program	**Flowing processes**	**Measuring**	**Success**
Knowledge sharing starts with a program that will give everyone value	Things change over time and processes are no different	There is more to measure than just productivity	Success can mean anything to anyone if there is no consistency across the team

Figure 8.4

Learning Program

Synchronization is important, and by now, you've likely understood what happens when teams are not in sync, both internally and externally. When teams are not aligned, it creates frustration and an "us versus them" attitude. To combat this, we must create a great knowledge-sharing environment where everyone understands what everyone else is doing. This doesn't require complete overlap; it just needs a bit of overlap to foster understanding.

One way to achieve this is by creating a learning program with flowing processes between teams and measuring their effectiveness. This leads to success. A learning program is crucial in an agile environment. For instance, there is a training backlog where courses are identified, and values are listed for leadership to review with the team and make appropriate decisions. Having a retrospective of training sessions is another valuable technique.

However, training retrospectives are often overlooked in many organizations. In a training retrospective, after a team or individuals take a course, they evaluate its value and determine how to apply what they learned. I've seen instances where a group takes training but then returns to the office without fully integrating the new knowledge. They might implement 5% of the course content, but the full potential is lost without a structured review.

To address this, we need one-on-one calls and group sessions. These help attendees increase their network and allow them to work together to understand and apply the course material. This collaboration ensures support and provides feedback to improve the course. Ultimately, this process enhances productivity, performance, efficiency, and the overall system.

- **Flowing Processes**

Improvements impact everything. A training or learning program doesn't have to be just a list of courses. You create mentorship and coaching opportunities, offer paid and free classes, and continuously assess everything to ensure that constant value is delivered. It's crucial to have flowing processes and evolving systems. The worst thing that can happen to any team is complacency, which halts evolution and maturity.

When teams become complacent, issues follow. They stagnate, becoming like stale water, no longer flowing or evolving. Teams may start using frameworks and agile techniques but get stuck if they don't strive for continuous improvement. Ensuring maturity and the desire to evolve is crucial.

All the components in creating an agile environment aim to prevent complacency by creating an environment where teams want to improve and push forward. This motivation comes from understanding the 'why' of an agile environment, which drives the 'what.' Ingrained in their minds and emotionally attached, this concept helps them regularly review and improve their values and methods.

Now, with this concept ingrained in your team's mind, you'll have a disciplined, agile team in delivery and their approach and mentality. This disciplined approach ensures ongoing improvement and alignment with agile principles, leading to sustained success and growth.

- **Measuring**

I mentioned this at the beginning of this book: an agile environment is about discipline. Being agile requires more discipline than the waterfall methodology. However, this doesn't mean agile environments are more restrictive than waterfall environments. There's a difference.

Discipline in an agile environment means continuously evolving and flowing while maintaining consistency. It's about striving to be 1% better than you were yesterday.

A mathematical equation can show what a 1% daily improvement will give you in one year.

$$1^{365} = 1$$

$$1.01^{365} = 37.8$$

Figure 8-5

Mathematically, just improving one percent a day leads to a dramatic change over one year.

To achieve this, it's essential to have measures in place. We need to measure progress to ensure synchronization, observe improvements, and witness the evolution of teams. This can be done through both quantitative and qualitative data.

By measuring these aspects, we can see the improvements and added value, which leads to success. Consistent measurement and evaluation ensure that everything in place contributes to the team's progress and success.

- **Success**

Many people have different ideas of success. However, being agile and pushing forward will meet everyone's definition of success. Success will be defined based on team agreements, charters, and partnerships.

Everything done until this point ensures you'll have a successful team, partnership, and leadership. All the elements are in place, and everything we've discussed and incorporated into your roadmap is designed to lead to success. By now, I hope you see that collaboration within the teams is essential to ensure it fits and makes sense when we get to the roadmap. It is vital to have everyone involved in creating the agile environment they will be a part of.

You'll work with your team to develop the foundation for the environment, which will then become a conversation point for moving forward. Remember, being agile is a team function. While you can be agile as an individual and grow, expanding that within the team is crucial. The organic growth of the environment through all the work will help the team improve, so they must be involved.

We must understand and review that this is about being in sync as a team. Each team is like a cell in an organism, evolving and striving to surpass expectations. To succeed in an agile environment, get the right behaviors, starting with basic behaviors and building on them. Ensure consistency across the team, moving from individual to group, tactical to strategic, and breaking through barriers to improve.

Creating an agile environment where teams can grow and succeed requires the right tools and frameworks. With over 30 frameworks available and too many different techniques to count, it's about using them effectively and efficiently to meet your organization's value. Doing so ensures continuous improvement and success for the team and organization.

AGILE VALUES HELP DETERMINE YOUR FRAMEWORK

While everyone wants to be agile, there's a more profound need to be agile to work more effectively and efficiently. I've experienced this over nearly 30 years of working in environments where we develop and produce products and services. An agile team is like an organism; it must evolve to thrive. This approach will help you evolve and succeed.

So again, your agile values will help you determine and ensure that the framework you choose is being used effectively and efficiently. This eliminates the confusion of relying on just one framework. You're adding to the toolbox, making the right decisions to have the right tools in place. With all that said and done, you will achieve synchronization within the teams through your learning programs and mentor coaching programs. You'll ensure knowledge sharing is in place so everyone understands what everyone else is doing, avoiding complacency.

Your behaviors will allow you to measure progress and evolve by constantly reviewing and improving. Ultimately, this leads to success within teams, departments, and organizations and improves employee and client satisfaction scores. The value and quality of work going out to the client will increase, as will the value and quality of the work being done by the teams. You will be able to use this approach to improve and evolve continuously.

A byproduct of all this is a competitive advantage. You might start surpassing the competition, potentially becoming the market leader. This adaptability is crucial in today's fast-paced environment, where changes happen rapidly. Without the ability to adapt and deal with these changes, you'll be left behind while others move forward. That's not what you want. You want to become the Zenith of your market.

By this point, you've taken accountability, worked through everything necessary, and made the right decisions for your teams. You're helping your teams become better at what they do. The agile environment you're developing with your teams will only lead to success. It will create the environment everyone wants and needs.

WORKBOOK: 08

What Constitutes an Agile Environment

In Steve Berez's article Q&A: The Challenges Agile Tech Teams Face.[54] He asks the question that many organizations seem to struggle to answer: "Agile teams are common in technology. Why are the results so often disappointing?" The Manifesto for Agile Software Development is over twenty years old, and organizations are still trying to figure it out. This inability to comprehend it has many negative implications for organizations and customers.

Some of the issues experienced will be:

- Us vs. them situations, either between teams or within the teams themselves. This holdover from a traditional management environment creeps in, adding frustrations as it clashes with the agile mindset.
- The traditional way of working hides in an agile environment. This severe clash in the way of working causes delays, firefights, frustrations, and avoidable stress.
- The Corvette-Chevette paradox. Agile teams clash with teams that are not agile. Either the loss of value of the agile teams slowing down to keep up with the non-agile team or obstacles when reversed.

One of the causes of all this leads back to Steve's article:

"The second pattern involves IT leaders putting too much faith in agile to solve their problems while underinvesting in necessities like modular architecture, automation, data management, advanced analytics, and engineering skills."

Blind faith that an agile framework will solve their delivery problems will not work. So, how do we fix this? How do we break free from the majority of organizations struggling to be agile? We need to adjust organizational behaviours. Frameworks are tools, and there will be struggles without the right behaviours.

---

[54] https://www.bain.com/insights/agile-teams-are-common-in-technology/

Treat organizations as evolving organisms. Different parts of an organism have separate functions yet are in sync with each other to adapt to the environment. Organizations are the same. Pre-2000, the evolution rate was slow, so a traditional way of thinking, behaving, and working succeeded. That is not the case today, and we see the struggles.

1. Does leadership feel the framework is all needed to be agile?
2. What areas we have discussed throughout the book do you feel are gaps within your organization that must be adopted for agile environments?
3. What could be implemented right away to help?
4. There is a big misconception about what it takes to adopt an agile environment fully. Organizations that thoroughly assess their agility find many gaps within their agile teams, let alone the organization. Take some time to think about your experiences with transformations, or if you have yet to go through one, what do you think can cause issues?
5. What barriers are in place that would impede going from adopting to transforming?
6. Would everyone agree to have a set of agile values to help teams and leadership exhibit the right behaviors?
7. Does leadership feel the need to stick with one framework?
8. This is what is meant to happen during an agile transformation. There is much focus on just the frameworks and keeping everything else in place the way it was. Doing so will create a clashed environment that will eventually cause problems. These problems are not catastrophic but are frustrating and create much stress. There is a reversion of how it was done before in that situation, which clashes even more. Take time to think about your organization and explain how this could be avoided.
9. An evolving agile team is not as simple as most think. As discussed throughout the book, it is more than just being able to deliver faster than when using a waterfall model. Write your thoughts on going from adopting to evolving and how you see it working in your team.
10. What has changed with your perception of being agile since the

start of the book?

Understand that Frameworks are only tools

Organizations must use agile methodologies to keep up with clients'/customers' needs and rapidly changing regulations and stay ahead of the competition. It is a natural evolution of business. Over the past 15 years, more organizations have started their agile journey.

As time passed, software development teams transformed to agile methodologies, and organizations started getting other divisions to transform. They saw the value of agile and wanted to achieve more with different groups. All parts of the evolution make sense due to the ability to eliminate red tape and bottlenecks. They would take the methodology used with the development teams and apply it to those departments. Unfortunately, that decision could create frustration and failure to use those methodologies effectively.

Reason? Agile frameworks are tools that meet the team's needs in an agile environment. Suppose the needs and flow do not fit what the framework can support. That doesn't mean that other departments can't be agile; what it means is that they need the right tool to get it done. Imagine an organization like this toy.

Each piece has a specific place to fit into, and departments within an organization are the same; they have differences. The size of an organization does impact; the smaller the organization, there could be less of a need to implement different methodologies. There is still a chance that multiple methods need to be in place.

Plenty of frameworks exist; depending on the list, a range of 20-30 doesn't include any mash-ups organizations may have created. They are all tools and need to be treated as such. What is essential is the behaviors, actions, and outcomes of those who use the tool.

1. How many frameworks did you know before reading this book? What are your thoughts on the mash-up of frameworks?
2. What is the understanding of leadership about agile frameworks?
3. Is there a general feeling that agile delivery is not working with

your team and leadership?

4. How difficult would introducing additional frameworks for different teams to use within your organization be?

Synchronization with everyone

People who talk about agile delivery tend to focus on software creation. This makes sense, as that is where it started with the Software Agile Delivery Manifesto in 2001. Now is the time for everyone else to adopt a more agile mindset.

Organizations realize this and have used the agile mental model to get leaps and bounds ahead of their competition. Look at some of the most successful organizations; Google is a prime example.

In 2008, Dan Woods[55], writing for Forbes, detailed how Google uses the agile mindset across its organization. Years later, they are still going strong and have entered other markets not imagined from their humble beginnings as a web search engine.

Organizations that use agile methodologies for software delivery will continue to encounter obstacles. When working with departments or vendors outside of the team, they will need to handle either not having the same agile values that are in sync with them or not working with any agile methodologies. These obstacles will cause pain points that will become commonplace, and complacency will take over.

There are websites now to help Marketing teams see how Agile methods can help them. Think about how well they can get work done while also having the ability to pivot faster to ever-changing market conditions.

10 AGILE IDEAS WORTH SHARING by Beth Stackpole[56]

Steven Eppinger, a professor of management science at MIT Sloan, recently argued that agile should be applied to development realms outside of software. Every company is trying to be more agile—it's become part of the regular engineering management lexicon," he said. It's shocking how

---

[55]   https://www.forbes.com/2008/08/09/cio-agile-computing-tech-cio-cx_dw_0811agile.html

[56] https://mitsloan.mit.edu/ideas-made-to-matter/10-agile-ideas-worth-sharing

quickly it's being adopted."

Apple is an excellent example of using agile methodologies to create hardware. Over the past few years, they have released multiple versions of the same phone with varying sizes and components to gain market share. Instead of going through a standard waterfall process and releasing products once a year or one product a year, they can see where the market is going and adapt relatively quickly to get that early jump.

Creating the right environment with the right behaviors and actions to achieve valuable output within any organization is within grasp. Whether they provide services, products, or both, the ability to show clients value and effectively adapt to change promptly will put that organization at the forefront of their market. Whether they create widgets, the software in the widgets, the services to sell or use the widgets, or even support the widgets, agile principles can improve efficiency and effectiveness.

1. How would you begin to achieve synchronization within the team and with other teams?
2. **What** would success look like to the team when synchronized with themselves, leadership, and other teams?

CHAPTER 09 | CHANGE MANAGEMENT PREREQUISITES

I want you to have the right mental model when I talk about pushing it out to all the teams. You started with building the environment for your team with the last eight chapters, or maybe you have started at an organizational level already; in either case, you have become an agile leader.

Now, you will set up the final part, the self-sustaining ecosystem that will grow. Your newfound knowledge will help identify how everything can make other teams create their agile environment and become more in sync with your team or department. This will enable overlap and mutual understanding.

Leadership and other teams must clearly understand what they must do with guidelines and guidance. You're moving away from the traditional management view and becoming a servant leader. You've set things up so others can succeed, allowing them to create team environments and agile frameworks. This will enable them to be in sync with your team.

WHAT ROLE DOES LEADERSHIP PLAY IN CHANGE MANAGEMENT?

Determine Agile Values

So now, you see how the example of cells in an organism applies; each has different functions but works in sync. You're growing and evolving this organism, the organization in the business context, by helping teams understand and adopt agile values for themselves and the organization. You're expanding the organizational vision and values to create team-specific visions and values to support them. These teams will build on the experiences and frameworks, aligning themselves with your team and the broader organizational goals.

There may be opportunities for shared agile values, where both teams want to work similarly and hold the same views. While there will likely be some differences in wording or emphasis, the context and overall alignment will be similar. Keep this in mind when working with other teams.

Understand Value Chain

Now, you will have a broader perspective of the value chain. It's possible that team members were already part of the value chain you identified but didn't fully grasp how everything interconnects. With this new understanding, they can align their actions with their values, providing you with a more straightforward framework to identify and expand on the customer's goals.

When you focus on expanding these goals, you uncover the underlying needs. Different teams may have varying methods of identifying these needs, which can provide diverse insights and approaches. This broader view allows for a more comprehensive understanding of the customer's objectives, helping you to tailor your strategies more effectively.

Understanding the value chain and how each part contributes can help you better align your efforts with the customer's aspirations. This alignment enhances customer satisfaction and drives more targeted and impactful results. As teams recognize their role within the value chain, they can contribute more meaningfully to the overall mission.

This broader view facilitates a deeper connection between your actions and the customer's goals. It enables you to see the bigger picture, identify needs more accurately, and leverage different team approaches to meet those needs. This comprehensive understanding will serve your customers and achieve greater success.

Understanding Innovation

When we talk about internal and external customers, they will understand what innovation means. You can now work with other teams to discuss what it means to be innovative. This collaboration will allow you to transform their behaviors and actions, helping them improve. The biggest aspect of an agile environment is to drive improvement, improve things, and become leaner.

Through continuous improvement, you have seen how to make processes more efficient and effective. Without this focus, you become stagnant, and neither you nor other teams want that. One of the benefits of this evolution section is that different teams will start seeing the value in your creation. Use the value of the insights from this book and how they can help them.

Understanding What You Deliver To Ensure Customer And Employee Satisfaction

The efforts made thus far are paving the way for significant enhancements. How can you connect employee and customer satisfaction to a larger context?

First, let's review what was mentioned in an earlier chapter. When employees are satisfied, they are more engaged and productive. This positive energy translates into better customer interactions, fostering a more pleasant and effective customer service experience when satisfied customers are more likely to remain loyal and recommend your products or services to others, creating a cycle of positivity and growth.

If you've applied changes to some of your discoveries, you should already notice an improvement in satisfaction scores, at least the general positive cultural shift. These scores are not just numbers; they reflect your employees' and customers' experiences and attitudes. An increase in these scores indicates that your employees feel valued and motivated, and your customers feel heard and appreciated.

You might be seeing a rise in value, whether it's through increased sales, improved retention rates, or enhanced brand reputation. This value increase signifies that your changes are making a tangible difference. Even if you're beginning to observe these improvements, it is a sign that you are on the right track.

This connection between employee and customer satisfaction and the broader environment will likely become evident to others. Colleagues, stakeholders, and even external observers will recognize the positive changes. They will see how your commitment to improving satisfaction is driving overall success. This recognition can further bolster morale and encourage continued efforts toward enhancing satisfaction, creating a virtuous cycle of improvement and success. This is how evolution starts.

Start With Servant Leader and Understand Self-managed Teams

When you see that increase in value, it signifies that everything is aligned correctly. You will naturally adopt a servant-leader style, with agile values created collaboratively, communicated, and understood by everyone. By leading through example, you will inspire others to follow suit. The initial apprehension towards self-managed teams will fade away as they witness your success firsthand.

This approach serves as a foundation for evolving teams. By demonstrating how your leadership style and values contribute to tangible success, you show others the path to their improvement. They will see that self-management is not something to be feared but rather an opportunity for growth and stewardship.

Your example will encourage team members to manage their roles and responsibilities, fostering a culture of trust and collaboration. As they observe the positive outcomes of your servant-leader approach, they will be more willing to embrace similar methods.

Setting the right conditions and leading by example will create a more dynamic and self-sufficient team environment.

Strong Trust Foundation & Understand Needs over Wants

Trust and respect are now firmly established and earned. This foundational trust fosters an evolutionary model within an agile environment, where the interconnectedness of all elements becomes clear. With an agile team, you can craft a clear vision for the product and the teams, addressing training, organization, impediments, and risks.

By establishing the right backlogs for the product and training, risk, and improvements, you have shown others how trust has grown with the team. They will want to emulate that to grow. This clarity guides the team internally and extends to interactions with external stakeholders.

Trust and respect allow for more effective teams that embrace change and continuously improve. This environment makes team members feel confident in their roles and contributions, leading to higher engagement and productivity. The shared vision aligns everyone's efforts, making tackling challenges and seizing opportunities easier, and transparency creates effective collaboration.

Adaptive to change

When team members start recognizing the importance of value, they transform from a development team into a discovery team. This shift goes beyond initial value recognition, enabling them to become more adaptive to change. Others will want to follow suit as they exhibit their agility in adapting to change easily. So, there is a collective effort to establish a strategic pathway for success.

They will see that becoming a discovery team means they are constantly seeking new insights and opportunities, not just executing predefined tasks. They become proactive in identifying potential value and innovative solutions, fostering a culture of continuous improvement and learning. This proactive approach lets the team stay ahead of industry trends and customer needs, ensuring their work remains relevant and impactful.

The team can respond swiftly and effectively to new challenges and opportunities by becoming more adaptive to change. This agility enhances their ability to innovate and improve, leading to better products and services. Organization leaders will be able to make strategic pathways more transparent so teams can align their efforts with long-term goals and objectives.

Strategic Pathway

When team members recognize the importance and value of becoming a discovery team rather than just a development team, they move beyond initial value recognition and become more adaptive to change. This transformation allows the team and interconnected teams to establish a strategic pathway for sustained success.

With a broader enterprise strategic pathway, there is a comprehensive understanding of how everything should be set up, along with a clear team vision. This clarity extends to a well-defined product, service, and team vision. These visions align with the broader organizational goals, ensuring everyone works towards a common objective.

From a measurement perspective, the focus shifts to continuous improvement. The teams adopt an incremental progress mental model by striving to become 1% better daily. This approach encourages constant learning and adaptation, fostering an environment where small, consistent enhancements lead to significant long-term gains.

The strategic pathway guides the entire organization, ensuring every team member understands their role and the collective vision. This commitment to ongoing development and incremental progress drives individual and team growth and propels the organization toward greater success and innovation.

Data Program

Establishing a data program at an organizational level is essential for creating a unified approach to measuring performance and progress. Like with your team you worked on throughout this book, identifying the data that serves as the baseline for your metrics, you can build a foundation that supports the entire organization.

It enables effective data sharing across all teams, ensuring everyone can utilize it in their processes. This organization-wide implementation ensures consistency across the value chain, allowing for meaningful comparisons and analyses. With standardized metrics, teams can compare apples to apples when measuring improvement, implementation, and overall progress.

Having a unified data program at the organizational level fosters a shared understanding and approach to measurement. It ensures all teams are aligned in their evaluation methods, enhancing transparency and collaboration. This alignment makes tracking progress, identifying trends, and making data-driven decisions supporting continuous improvement easier.

Standardization facilitates consistent measurement and comparison, driving better insights into improvement, implementation, and overall progress. Such an approach enhances the value chain and supports the organization's continuous growth and efficiency goals.

Improvement Identification Process

Collaborating to identify process issues and pinpoint root causes is essential. Now, it is about doing it on a larger scale. Rather than holding a large meeting, you want to keep the effort small by addressing process issues within individual teams. Each team focuses on identifying and resolving its process challenges.

As previously discussed, you can implement team retrospectives and heartbeat meetings to facilitate this. Additionally, introducing broader meetings such as a "scrum of scrums" allows representatives from each team to come together. In these meetings, individuals share insights, discuss improvements, and gain a comprehensive understanding of what is happening across the organization.

This approach helps identify and implement necessary changes and fosters better team communication and collaboration. By enabling teams to focus on their specific issues while participating in organization-wide discussions, you create a dynamic environment where continuous improvement is a collective goal.

Where Leadership Fits in

Now, your leadership across teams shows that they are becoming more strategic. They've given the teams trust and removed the fear of self-managed teams for both themselves and the teams. The teams can grow and evolve, with leadership to guide them to succeed and achieve the value we expect from being agile.

You've built the foundation of trust and are building more trust as you expand your ripple. You've provided an ecosystem for self-managed teams, and now you're growing the trust across the board by removing fears and helping the teams improve. Everyone now understands what's needed and the expectations. Dealing with escalations no longer becomes a contentious issue but a collaborative effort to resolve the problem. There's no point in getting angry about something if it's due to a process break that no one understood. You've identified those issues and have an environment in place to resolve them, and that's all that is needed.

Communication Program

Now, the focus shifts to understanding how these teams collaborate and communicate. Determining the most effective communication methods within and among teams is essential. Do we have the appropriate tools to facilitate effective communication and add value to our interactions?

It's about ensuring everyone understands the goals, processes, and expectations.

By evaluating communication methods and tools, you can identify areas for improvement and implement strategies to enhance collaboration and productivity. This might involve leveraging project management platforms and communication apps or establishing regular meetings and channels for sharing updates and insights.

Working with other teams to create a broader and more effective communication program allows alignment, transparency, and productivity across teams. It ensures everyone is on the same page, working towards common goals, and can address challenges efficiently.

Guidance to Team Collaboration

Next, you want to ensure that there is guidance on how the team should work together. You have your team agreement, which will improve as it allows the teams to collaborate most effectively. Leadership provides guidance, ensuring the teams deliver value and achieve measurable goals. They must be disciplined and trust their ability to move forward while adhering to agile values. We've discussed agile values in every chapter as the guiding principle.

When you first created those agile values with your team, you secured their buy-in. Everything leading up to this point should now reflect those values. Teams should recognize, "Hey, I created those agile values; I can see how this fits in." Or perhaps they might think, "Maybe we need to adjust the agile values a bit," or "We need to change how we communicate to fit the agile values better." However, any changes will not be drastic because the groundwork has already been laid.

As you evolve this to other teams, the guidance and understanding of expectations will be clear. Everyone understands because they own those agile values, making the expectations straightforward and easily comprehensible.

Definition of Quality Assurance

Ensuring quality is not solely the responsibility of a specific department or role; it is a collective effort that encompasses every aspect of the organization. Quality assurance extends beyond testing; it includes the quality of the product, service, development, and every individual's work.

It is essential to instill a mental model where everyone understands their role in upholding and enhancing quality. This means exhibiting behaviors that prioritize quality in every task and interaction. Whether crafting a product, delivering a service, or contributing to development, each team member plays a vital role in ensuring quality.

Fostering a culture where quality is ingrained in every aspect of work is crucial to the transformation process. This involves changing behaviors and promoting a deep understanding of quality assurance principles. Team members should be empowered to take stewardship of quality in their respective areas and strive for continuous improvement.

Organizations can enhance overall product and service excellence by emphasizing the importance of quality assurance and encouraging proactive measures to uphold it. This cultural shift improves customer satisfaction and fosters a sense of pride and accountability among team members.

Quality assurance is everyone's responsibility, and everyone should help make others better at what they do. It requires a collective effort to prioritize quality in all aspects of work. Organizations can drive significant improvements in product, service, and overall work quality by fostering a quality culture and empowering team members to take stewardship.

Understand Changing Priorities

We all must acknowledge that priorities can shift over time, and how teams navigate these changes significantly influences the quality of their work and the products they deliver. Without a plan to manage evolving priorities, the overall quality of products and services can be compromised in the long run.

Understanding the dynamic nature of priorities is essential for maintaining high-quality standards. Teams must be equipped to adapt to changing circumstances while still delivering outcomes that meet or exceed expectations. This requires effective communication, strategic planning, and agile decision-making processes.

Organizations can safeguard the quality of their products and services by proactively addressing changing priorities and implementing mechanisms to manage them effectively. This may involve establishing a broader set of prioritization frameworks and guidelines, maintaining open lines of communication, and regularly reassessing objectives and timelines.

By staying responsive to evolving needs and challenges, teams can continue to deliver value and maintain a competitive edge in the marketplace.

Product/Service Value is a team event.

Ensuring that every team member comprehends their role in delivering value is essential for the success of any endeavor. Regardless of their team affiliation, everyone contributes to the outcome, and they must recognize and embrace this responsibility. This sense of stewardship empowers individuals to actively engage and contribute their expertise and insights.

Integrating agile practices goes beyond increasing speed; it's about fostering a deep understanding of the environment and cultivating collaborative behaviors. It involves transitioning from accepting practices to a change journey toward continuous improvement.

By instilling a culture of continuous learning and adaptation, organizations can ensure that they achieve their goals and evolve and thrive in an ever-changing landscape. This involves creating an environment where experimentation and innovation are encouraged, and teams are empowered to iterate and refine their processes iteratively.

Ultimately, organizations can drive meaningful transformation and achieve sustainable success by emphasizing the importance of every individual's role in delivering value and embracing agile principles. This journey towards continuous improvement enables teams to remain responsive and adaptable, positioning the organization for long-term growth and innovation.

Understand that Frameworks are only tools – Synchronize with everyone

We want to understand the tools to get where we need to go. Are we using the right tools? Are we using the tools correctly to achieve the value we provide?

When we have the right toolbox combined with the behaviors we've discussed, synchronization will happen organically; it won't be forced. The roadmap will lead to organic changes in behaviors and actions within the team, allowing for natural growth. This system is not just for one team but can also extend to others. It guides creating in an agile environment independently of other teams.

In each chapter, we worked through the details of creating your special agile environment. The workbook provides additional insights on how to improve in each of those areas. The final step is building out that environment. You should now know what it will look like for your team. It's important to understand that this roadmap flips the Golden Circle. Previously, almost 95% of most organizations looked at agile from the "what" into the "why." By the time they got to the "why," the message was lost, and the work became redundant and difficult to mature. This book has flipped it.

Now you're going from the "why" to the "what." We're not changing your framework; we're completing the transformation of behaviors to be agile. You've stuck through the building process, and we're almost done. Now, the door is open. It's time to take action. Review the workbook at the end of each chapter and review your answers. See the gaps and opportunities you identified. All the information until this point will feed into what you will do next. You've taken the information, and now you can go out and improve.

You'll take everything we've learned, the three phases: your foundation, your system, and your scale, and create the beginning of a beautiful, agile journey.

CHAPTER 10 | GROWING

Evolve your organization to surpass the completion by taking the roadmap process to them

Goals	Why	How	What
Grow agile values	Evolution of the organization	Taking teams to the next level of achieving value	Growing agile behaviors and actions
Improve flow	**Adaptive**	**Strategic leadership**	**Innovation**
Synchronization equals smoother flow of information	Improved adaptability with changes.	Leadership focused more on strategy and less on tactical.	More opportunities to innovation

Figure 10.1

So, finally, we have reached the last step: Evolving. Everything up to this point creates an environment where teams and the organization will thrive. You have started a new ecosystem where the opportunities have no bounds. This final step is essential for tying everything together and building more. Think of it as throwing a pebble into a puddle of water, and the ripples expand and reach the edge. This chapter will get into how to get those ripples to expand.

You are about to take this ecosystem and make something unique. It's how you will develop the environment we've been discussing until now. The workbook section at the end of each chapter is an information source for growth. I am sure you've been taking many notes and writing down all your answers. With all that information, it is time to make practical improvements. This involves planning to outline each step, specify the tasks, and set goals for everyone to achieve. Any transformation and culture change will take time and more. We have to determine what that "more" is.

If you search on the internet, you will see different failure rates of agile transformations: 47%[57], 70%[58], or even a range of 50-96%[59][60]Regardless of the varying numbers, they are all extremely high. What you have learned through this book can help improve your odds, as you are now keen on finding deep-seated issues that impact such a change.

Certain important things are not taken into account when going through change management. For example, what motivates others? How do others disseminate information? And what can be done to help get them on board?

This chapter gives ideas on what to consider as you go through change management. It aims to help you resolve the answers you provided before and implement the solutions you've documented in each question.

Let's see what we have learned so far.

WHAT DO WE HAVE

A. Your View

Throughout this book, you have been given ideas and guidance on where to look and provided your perspective on those answers. Does that mean your view is the right one? Maybe, maybe not. As an agilist, one of the things we all need to know is that it is a collective intelligence effort. It's not just about how you see things but how everyone sees things. Remember, an agile environment is about what is best for everyone. Even with your positive views and the right intentions to make and identify these changes, you still need to work with others to address those issues.

B. Confirm with Others

As you've seen in previous chapters, it's all about communication and dialogue. You want to work with others and have them see and understand

---

[57] https://www.scruminc.com/why-47-of-agile-transformations-fail/
[58] https://www.bcg.com/publications/2022/what-employees-say-about-agile-transformations
[59] https://innovify.com/insights/why-agile-transformations-fail/
[60] https://www.netsolutions.com/insights/how-to-prevent-agile-transformation-failure/

what needs to happen, confirm what needs to happen, and identify where the gaps are. When changes are prescribed from the top down, sometimes those at the top may not realize that other teams or groups have already improved their value or productivity. However, these improvements may not be fully recognized if other teams face issues.

To succeed, we need collective intelligence and knowledge sharing to understand where the gaps are and what others feel needs to change.

Now, let's discuss what challenges you will likely face in the final step of this whole framework.

GROWTH STRUGGLES

Now it's time to expand.

It's time to expand agile delivery methods and behaviors to those outside the team. It's also about evolving the team itself. You want to have the team evolve and grow with agility. We want to grow these agile values and improve the flow between teams. Adaption, strategy, and innovation are the final components that lead to evolution.

As agile environments evolve, problems arise, such as department bottlenecks. Issues like "I don't want to do it that way" or traditional attitudes like "first in, first out" can cause friction. Teams not recognized within the value chain or have misconceptions about agile delivery, thinking it's just for software, also create challenges. As discussed throughout the book, an agile environment is not just for software. This brings us back to the "us versus them" mentality.

So, how do we effectively grow an agile environment for other teams? How do we create those additional ecosystems?

Team 1	Team 2

Figure 10-2

The pictures I've chosen here serve as examples of the tools. One team might use one tool, while others use different ones. Yet, you can set them all up to build something great, not just a product or service, but an entire organization. It's not just about a framework; it's about growing the teams.

When we look at the following sections, you'll notice no user stories for each, unlike other chapters. The reason is that you're now taking all the user stories from the previous chapters and expanding them. We want to create that adaptive environment using those user stories as the context. Look at all the last adaptive user stories and organically grow an agile environment for other teams. Consider all the user stories about behaviors and actions and grow the team to have the right ecosystem.

For an agile organization, your role is to be that change champion for all those user stories and supporting items throughout the book. That's why it's not written out here. One, it would be repetitive. Second, it allows you to review the chapters and questions with a frame of mind on the organization. It's about having the "why" and pushing it out to all the teams.

WHAT'S NEXT?

Now that you have gathered all the documented information and are aware of the challenges ahead in the implementation process, what comes next to actually bring about change?

The pointers you have written down indicate that significant work is required behind the scenes to effect positive change. I have emphasized this several times and must reiterate that implementing a framework does not automatically create an agile team or organization environment.

Biases can creep in unnoticed, creating gaps that affect decision-making and transformation. While biases make decision-making easier, they complicate transformations because addressing deep-rooted issues takes effort to achieve the final goal.

To ensure your journey is effective, it must eliminate cognitive biases and logical fallacies regarding various aspects of an agile environment. This will enable you to create an environment that flourishes and evolves.

Revisit the questions and answers provided to identify any biases or fallacies within your organization or team that could negatively impact transformation. Recognizing and addressing these biases is crucial for successful outcomes in agile transformations.
Here is how you can begin:

- **GAPS**

The notes you have prepared reflect the identified gaps. But are they all the gaps? That is for you to determine because this is where significant change management needs to happen, and fully understanding what it means for your organization is crucial.

When transformations occur, one of the unknown blockers or unseen impediments to their success is the failure to understand or identify all the gaps. This is where cognitive biases and logical fallacies come into play. For example:

The Cognitive Bias: Anchoring

Anchoring occurs when initial judgments significantly influence subsequent ones. Due to our minds' associative nature, the order in which we receive information plays a crucial role in shaping our judgments and perceptions. In an agile environment, where adaptability and collaboration are paramount, understanding anchoring is vital for effective communication, collaboration, and decision-making.

The Power of First Impressions

The initial encounter with a new project, task, or team member for agile teams sets the tone for the entire collaboration. This first impression is an anchor, shaping how team members perceive and approach subsequent interactions. Imagine a scenario where a team is introduced to a challenging project with a negative tone. This initial reaction can create a mental anchor, influencing how team members approach problem-solving, collaboration, and the overall project.

Despite agile methodologies advocating flexibility and continuous improvement, the human mind tends to latch onto initial impressions. Anchoring can either be a catalyst for positive collaboration or a stumbling block hindering progress. Recognizing and managing anchoring biases is essential for creating a healthy and productive agile team environment.

Setting Positive Anchors

Creating positive anchors within an agile team involves careful planning, effective communication, and nurturing a culture of open-mindedness. Onboarding new team members provides a prime opportunity to establish positive anchors. A warm welcome, clear expectations, and camaraderie can set a positive tone, influencing the newcomer's perception and subsequent contributions to the team.

Similarly, initiating a new project or sprint offers a chance to create positive anchors. Project kick-off meetings emphasizing collaboration, shared goals, and a can-do attitude can set the stage for a successful endeavor. Positive anchors elevate team morale and contribute to a more resilient and adaptable team culture.

The Ripple Effect on Decision-Making

Anchoring significantly impacts decision-making within agile teams. The first piece of information or an initial proposal serves as a mental anchor, shaping subsequent discussions and decisions. This influence can be a double-edged sword, potentially leading the team down a path that may not align with their best interests.

Agile teams can adopt practices such as divergent thinking to mitigate the negative impact of anchoring on decision-making. By encouraging open dialogue and considering various viewpoints, teams can break free from the constraints of initial anchors and make more informed, unbiased decisions.

Managing Anchoring in Retrospectives

Retrospectives involve reflecting on processes and identifying areas for improvement. Anchoring can influence how team members perceive the success or failure of a sprint or project. Managing anchoring in retrospectives requires approaching the review with an open mind and a willingness to challenge initial perceptions.

Facilitators can guide retrospectives by encouraging team members to share their perspectives without judgment. This creates an environment where the team can collectively reevaluate their initial anchors and consider alternative viewpoints. Managing anchoring biases in retrospectives allows agile teams to foster continuous improvement and adaptability.

Recognizing Anchoring in Daily Stand-ups

Daily stand-up meetings can either add value to the day or cause discord. Anchoring can subtly influence these meetings, especially if the first team member to speak sets a negative or overly optimistic tone.

To counteract the potential impact of anchoring in daily stand-ups, teams can establish guidelines for maintaining a neutral and objective tone. Emphasizing data-driven discussions and focusing on facts rather than emotions helps mitigate the influence of anchoring biases. Creating a culture of transparency and objectivity ensures that daily stand-ups remain a constructive and forward-looking practice.

CHANGE MANAGEMENT IS BIG THING

Most organizations don't neglect change management, a considerable aspect of any transformation. However, they often miss critical points when following a generalized process.

Generally, change management practices are successful and can facilitate organizational change, including implementing new services or products for clients. However, for change management to be effective, it must be tailored to the organizational needs to extract the full value from the transformation, ensuring that everyone involved is aligned and supportive of the change.

General Practices

One of the most influential figures in the discussion of general practices for change management is John P. Kotter. He is the author of the bestselling book Leading Change. In it, Kotter outlines an eight-stage process designed to transform organizational culture effectively.

These practices focus on achieving the overall change goal by using various techniques to empower teams and ensure successful implementation.

SOMETHING TO CONSIDER

Another important aspect of change management is recognizing that everyone is different. People absorb information differently, are motivated by different factors, and have unique ways of working with others. Understanding these differences in detail is crucial for effective change management.

Many change management processes overgeneralize how individuals perceive and adapt to change. The DiSC model, developed in the early 20th century, is a useful framework that helps us understand different personality types and how they interact with change.

American psychologist William Moulton Marston first developed the DiSC model. Marston introduced the model in his 1928 book, "Emotions of Normal People," where he described four primary emotional types:

- Dominance (D)
- Inducement (i)

- Submission (S)
- Compliance (C)

Marston's foundational ideas laid the groundwork for the modern DiSC assessment, which was later refined and commercialized by industrial psychologists and organizations. Companies like Wiley (formerly Inscape Publishing), which specializes in psychometric testing and personal development tools, have further developed and popularized the modern version of the DiSC assessment.

While Marston is credited with the foundational concepts, the specific DiSC assessment tools used today have evolved through contributions from various psychologists and organizations over the decades.

The specific DiSC assessment tools help us understand the behaviors of the teams, especially during a transformational phase, and how they take in and accept information. A small element often keeps the old ways alive when things don't go as planned or the change isn't implemented effectively throughout any change management process. This was quite clear in an organization I worked for, which another company had just acquired. Under new leadership and a new name, the teams from the previous organization struggled. They constantly compared the old methods, insisting they were better than the new processes and ways of the acquiring company.

During this transition, I noticed a symbol of resistance in the kitchenette: a cup still emblazoned with the old company logo. This cup represented a reluctance to let go of the past. It was a small but significant *anchor* to the old company's values and methods, which hindered progress and adaptation to the new organization.

The previous organization had been struggling, so it was bought out. The new company aimed to improve upon the existing value. I took the cup and smashed it on the ground in a meeting with everyone present. This action, though blunt and perhaps a bit harsh, was symbolic. It demonstrated that clinging to the old ways was not productive, and the new organization's methods aimed to better everyone's work experience and efficiency.

It could have been avoided if the leadership had fully understood how the teams worked together and how they dealt with different situations. With that knowledge, they would have a roadmap on how to effectively introduce change, have positive conflict, gain acceptance and gain stewardship through accountability to get the results they were expecting in a smoother transition.

THERE'S MORE

In setting up their foundation to create an agile environment, people often assume that team collaboration will automatically improve or is already optimal. This assumption is a cognitive bias because it overlooks the current dynamics of how the team works together.

In an agile environment, a high level of discipline is required among individuals and within the team throughout the organization. This discipline ensures proper collaboration and smooth teamwork, essential for reaching the end goal.

To ensure this discipline, it is crucial to have a structured environment where teams feel psychologically safe sharing ideas and suggestions and holding each other accountable. This environment is not about finger-pointing or blaming individuals but about working together as a cohesive team towards a common goal.

KEY TO SUCCESS

Ultimately, we aim to make a positive impact through change. Identify what we need to change as a group. In an agile environment, unilateral or top-down directives for change often struggle to succeed. Understand the people affected by the change. Some individuals may resist or follow their path. They might need the change communicated in a way that aligns with their thinking.

As John P. Kotter emphasizes in step six, focus on achieving short-term wins. You are not trying to change everything at once. Have a plan where quick wins build on each other to reach the final goal. Avoid getting fixated and let go of biases in decision-making. Keep the organization's best interests in mind and collaborate with others to make decisions that benefit the teams.

Remember, what works for one may not work for others. Be prepared to adjust and ensure synchronization remains intact.

Final Thoughts from The Author

Writing this book has been a profound journey for me—one that has been both long and deeply rewarding. Capturing my thoughts on building a foundation for an agile environment wasn't easy, nor should it have been. I aimed to create something that could inspire others to cultivate something truly wonderful within their teams and organizations.

I am incredibly proud of what I've accomplished. The sections, chapters, and workbooks are all rooted in my experience and learnings over the past two decades. As an agilist, I'm always evolving, and the creation of this book is a testament to that continuous journey. Over two years of gathering information and organizing my thoughts, followed by another two years of writing, have brought us to this moment, and still many changes in the last two years.

This journey began with a conversation about maturity models with my mentor and friend, Tom Cagley, many years ago. From there, the idea of evolution, inspired by Pokémon, set me on a wondrous path to enlightenment.

I hope this book provides you with valuable insights and helps you and your team discover a path to growing into a thriving agile ecosystem.

Best wishes on your agile journey,

Jeremy Berriault

The Evolutionary Agilist™